Inter-Temporal Cheating

Nathan Coppel

Contents

Chapter 1

Standing in front of the temple, Anthyren Hyiressen let the brisk wind to cool his reddening cheeks. Little clouds were made by his sigh, although the cold had nothing to do with the way a shiver ran down his spine. Though his mind was far from what he was seeing, his eyes swept the horizon that was clearly visible.

He exhaled, "Finally," and threw his head back as his joints assuredly cracked. His fingers lingered near the hilt of the sword on his belt as orange street lights added intensity to his already menacing appearance. His shoulders stiffened like a well-knotted spring, ready to erupt into utter mayhem. Something," he pondered. There is something to stop this. Amp up the flavour.

Anthyren caught a glimpse of the heavy temple doors opening just slightly, enough to let a very thin figure pass through. His fingertips touched his sword as he extended his neck. As he observed a young man, perhaps twenty years old, enter the room via the entrance and into the chilly night air, curiosity took over his face.

The young man stood next to the older man after poking his collars and giving him a curt nod of the head. He retrieved a cigarette from his pocket, squeezed it between his lips, and lit it while keeping his flame hidden from the wind. His eyes were also now examining the nearby horizon. Even before he could take his first breath, the smell of tobacco blended perfectly with the cold, with ashes strewn about. The guy flickered the ash once more, but this time he wasn't sure if it had come from the sky or the child's cigarette.

The youngster greeted Anthyren, "Good evening to you, my good sir." "Are you, by any chance, a guard?"

You were granted your request. Anthyren chose to make fun of him. "Or something like. a newcomer?

The youngster hung his head in dismay. Oh, to think I tried my hardest to fit in.

Yes, that's the wrong guard and the wrong night to strike up a discussion with. He had never heard his own laughter before; it was loud but unprofessional. "If you were from around here, you wouldn't need to ask who I am."

I'm assuming from this that you are well-known. The child held out his hand. "Damien," he murmured.

Anthyren smiled back, "What a strange name." He did not, however, extend his hand to Damien. The third Anthyren Hyiressen.

"Nice to meet you, Anthyren Hyiressen." He grinned with unadulterated satisfaction. Damien's eyes became brighter, as if the continuous ash rain wasn't enough to make him unhappy. It was unexpected because Anthyren wasn't used to seeing sincere smiles. Only masks, such as those used to cover up hatred, nefariousness, or fear, were intended for smiles. A smile would never be followed by something positive.

The question "Are you listening to me?"

Anthyren shook his head to clear his mind of the visions, "Honestly, no," he said. He tightened his grasp on the sword's hilt in an effort to cut himself with it and possibly return to this reality. "Where are you originally from?"

"To be honest, I have no idea. Isn't it intriguing? Anthyren felt himself taking one cautious step backward after hearing him laugh. Oh, fantastic, he said. Either he's insane or high. "I woke up, and I was here." Damien cocked his head to the side while opening his arms widely. The way the cosmos functions is truly enigmatic.

"Oh." Anthyren gave a solemn nod. "So, why are you here? What route did you take to get to this temple?

He shook his head and threw his cigarette to the ground, stomping to put it out. "I was looking for an old acquaintance," he said. I was informed that he would arrive. Instead..." He groaned and fixed his intense gaze on Anthyren's face.

A: "Was he here?"

"Oh, yes." Damien grinned once more, albeit more feebly. I'm waiting for him to emerge as the centre of attention and everyone's fascination.

Damien scowled at that. , "The priest?"

Definitely not. The youngster's head jerked in disgust. Priests are the worst. They make my blood boil.

Anthyren said, "You and me both," as she observed Damien light yet another cigarette. "Then who?"

"Alexei," he responded, turning his head away. "Or, as you probably already know him, Sylen."

Anthyren was left speechless in response to that. The question "Who exactly are you?"

We're friends, I told you," Damien remarked. "However, I'm not really sure how or where. Please, if you'd be so kind as to introduce me to him.

Why do you believe I am familiar with him?

Of course you do, I say. With a mournful shrug, Damien replied. He left handprints all over you, I can see that.

Anthyren had neither sought for nor anticipated this. The words "His handprints?"

If you know how to look, significant. Yet another large cloud of smoke was expelled by him. Will you assist me?

Anthyren relished the opportunity to hesitate for a considerable amount of time. He then raised an eyebrow before turning and approaching his master to inform him of the familiar friend with a new appearance. "Wait right here."

He took a moment to look back before entering the temple through its massive wooden doors. exactly level and embellished with scales. They cut off all communication with the outside world, which was chilly, wet, and dark, when they closed behind him. No. Chandeliers draped in gold hung from the walls, lighting up the room like it was noon. On the gleaming marble flooring, lights danced.

In all honesty, he detested the hideous acts of worship to the gods, including the overly dramatic speeches, the temples that were flowing with gold in every direction possible, and the gold-en-cloth-clad priests and their ilk. They gave him the need to throw up his insides, and he frequently worried that if he did so during a worship service, the anger and hatred would be so intense that it would melt through the pavement.

The geometry and scales were intricate symbols, and something about them made the hairs on his arms stand on end. He wouldn't even understand what terror is or feels like; this was not dread. No. This was different; it was the constant ringing in his ears. Everyone, even the young children, gave him a brief moment of big eye contact before turning away and scurrying away. His stomach tightened, and he felt the want to cover his face with his hands.

He didn't, though. He could constantly hear Sylen's voice in his ears saying, "This is what I wanted for you — for them to know you, and to be terrified of you." It didn't, however, make him feel any better.

He observed the God conversing with the human king and anxiously awaited attention. He took the time to look at the man, noting how worn out and pale he was as he scratched his wrist and noticed how his nails stuck on the bumps and lines. Even in the bright candlelight, his typically golden hair appeared practically platinum. A needless wave of anxiety attempted to ascend from his heart to his throat and demanded to be let out in the shape of meaningless words said. He was more aware of where he belonged. He was even more aware of the need to respect his master.

He was a leytian, that much was clear. Although the young boy Damien was correct when he referred to him as the "very sharpened blade," being a Leytian meant more than that. At least it was in the past. At least that's what the children's stories said. He was meant to be the secret keeper. Not a pointless tool.

Yet.

The God soon turned his attention to the leytian and grinned generously as he did so. He said, "Tell me, Anthyren."

Anthyren responded, "There's someone asking for an audience with you. He describes himself as a friend.

Sylen exclaimed, "Oh," raising his eyebrows in surprise—but not in a good way. Anthyren gritted his teeth. Did he reveal his name to you?

"He said Damien, master," I said. When he said the last word, he couldn't help but feel genuinely sick. Every time he uttered it, something in his heart compelled him to feel it, and this time was no exception. But there was never a time to heed those cries, particularly not now.

I've never heard of this name before. Smiling, Sylen. Anthyren was accustomed to seeing smiles like that. Uncomfortable, expertly concealing discomfort. Where is he right now, kindly?

He is outside, waiting for you.

Sylen inhaled deeply. He said, "Thank you, Anthyren. His voice had a different tone than usual; if he dared to believe it, a shadow of fear crept through its fissures. You're free to go. I'll see you tomorrow in Court.

Gods both take and give. This was an uncommon instance of gratitude for Anthyren. It was an accomplishment to be let go without a one-on-one meeting with the man.

When the guy of the night eventually emerged, Damien was shocked by how elderly he appeared. His face had deep wrinkles that appeared to have been permanently inscribed by a bad artist on the lovely marble. His eyes were narrowed and filled with uncertainty, mistrust, and terror as he looked over Damien from head to toe as if looking for a concealed danger.

Alexei murmured, "Damien," before he added, "Damien."

Damien found himself staring at him in awe. His heart was hammering like a drum as doubt crept in. He recalled Alexei as having a boyish charm and youthful innocence disguising the constant mental churning. Now the man in front of him had lost all the brightness that he had been carrying, even in the most severe circumstances. Even so, are they the same person?

"You look different," he remarked.

One brow was raised by Alexei. It was impolite of you to say that before making an introduction.

"Oh." Damien nodded while losing his smile. "I figured you'd recognise me," He ran a hand over his dark hair as he cleared his throat. "My name is Ashren,"

He observed Alexei's face as reality began to set in. If it's possible, he appeared paler. His knuckles turned white as his hands tightened into fists. Too worn out to utter things into people's brains that would become truth, his left upper lip twitched.

He said, "Ashren," once more. His tone was venomous. I haven't heard that name in a very long time.

Damien responded, his lips rising upward once more, "If the one before me met the same fate at your hands, too." "A long time must have passed."

"Are you who you say you are really?"

Are you sure you want to participate in that game? He tossed his cigarette's ashes aside. I had assumed that ilk would recognised ilk.

Alexei scowled at him. I asked, "What are you doing here?"

I wanted to speak with you to obtain your perspective. To check if you are aware of what I believe almost everyone is by this point and to see if you are taking any action.

Alexei's lips became just a line. He spoke in a voice that was incredibly crisp. I'm positive I don't understand what you mean.

"So you are even more foolish than I thought you were. Even here in Lanenketer, a man who pays great attention to everything would undoubtedly notice the continuous ash rain.

The twitch reappeared there. Why are you here, exactly?

Damien leaned in and said, "Look. "When I opened my eyes, I found myself in this dying cosmos. We don't have much time left, so let's get right to it.

"Which one is?"

Damien searched for something by tracing his index finger along his own throat with one hand. "Alexei, your universe is ebbing away from you. No need to lie right now because we all know it.

"Let's say that it is." He had his arms crossed and his chin elevated. He didn't sound assured, though. What are your options?

I'm not sure right now," Damien said. "I want to learn about the players first. Then we may discuss our options and our obligations. Alexei's throat drew his eyes. He stopped, concealing his brief reluctance behind his cigarette. What say you, then?

"In the morning of tomorrow," Alexei said. His statements had an air of urgency about them. "I think you know where to go,"

Damien put out his cigarette as he vanished.

Chapter 2

After settling into a chair at the table, Damien wasn't overly impressed with the morning assembly. He could come up with a justification for the meeting that morning, but for any other meetings? These folks placed an excessive amount of value on themselves.

When Alexei introduced him to everyone, he received only four shocked stares from people he had previously known well.

"Why?" One of the four women inquired, her large, blue eyes fixed on him. He remembered her from when she was younger and had her long, black hair in braids. It seemed like yesterday. She appeared slimmer, unhealthier, and nonetheless equally stunning. With her frown, Juventas' line between her brows grew deeper. I ask, "And how?"

Damien spoke before Alexei could respond, saying, "I wouldn't be able to answer how." I'm here to make sure you still have a universe, I would say, for that reason.

She remarked matter-of-factly, "You're pandemonium. Your existence and your actions are at odds.

To bite down several of the words he wanted to utter, he clinched his jaw. Then halt. It is ineffective. Instead, he took a long breath. He leaned closer and continued, "I would much rather be the one ending everything. It was difficult not to bring up numerous topics that she probably wasn't even aware of. However, I'm not. This was not intended. Do you not see a problem with that?

She reclined in her seat. Then, please tell, she said icily. What are you anticipating from us?

"I assumed you'd know the obvious response to that," she said.

I'm more interested in how you found out.

While hopping one leg up and down, Damien inhaled deeply once more. His gaze swept the faces of everyone seated at the table. He observed uncertainty, dread, and—most important-ly—complete focus. Damien was conscious of being heard. He fo-cused on one young but intelligent face among the crowd. Damien said, looking at this youthful god, "Go ahead." "Say whatever you want to say."

Alexei muttered, "Leave him out of it.

"Why?" Damien kept staring into the stunning blue eyes of this blonde man. He will also be impacted, won't he? Why should he be left out?

"I won't say it once again. Let him be excluded.

He said, "Father," the one in issue. He is correct.

"I am usually." I saw Damien nod. It's great to see the young prince expressing gratitude.

When the prince got up from his chair, he nearly had everyone look his way. He ignored everyone else and stated, "I request a private audience with you," pointing at Damien. "Now."

He rose from the meal and walked over to the door, defying his father and everyone else's objections.

Damien put out his cigarette and added, "Kids." He pushed his chair back and grinned as he observed the stunned group. Parents are never listened to by them.

He also stood up. He walked carefully despite the fact that the distance between where he was seated and the massive wooden doors looked insurmountable. I'm not in a rush. He was expected to be rushing. Unconsciously, he turned his gaze to the leytians manning the door. Anthyren Hyiressen was standing there with worried-looking lips. He believed that something was wrong with him. Deeply. And it most definitely wasn't the scars he made no effort to conceal.

When Damien came out, the prince took him to an adjacent chamber. He turned and spoke, locking the door behind them.

Isn't it over now?

What being?

"The cosmos. It is done. I can sense it.

Damien then noticed. His shaken hands appeared almost black, and bruises were moving towards his throat. "You're Haylen," he declared. It is "The Universe."

He received a curt nod as an answer. You don't know who I am?

Although I have a feeling Ashren and Haylen had already met, those memories are not mine. He took the opportunity to turn around and look at Haylen to see if there was any obvious harm. Damien sighed and leaned against one of the bookcases after two turns. Do you prefer the comfort or the truthful response?

The question is, "Are they different?"

Depends on your response.

"Truthful, then."

It's really near, he declared. "You also understand it. Ashes fall, as the weather warms. There is a fire everywhere.

"Dad says it's all right. This hard to uphold order is what he insists upon.

Despite the altered terrain, he keeps everything moving following the planned course. Haylen bowed his head as Damien sighed once again. As he went on, he lowered his voice. You are aware that this can be resolved, right?

Your father must pass away, Haylen.

Right, yeah. He laughed once more, but his face became pale as he saw Damien's reaction. Say something like, "Tell me there's another way."

"Not at all. He holds the key to everything.

"You cannot,"

Either someone else or he himself will do it. Once, it was I who passed away. or mayhem. It's now his turn.

Why do you say once? How did you learn all of this?

He responded, placing one hand on Haylen's cheek, "There had to be a chaos before me." The question "What happened to them?"

"You..." Shaking his head, Haylen. You're lying, I say.

"Haylen, you know it's true deep inside."

"My dad wouldn't ever-"

You don't think of him as being unkind. Haylen, there is, however, always a chance that he is. He shifted his weight forward and whispered. "You can see that even in his leytian."

The phrase "that was—" Haylen put his palm over his mouth.

"That was what?" you ask. Damien made a push.

Father claimed that there was no other option except to teach him. Haylen once more shook his head. The attention was evident, so evident. "I begged my father to keep him alive, and he said—"

"He was too rebellious, he would have been killed otherwise." He paused mid-sentence before opening his eyes in genuine shock.

Damien cocked his chin and said, "Haylen, your father needs to die. "Your father needs to pass away if you want to survive and if you want everything else to survive. It doesn't matter who did it, though I would like it if it was his own.

You're promising to murder him, right?

I doubt I will be successful. He moved towards the door while turning around. "Consider it, get advice, and speak with your father. However, the clock is running out, and each second that goes by takes something from your life.

He turned and walked away, stopping in front of the leytian from the previous night, staring at him in quiet.

"Anthyren," he responded. He thought he heard whispers or a buzzing in his ears. He strained to comprehend as his eyes contracted. How can I help you, exactly?

"Sylen needs to speak with you,"

"As anticipated." Damien indicated the hallway. Please show the way.

But Anthyren remained still. "Wait." He ascended, shoulders back. "Can I put my trust in you?"

You don't need to, but you should.

"Is he going to be okay?" His gaze briefly rested on the door Damien exited through before returning to the young man. Damien's heart was torn to pieces by Anthyren's expression, which was marked by utter despair, fear of hope, and a little trembling in his voice.

Damien said softly, "I would make you promises, but I won't." I would, but I'm powerless to inform you. Actually, Anthyren, I have no idea. Bring me to your deity, and no matter what he says, tell me to leave. Escape. It'll probably turn out ugly, I'm pretty sure.

You'll murder him?

I vowed not to hurt Haylen.

Anthyren had his sword in his hand, and his hand was firmly grasping the hilt. He gritted his teeth. "You know I'm not talking about him,"

Damien groaned. All of this was a huge waste of time. "Anthyren, respond to me. Do you have a ringing that never stops in your ears?

"What?"

"You caught me,"

Anthyren's face turned white as paper. The question "How do you—"

"Permit me," The leytian's face briefly became expressionless as he snapped his fingers. a brief moment. In its stead, a terrifying image appeared. He said it again, "Escape, Anthyren." "If you must, go to Haylen, but don't enter the chamber you're taking me to. Promise?"

What happened was?

Nothing matters. Simply promise.

They travelled in silence to their destination, and when they got there, Damien told the leytian once more that he should leave.

Why are you concerned about me? Leytian enquired.

Damien believed he could have spared the leytian a few seconds to take in his features. His hand was once more on his own throat, fingers fumbling for anything while his heart raced in his chest. He shrugged, "I am just one of those." "Romantics who think that love overcomes anything. Now go."

He entered the throne room after opening the door. He prayed, wished, and thought, "Please make it easier." Make the wise decision, please.

"Here I was," said Alexei. I believed you were actually there to assist us.

That was the most impressive thing Damien had ever seen, to be honest: A grey-clad monarch sitting on a golden throne with an equally golden crown on his head. Shamefully, he had no golden staff in his hands. Why hold back when one may go all the way?

But he had a sword. That undoubtedly wasn't gold.

"So, what will it be?"

"You suggested that I should die to my son,"

"I'm shocked. You don't have enough faith in him to be discreet. Take caution, Alexei growled. "Or I'll—"

"I'm yours to kill. This time won't be the first. He inhaled deeply as he considered the best phrase to use. However, if you live, it is you who will be responsible for your own son's death. You won't escape the calamity that results from this. Everyone passes away along with the universe.

I said, "I was doing..." Alexei took a moment to consider his next phrase. "I was doing what came naturally to me."

Damien nodded, "I know. You're mistaken because your nature goes against what the cosmos intended for your heart to desire. Alexei tightened the hold on his sword. "I always did what it asked of me."

"You don't need to show me that you were following instructions. A long time ago, the environment altered.

They exchanged silent glances with one other. Damien observed Alexei's eyes widen and his mouth open almost in slow motion. He could almost picture every justification the man in front of him would offer, down to the last word and sentence. Nevertheless, the gulf of quiet between them widened.

Until Damien made the decision to shatter it with a single fact.

"I was there," he admitted. "Once, at the beginning, I was there."

The answer is "No, you weren't."

"I was somewhere else," He succeeded in forcing a sterile smile into his nostrils. "We walked away together. We got going together. You later murdered me. Everything is currently dying at your hands.

What occurred here wasn't up to me, Alexei said. I would not have preferred this.

"I know." So he did. I'm not even furious that you killed me. The corners of his eyes started to get wet, and he could feel it. But Alexei, you know what to do if you want to stop it.

Alexei got to his feet and moved cautiously towards Damien's direction, dragging his blade in his wake. Neither of them covered their ears as the sharp metal's spontaneous passage through the marble rang a wail from the walls. They kept looking at each other.

As soon as they were nearly face to face, Alexei started speaking. Damien wanted to take a step back but couldn't bring himself to do so. He could see what was approaching yet he was unable to turn his head.

Alexei sighed and began, "It is hard," briefly closing his eyes. "Trying to swim against the current and the approaching doom is difficult where I am," the speaker said.

Damien noted, "It's already at your door."

The "merciful ending" would be the end of the universe as we know it. He smiled shakily while shaking his head. "You claim to have been there at the start. You need to be aware of that.

But this is your universe. Your son is the first to pass away—this is your warning.

"Don't you know it..." Again, Alexei sighed. "On each occasion. So initially... He raised his sword, his eyes completely darkened by a malevolent glint. Initially, I'll take care of you.

Damien stood tall in the comfortable space of helplessness as fear gripped his heart. He slid his eyes shut and remained still.

CHAPTER 3

He thought there were shards of glass or shrapnel in his lungs, for it was the only way he could explain the immense pain each breath brought him. He coughed, in an attempt to dislodge them, body convulsing with the power of each spasm, thrashed beneath the soft, silken bedsheets while his eyes remained closed.

"It's all the cigarettes," came a soft voice from his right, heavy with sleep. "I keep telling you. Not only they smell awful, they also hurt your lungs."

Damien opened his eyes, struggling to focus on the ceiling through his blurry vision. The pain in his lungs subsided gradually, replaced by echoing of his heartbeat. Everything settled in what felt like an eternity, clarity not only in his vision but in his mind, too. "I am alive," he breathed.

"Yeah, I would assume so." This time, the voice was clearer. "Are you alright?"

Damien shook his head, trying to calm himself down. He basked in the familiarity of the voice, slowly turning to look. He took in the sight of the handsome man laying next to him, running a hand through his disheveled silken blonde hair as his bright blue eyes slowly filling with worry.

"You're alive too!" Damien blurted out.

"Did you..." Haylen chewed his lip with a frown. "Did you hit your head or something?"

"We can say it was a brush with death, yes." He rose from the bed, almost laughing. His eyes lingered over every corner of the room, in a state of ecstasy he had never experienced before. It was a nice room, comfortable, with sky blue walls. Sunshine painted them into a most cozy tone, adding warmth to peace. He was aware he wasn't wearing anything, but Damien didn't feel cold. He didn't know where this room was, how he came here, or why he was with Haylen in the first place, but they were both alive, and everything seemed fine.

"Okay, though," he said with a wide enough smile. "What happened?"

Though in contrast to the joy he felt in every fibre of his body, Haylen grew worried with each passing second. "When?"

"I don't know!" He stopped containing his his laughter. Every part of his body buzzed with electricity, it took great amount of power to stay where he was, leaning onto one of the drawers. His muscles relaxed in relief. "Give me the bullet points!"

Haylen looked worried as he raised himself on his elbows, and examined Damien's face. "You look terrified."

"Fear and excitement, they are close neighbours." Damien blinked rapidly. "Okay, let's start from how we ended up here."

Haylen once again was chewing his lip, eyebrows furrowed. "You were helping me with the seams," he started, but then paused shortly. "As you usually do."

Damien felt the cold, taking ahold of his body. As you usually do. The words echoed in his head. Everything paled as he leaned a bit forward, his throat closing down on any sound he could make. "Seams..." His voice was raspy, barely coming out. "Continue, please."

"We were here — you, me, Antenyr. We drank, we talked, we laughed, and you stitched me." He sounded more certain now, his eyes even larger with worry. "Damien, please sit down."

Damien did as he said, taking a few halting steps, then collapsing onto the bed.

"Tell me you just injured yourself and I helped you out with that."

"I was injured, but not like that... You really don't remember?"

"Clearly not." Impending doom beat its drums in a speeding rhythm.

"I'm bursting, with light," Haylen said. "You were the one who told me it's the sign of general issues with the universe itself, the fabric of reality as you called it. That's where the stitching idea came along. How did you forget all of these overnight?"

But Damien had already stopped listening to him. "And I thought I did it," he muttered, more to himself than to Haylen. All the energy he had drained from him, he was cracking his fingers one by one. His shoulders rolled forward with the weight of what he heard. "I thought it was all saved!"

Haylen threw his hands in the air. "What was all saved?"

"The universe!" Damien looked straight into Haylen's eyes, hands curled into fists. He was shaking now. "You!" Then, he buried his face into his hands, shaking his head. He felt so small, so inconsequential. "Your father, Alexei, he was about to kill me and I woke up here! I thought it was because, because..." He wanted to curl up under some blankets and cry his lungs out. "Why is this happening?"

"Uh..." Haylen nodded, unsure. "Do you need to talk your mother?"

"My mother?"

"Aunt Juve?"

"Juve?" Damien raised his head in disbelief. "Juventas is my mother?!"

"Okay, this is beyond my abilities," Haylen sighed. "Let me call Aunt Juve, and we can figure out what's wrong with you."

A summary, Damien thought to himself. That's what I need. He raised his hand to stop Haylen, and closed his eyes. Something tugged him forward from his chest. He heard his ribs croaking, feeling their struggle against his skin, trying to get out of there with little care for what they were destroying on the way. He breathed in and out, clenching his eyes even tighter, hands placed right on his heart to keep it there. Gossamer threads flooded his vision under his eyelids, extending beyond eternity, tangled in impossible knots. All he needed was the trigger, so he simply snapped his fingers.

Pain clouded his vision when he opened his eyes back. His body was frozen in an uncomfortable state, for a moment he feared if he looked down, he would see a thousand knives going through his ribs. He whimpered, pressing his lips to stop any more sound coming out.

"Damien," he heard Haylen's worried tone. He let a shaky breath as Haylen gently placed a hand on his back, moving his eyes to meet Haylen's. "What's wrong?"

"Everything," Damien whispered. "But I will be alright. You don't need to worry about me."

"What just happened?"

"I don't know." He was surprised at how pathetic he sounded. He just wanted to collapse in himself, hide from everyone, try to forget all of these even happened. "But we don't have much time."

"For..?"

"Saving you." Damien shook his head. "Just... Go, okay? Give me some time, I will be fine."

"Damien—"

"I mean it. You have to leave me alone." He opened his hands, spreading his fingers, and closing them again. Piece by piece, pain dispersed and he gained some mobility. Nausea rose from his stomach so fast, he had to swallow hard to stop it. "I need to think."

"Okay," Haylen said, quietly. "We can think together."

"No." Despite the struggle, he managed to sound curt. "I will see you when I see you, and I will be in a better place to talk to you."

"I understand." Haylen's eyes grew darker. "At least come for breakfast, Damien."

"Breakfast?"

"Us, our distant cousins, The Quarter Century Gathering?" Haylen replied, holding Damien on his shoulders. "You need to eat something. Then someone needs to check up on you, because you don't seem remotely fine."

Damien nodded, just to get him out of his hair. "Okay," he said. "Fine. I'll come down for breakfast. But now, please go."

*

Damien walked into the garden to make his promised appearance at the breakfast table. He knew he couldn't stomach anything. The acidic taste of vomit still burned his nasal passage, and tears stung his eyes despite his attempts to wipe them away. He managed to get himself dressed enough to be presentable, but there was nothing he could do for his whiter than paper face and his eyes, bloodshot due to the strain.

Not the beautiful spring sky, nor the beautiful flowers surrounding the table mattered to Damien as he made eye contact with some people around the table. Their faces changing immediately to pity stung more than anything. Watching these people he was supposed to know but didn't trying to show sympathy exhausted him. Especially because it was difficult to concentrate and remember them, for his mind felt like a horribly made soup of information with limited meaning and context attached to it. All the faces he saw there corresponded to something in his mind, but damned if he could reach to that something and react accordingly.

Haylen immediately got up from his seat, worry etched into his beautiful face. More eyes focused on them now, whispers coming from all sides like a gentle spring breeze caressing grass. Damien found himself wanting to scream at them, scream that none of it mattered and everything would be over so quickly. He swallowed the urge as he sat down. There was no need to cause a scene, after all. Instead, he quickly filled a glass with water and started sipping it.

"Feeling better?" Haylen asked.

Damien raised his head to answer him, but his breath hitched in his throat. Before Haylen, he saw two identical faces. He froze with his glass half way up, and stared at the twins.

"I would guess not," one of the twins quipped. "What happened to you, Damien?"

You really wanna know? Damien slowly put his glass down and shrugged. Every single muscle he had screamed at him as he did so, his bones aching like someone gave him a great beatdown, yet, he kept his composure. "Life," he said shortly. It was better than the real answer.

"You were fine last night," the other twin commented, his eyebrows raised. He had to be Antenyr. "Did you hit your head?"

"Hilarious," Damien replied weakly, watching Antenyr look at Haylen and then wink. The starstruck expression in Antenyr's sea green eyes were unmissable. His one hand was on his neck, fingers running up and down through his shortly cut hair.

Taste of a familiar realisation took over Damien's palette. He inhaled a sharp breath through his teeth. His eyes darted from Antenyr to Haylen, a weak smile slowly forming on his face. He took another sip from his water and leaned back in his chair.

Haylen's eyes went slightly wider, clocking what Damien was looking at. "He will be fine," he said, to assure the twins. His eyes, too, lingered a bit longer on Antenyr. "I believe all the drinks and the events got to him."

"If you say so," Antenyr murmured, casting a side eyed glance at Damien. "Just long as he doesn't collapse on us."

Before Damien could reply to him in a very brightly coloured language, someone put his hand on Damien's back, a gentle act though it startled him all the same. A sense of security and familiarity perked in his chest, as he looked at the wrinkled face of the man who asked for his attention in the quietest way, he had no conscious idea who he was.

"Can I borrow you?"

"Of course." Damien knew he was supposed to know this man, and he wasn't gonna let others realise he didn't. Matters of absent knowledge were best discussed in private. He made sure bidding the people in the close vicinity bon appétit, and followed the man.

They reached inside of a house. Damien couldn't help but appreciate the taste that went into creating such a spacious, yet comforting place. The way sunshine was invited through the large windows warmed the place and all the marbles in it up. Furnitures were a warm tone of white, pairing well with the natural lighting. There was a part in Damien that felt at home here, safe, untouchable.

The feeling was a fleeting one, however. Once Damien actually sat on one of the armchairs, the man turned to Damien. He didn't look mad, just an inquisitive, searching expression in his coffee brown eyes, but his voice when he said "You are not Damien," was terrifying enough.

"I am Damien," Damien replied. "No, I am. I might not be the Damien you know, but I'm Damien nonetheless."

The man didn't look like he believed in him, still. "You don't know who I am?"

"Unfortunately, not. My memories don't work in the way they're intended to work." He didn't know why he was talking this much. "So, I'd be glad for an introduction."

"My name is Martyn," he said. "And I am your father. Or rather, I was."

"And you'd be the God of..?"

"Fate." Now he looked somber. His lips slightly curled downwards, his eyes losing their light a bit. "Are you going to tell me what you are doing here?"

"If you're fate, you must know that this universe is about to explode in itself. I'm trying to prevent that from happening."

"Trying?"

"Last time, I failed. Usually Alexei kills me at the end."

"Yeah, he has a habit of killing the chaos," Martyn sighed. "And this is the first time you're meeting me?"

"Yeah." Damien lowered his eyes, focusing on the shapes and patterns on the carpet. "Sorry about your son."

Martyn inhaled deep. "Let's have a tea, shall we?" He asked. "We have a lot to discuss."

He rang a small, porcelain bell and announced to the room that he wanted tea, then leaned back in his armchair and gestured with his hand at Damien. Go on, he clearly wanted to say. Tell your story.

So, he did. As much as he could remember, which was not much, granted. He remembered the facility, he remembered Alexei's palace and he remembered death. Damien told him, in a monotone voice, as if it didn't happen to him. As if he watched all of it from a distance and not lived through it. His eyes were still on the carpet, drawing imaginary lines on the patterns.

A servant came in and brought a porcelain teapot with two teacups, all of which are adorned by beautiful blackthorns. They both fell into silence as they watched the servant pour tea into the teacups, then serve them. Martyn first, Damien second. Neither of them said anything other than offering their thanks to the servant.

"How many times?" Martyn asked, once the servant left. "How many times do you think this has happened?"

"I don't know," Damien replied, his eyes still on the carpet. "I don't remember. I distinctly remember the last two times, but it feels like it happened a lot more than that. I try, die trying, wake up somewhere else. Players remain the same, their roles not so much. It's confusing."

Martyn took a long look at him, a careful one — Damien hoped it lacked disdain. He wasn't ashamed of his thoughts, however, no matter how horrible they sounded. It was a cycle that everything should go through: Birth, life, death. Start, progression, end. It could be in ten years, ten thousand years, or ten million. It didn't matter. Chaos existed before all, and everything would return to it eventually. He was just trying to give everything one more chance, because every time this stupid universe died, it took him with it. Entirely selfish motivations, he thought to himself. Nothing about survival is selfish.

The way he carried himself, the way he spoke and offered his thoughts on things — Damien thought he'd be happy to have Martyn as his father. Whichever version of himself he replaced here, was a lucky person.

"You're certain it's him, then," Martyn said finally.

"It's the only theory I have." He shrugged. "It's his purpose, isn't it? Final balance, nothing comes in, nothing comes out, nothing moves. It only makes sense."

"Same argument could be made about you, too." He folded his arms, leaning back. "What makes you so sure it's him?"

A good question. "I can't precisely tell. I just feel it."

"That's not so convincing, is it?"

"If you are fate, you can check it yourself, too."

Martyn let out a cold chuckle. "I'm touched that you assumed me to be an all-knowing being, but my vision is as far as I can track the threads."

"What do the threads tell you, then?" Damien raised his head, leaning forward. "I want to kill him and see what happens. At worst, I'll die again. Not gonna be the first time."

One eyebrow raised, Martyn tsk-tsked. "You seem awfully comfortable about it. Lives of others don't mean much to you?"

"Should it?" Damien shrugged again. "They would have died without me. Things are going to end regardless of my intervention."

"Why are you here, then?"

It was a simple question. With no simple answer.

"I don't know," he replied, eventually. It was repetitive at this point and yet, the truth nonetheless. "I opened my eyes here. I wasn't given a choice as to where I will wake up. Damned if I have the choice of giving up. I die, I wake up somewhere else. This universe just doesn't want to die, and I'm intended to grant its wish for it's been pretty fucking insistent."

"So you will kill Alexei."

"I will try if I absolutely have to," Damien sighed, his blinks slow. "But I don't want to. I don't know why but he's just that good at convincing people and getting the upper hand on me."

"You see," Martyn said, sipping his tea. "Alexei and the rest have gone through a lot together. They have their disagreements and betrayals, of course, yet..." He put his cup on the coffee table and leaned forward, his voice dropped to a whisper. "You can say he has a lot of experience on getting the upper hands."

"So my chances are slim, again."

"Unfortunately so."

Damien finished his tea in a single gulp. "Well, we're fucked then, to put it mildly."

The God of Fate simply shrugged. "Maybe. Maybe not."

CHAPTER 4

The moment he stepped out of Martyn's house, Damien came face to face with one of the twins. He did not dare assume he could tell them apart, yet, he wanted to roll the dice and go on the offensive. "Antenyr," he saluted him, lowering his head.

"Damien," the man replied, saluting him back. "Walk with me, please?"

Of course he wasn't going to say no. He watched Antenyr turn his back and start walking, then he trailed him. Catching up wouldn't be easy if Antenyr didn't slow down just enough to match Damien's pace, even though the advance he had were mere seconds. The man walking right next to him in utter silence hid his true emotions behind a perfectly cultivated mask of calmness. Damien expected to see him gripping the hilt of a sword in his belt, until his knuckles went white. There was not a sword there. He wasn't wearing a soldier's uniform. Instead, it was the blacks of the soldier merged with royal purple, some buttons loose. He was so different than Anthyren Hyiressen, yet they were also so similar, and not just because they shared a face.

"Will Axel be alright?" Antenyr asked, in a quiet voice.

Damien sighed. Axel, he repeated to himself. Haylen. That's one knot undone. He didn't need to look into Antenyr's eyes to see that same mixture of desperation and hope. He couldn't help but smile. His own death maybe wasn't the only constant between different… timelines he woke up in.

"Do you want honesty?" Damien asked once again. "Or do you want to be consoled?"

"I already got my answer." Antenyr's left eye twitched. "What can I do?"

"All we can do is convincing Alexei to kill himself. I failed twice, as far as I can remember." He shrugged. "If you think you'd be successful, by all means, be my guest."

"Can't I do it myself?"

"You probably can."

Antenyr nodded. "Will you be alright?"

Damien stopped and closed his eyes. This question Antenyr was bold enough to ask was a very simple one with a very simple answer. If only the words could leave his lungs first, then his throat, then escape through his teeth…

"Damien?" Antenyr leaned, gently, placing one hand on Damien's shoulder. His face stayed as calm as it had been, yet his voice did a bad job at hiding the worry.

"I hear you," Damien replied, his voice barely audible over the whistling of the trees and the grass. "It's just…" He took a deep breath, tears pooling at the corners of his eyes. "I don't know."

"It's okay. Just, breathe."

Antenyr pushed him down a little, causing Damien's knees to buckle. Damien found himself sitting on the ground and opened his eyes. He wasn't surprised to see Antenyr sitting right across him. Damien smiled weakly, his eyes wet with tears.

"Sorry," he said. "I was hoping I would be able to maintain my composure."

"Whatever happened to you last night whilst you slept," Antenyr replied, his voice soft. All the traces of the soldier disappeared from the way he stood and the way he talked. "It must have been a lot. You still don't remember anything?"

"What I remember is a long story," Damien replied. "One I would not rather retell. But answer me this." He wiped away his tears. "Would you really be willing to kill Alexei?"

"If that's the only way I can guarantee Axel's safety, I wouldn't hesitate."

"He loves his father," Damien pointed towards the general direction of the breakfast table with his head. "He might not take it well."

"I would talk to him. Tell him." Antenyr turned to look in the same direction, and paused before he continued. "We all succeed our fathers. Either in accomplishments, or in terms of the time period we live in."

Damien's smile appeared again on his face, this time a bit stronger. "You're a wise man."

"Oh, no," Antenyr chuckled, blushing. "That's my brother Anthony. I am just a simple man." He, too, smiled. "Here is another question. Do you plan on attending the evening events?"

"What events?"

"You don't remember, of course." Antenyr bit his lip. "It's the Night of Debauchery. An endless flow of food, booze and music. Everyone wears masks and just finds a partner to spend the night with and disappear to a far away corner to relish pleasures of the flesh." His eyes gleamed as his lips curled upwards. "Will you be there?"

Damien frowned. "The universe is about to explode in on itself and you're asking me if I'm going to get drunk and find someone to have sex with?"

"If everything is going to end, we might as well enjoy ourselves." Antenyr winked. "If you asked Axel, I'm sure he would agree with me."

"How?" The question seemed so necessary, yet he didn't mean to ask it. "You know what's at stake. How can you be so calm?"

"You see, my friend," Antenyr replied, his eyes up in the sky. His voice was raspy, he blinked his eyes rapidly. "We will do what we have to do and leave the rest to the hands of fate."

Damien could only admire that.

*

The Night of Debauchery marked the very last night of the Gathering. All the gods and goddesses would don their masks, and would find themselves companions for the night as the wine was consumed like water. It was a disaster recipe, in Damien's opinion, really, drunk people and unlimited power at their fingers were never a great match. That didn't stop it from being glorious however, or enjoyable. It bothered him how guilty he felt for actually being somewhat happy about something for once. Still, it was too easy to get carried away from all the worries here, surrounded by this grandeur and extravagance. Hundreds of flickering candles lit the room in rich, warm tones. Their light bounced off from the marble floors which were polished to high shine. It seemed as if everyone glided across a sea of diamonds as they walked.

Under the masks they hid their identities and intentions mostly. Damien noticed one in a beautiful butterfly shape, with shimmering vivid blue and purple over the black base. Another was made with crystals and silver wire. Some skilled hand had bent the wire into intricate shapes, crystals catching the candlelight and refracting it into million tiny rainbows.

In all fairness, he felt thankful to the person who came up with the masks idea as he nursed his drink. Yes, underneath it, it was uncomfortable. But at least he didn't need to keep his composure at all times, or pretend he wasn't listening to the footsteps of destruction coming. They did nothing to hide the eyes, though. Even though his face was mostly hidden, Damien could see Axel's clear annoyance.

"What?" he asked, finally.

Axel shook his head in disbelief. "Still cannot believe you told Antenyr to kill my father."

Damien finished his drink first. "I didn't say that."

"You cannot be that amnesiac."

"I do remember what I talked with your boyfriend," Damien rolled his eyes, gesturing at one of the servants for a refill. "I didn't tell him that he should kill Alexei. But I am not going to weep if he does it."

Axel's voice was cold when he spoke. "That's my father you're talking about."

"He's killing you." A servant put a wine filled glass in front of him. Damien lifted his mask slightly to take a throat burning sip. "He's killing the universe. He's going to kill everyone. He has to die."

"It's so black and white for you, isn't it?"

"Instead of my perspective," Damien said, finishing his glass in one go. "I would suggest you to question if your father is more important than literally everyone else combined. Because it's either your father, or everyone else, Axel."

He put his glass down, nodded slightly and moved away from Axel as quickly as possible. It took him some steps to get to the bar. He asked again for a drink and leaned back to see the entire room. He could see clusters forming between the guests, hands quickly placed on other bodies to signal what the intentions were. There was a cluster that drew his attention much more than the others, however.

Alexei had already taken off his mask, looking intently at the man in front of him. The man whose face Damien couldn't see also wasn't wearing his mask. Alexei had a smile on his face as he spoke, yet, the light of that smile didn't reach to his eyes. Whatever he was saying, he clearly didn't let the other person get an edgewise. Damien turned his eyes on the other partiers. It didn't take him a minute to find Axel and Antenyr together, masks already off as they were kissing. He nursed his drink with a smile before his eyes drifted back to Alexei again.

Alexei stopped talking, which, in Damien's opinion, was good for the poor guy listening to him. But then, the man turned. It was a familiar face, no doubt, but that face carried no expression. As he walked, he paid no attention to other people, as he ran into them often. Damien's eyes caught Alexei's. Alexei raised his glass towards Damien and shrugged, as if to say, what can you do?

On his way out, Anthony had to walk past him. Damien waited for that moment, his entire focus on him. There were only a few feet between them when he heard it. The ringing. So intense, so high, and so deafening, he had to turn his head away.

He followed Anthony, descended the stairs almost in a ghostly fashion — as quiet as he could be, as calm. Night sky was beautiful, so beautiful. All the stars were so close and so bright, Damien actually wanted to watch them for a while. Grass whispered in its own language with the wind, trees joining their chorus. There was no time to pay attention to them, though.

Anthony was standing in the middle of the garden.

"Hey!" Damien called out for him, as he sped up. "Anthony!"

Anthony didn't look like he heard it as he fell onto his knees and pushed his hands into the ground. His eyes were closed, his lips moving silently. There was a few seconds where nothing happened, then Damien felt it in his bones, a wave of nausea overcoming him. He started running this time, to make him stop.

The ground where Anthony touched shone red and orange, as if someone set it ablaze, but he just kept his hand there.

Damien was running towards while every part of his body screamed at him to run away. They had ten steps between them when he felt hot blood trickling down on his face, so he had to stop. "Anthony!" He yelled once more, to no avail. The ground started to shake beneath them, and the ringing got even louder, and louder.

He raised his hands, and snapped his fingers. All the threads everything and everyone were connected through appeared before his eyes, and he did what he always did best: Played with the threads. Antenyr's words ringed in his ears: Leave the rest to the fate's hands. Well, sometimes fate needed a little push.

Two threads got themselves wrapped on Anthony's wrist, and Damien used them to disconnect the man's hand away from the soil he was touching. He straightened and started walking again, ignoring his vision going blurry, his nose bleeding. I will pry your hands away myself. His stomach threatened with a strong wave of nausea, but he didn't stop. Get it together.

He directed the threads once again to wrap themselves around Anthony — and pushed them to steady him. Anthony was panting as if he was running, and his skin looked thinner already. His eyes were open now, glassy, pupils dilated. The ringing sound replaced itself with a scream, but Anthony didn't seem to be bothered by it. He was staring at Damien, without acknowledging his existence.

"What's going on?" He heard Antenyr's voice, loud and clear, carrying through the scream. Anthony kept his current focus. Damien had to turn to him.

"Alexei," he managed to yell, scream, or whisper. He couldn't hear himself. "I'm trying to—"

He inhaled, and ignored all the ways his body was begging him to get away. He snapped his fingers, and kept snapping them until the scream got quiet, trying to push with his own energy through the wall Alexei built around Anthony's mind.

Eventually, it stopped. Everything stopped. Anthony shook his head and looked at Damien, all crazed. "What is going on?" He asked. "You're bleeding!"

"Side effects" Damien laughed, collapsing on his knees. The ugly red light disappeared, and he felt someone was handling him, laying him down — gently, but like one would treat to a potato sack. He didn't have to raise his head or open his eyes to know who it was. "Is Axel okay?"

"Fainted, but I am assuming he will be." Antenyr's tone was curt. "What happened?" The question was to Anthony.

"I haven't got the faintest idea," he replied. "Something in me just kept saying I should let the energy go, and this was the best way. It was stupid, I couldn't even stop myself—"

"Alexei," Antenyr said, and Damien raised himself up. Everything was aching. "You said Alexei-"

"Alexei made your brother do this," he replied. "He has a thing where he can just say something to you and hypnotise you."

"How did you know, then?"

"I heard the ringing. It's a distinct sound, closer to a scream or a screech when you get close to it."

"This is betrayal," Antenyr said, he stood even taller in that moment. "I do not accept this, and I'm pretty sure nor will our father."

Before Damien could answer, they heard the screams, and turned their heads to the palace. The stars were even closer now, breeze was no more.

"Oh," Damien sighed, softly. "So much for having some time to enjoy myself."

Antenyr had already started running towards the palace. Damien had no choice but to follow him, knowing Anthony trailed not so far behind. With every step, his muscles and lungs protesting in sharp stabbing pains. He heeded no attention to them.

Once they were back in the ballroom, they found it different from how they left it. People were speaking in hushed tones, all standing in a perfectly formed circle. Antenyr ran there before the remaining two could, and as the circle parted to allow him passage, he froze.

Alexei was crying, so was everyone else.

"He's —" Antenyr started, his voice barely above a whisper. "Did he—?"

"Axel is dead," Alexei announced, tears in his eyes. "And it was your brother who caused it, Antenyr."

"No, he didn't," Antenyr stumbled backwards. "No this doesn't make any sense, he didn't do anything."

Silence befell into the room.

"Father," Antenyr turned to a man. Damien didn't know his name, but the similarity between the man and the twins was rather striking. It was like seeing Antenyr and Anthony some long years into the future. "Anthony didn't—"

"I know," the man replied with a cold voice. "I leave it to you to deal with it as appropriate, Antenyr."

With that, he stood, strong. "What did you make my brother do?" He asked Alexei.

"I didn't—"

"Don't lie to me," he spat. "Damien said you did, and I believe him more than I believe you, that's for sure."

Damien, standing as tall as he could, walked to the circle. "Yes, I said so," he said. His eyes were glistening red, his face still stained by blood. Gasps came from every section of the circle. "You've been playing this game far too long, Alexei," he turned to the man in the middle, cradling his own son's corpse. "You should've seen it was your fault."

"You don't know what you are talking about."

"Fuck off with that!" Damien felt his entire body shaking. "It's always the same with you. Always playing the same game, ending the same way!" He took a deep breath, pointing at the windows. "We're all going to die in a very short time, so fuck off with that!"

Everyone started yelling at the same time, with two notable exceptions.

First exception was Antenyr, now on his knees. His eyes were on Axel's face. He took the body from Alexei, and with trembling fingers, he combed Axel's hair, still soft as silk. His lips moved, but through the noise, it reached no ears.

All the screams and shrieks and cries increased as it started to look like day time out there.

Second exception to all was Damien. As everyone tried to find something to fix it, he simply walked to the bar. He, too of course, noticed the sky above. Everything felt a lot hotter, second by second. His face was slick with sweat, his skin already feeling hotter. He ran a hand through his hair as he looked through the endless bottles in front of him, trying to pick an appropriate one for the end of life as he knew it.

Yet when he found the one, he paused before opening it. He needed to toast to something. Nothing came to mind until he looked through the windows to see the stars on fire. "To the stars!" His own body felt like it was boiling up from inside. "It was a pleasant—"

CHAPTER 5

His lungs were aching when he woke up, on the cold hard ground. Not a good start, he thought, trying to cough them out. You wanna go, go. Not like I need you. He gave himself some time to stay exactly as he was, passive — aside from the coughing that would've attracted all sorts of unwanted attention — and ignorant. His organs and his muscles agreed with the decision, and it baffled him why on earth this new body that supposedly belonged to someone else was as tired as him. I'm the one who died, he thought bitterly. Why are you tired?

Eventually, and quite reluctantly, he opened his eyes. This is it. It was hard getting up, but he did. Everything was washed with an orange light, he figured it must be getting late. I'm no more chasing after anyone to save the universe. The air was stale, it was plain fields as far as the eye could see in all directions. Where am I? He started walking towards somewhere, though it didn't specifically matter for everywhere looked the same. He walked until his legs hurt, but the sky remained disgustingly orange, and

Damien noticed he couldn't see any progress. It was as if he was on a treadmill.

The body he came to invade was fully clothed, luckily, though it lacked anything to show time — not that he believed it to matter. He snapped his fingers to make a watch appear, and he had no problem there — the problem was in making the watch work, which made no sense, for it had to work, it was all mechanic after all. But it didn't, so Damien shrugged, and continued walking in the same direction. Where the fuck am I?

He kept walking, and tried to make some sense of everything so far. I died, nothing new. He couldn't shake the crashing loneliness. I had a family. A father who was willing to stand up for him, a mother who would try to help him. It was a stupid feeling, really, but he didn't even own a body. Even his body wasn't his own, he was just a passenger, walking in ghosts of the universes, watching them die in several different ways, over and over again. He witnessed the love, the hate, he suffocated in loneliness and sometimes found companions to take the edge, but in the end the self assigned mission was his, and his alone.

He kept walking, and he kept walking, and he kept walking, until finally he saw a building that looked like it was hardly standing up. Damien raised his left wrist to look at the time, almost out of habit, but he saw that it was all rusty and cracked now. Okay, seriously, what is going on?

Against his better judgement, he walked in. It felt like a trap with each step, but the interior impressed him as well. Everything was dusty, but underneath that dust, there laid some pretty marble. It had to be a palace, he was sure. Or a museum. It must have been all so pretty, so carefully made before it was turned into rubble, and dust, and rendered unrecognisable. It had a familiar feeling to it, one that he couldn't quite name. Wait. He was standing still, as did the universe around him. Nothing moved. No breeze, no sound, not even time. Everything waited for him, as he stood in the middle of the once-grand entrance, trying to remember. Wait. For what, though? What am I waiting for?

In another life, he stood there. I know this place. He walked the beautiful halls of it, making fun of the stupid portraits that filled its walls. Isn't this... He walked to the staircase, with careful and quiet steps, and even though the correct course of action was to run away, to get out of this building and keep walking somewhere else, he started ascending it. The steps carried him without giving beneath his feet, they didn't turn into rubble, which was welcome. What happened here? How am I supposed to save it?

He found some comfort in seeing the portraits there. Some-things never change. They were ruined, almost all of them. Almost. There was a single one, as intact as it could be in the conditions. It was way less dusty, even though its frame was already falling apart. Someone must be cleaning this. Is there someone here? Even with the pressing questions, though, he couldn't help but smile when he took a careful look at the face.

"Good to see you, Haylen," he said, the paint rough beneath his finger. "Who ruined your house like this?"

"I did," a voice came from his left. "Care to explain who you are?" It was rough, almost a croak. As if taking the words out was a struggle. Damien turned his back to see the owner of the voice. His smile got even wider.

"I am Damien," he said. "Ashren. Chaos. And I know who you are."

"If you did, you'd be running away from here, kid." He turned his back and started walking through the hall. Damien almost ran behind him, to catch him. "And you certainly wouldn't be following me."

"Oh, but I really do!" He couldn't contain his excitement. "You're Anthyren," he said. "Or Antenyr. Normally I would also guess Anthony, but looking around, clearly you're not him."

"I am neither," the man who was supposed to be one of the three replied. "The Destroyer, is what I am. King of Ashes. And your name isn't who you are."

"Tell me your story, and I'll tell you mine?"

"Do you think you're in a position to bargain? Do I look like someone you can bargain with?" The man turned, in light speed, and grabbed Damien's wrist. For the first time, he had a good chance to look at the man thoroughly. A single line went from his eyebrow to his cheek, a shiny scar that should've gone through his glassy left eye as well. "Walk." He almost threw Damien forward.

Okay, definitely not the gentle prince, Damien thought, walking. The hall was different, in there were no other doors on the surrounding walls. It was just a long corridor with one door at the very end. Isn't this Sylen's palace? Damien knew the palace very well — after all, he died many times there — but the certain eeriness of this place was something he never encountered before. Maybe it's the decay and the dust. It wasn't the decay and the dust.

Eventually, they reached to the end of the corridor, to a room guarded by heavy wooden doors. The man swung them open, and without taking a second glance back, he walked forward, to the throne in the middle. Like everything else surrounded it, it was a rusty, dirty throne. No doubt it was made of the prettiest metals once, shining. Now, neither the man sitting on it, nor the throne itself was glorious — far from it. The ground beneath them wasn't the exquisite marble, it was charred to the point of invisibility. What happened here? How did this guy survive? Damien knew he was supposed to be afraid.

He was not afraid.

"My story?" The man inquired, interrupting Damien's thoughts, one eyebrow raised. There was a certain intensity in his face. This wasn't fear, it wasn't even curiosity — this was panic, panic of getting caught redhanded. Damien felt examined, when he should have been doing the examining. We're now at a stalemate, he wanted to say. Your story in return for mine, stranger who isn't supposed to be one.

"This was Sylen's throne room, wasn't it?" He asked instead.

"You're familiar."

"I've died here once." He returned his looks back to the man. "Or more than once, I can only remember the most recent one. Still a fresh wound, on my pride."

"So are you a ghost?"

"I'm not, at least I don't think so," he shrugged. "I'm travelling from timeline to timeline to stop this from happening. I've never seen the after, though."

"After of what?"

"The death of the universe, of course." Damien smiled, and the man was surprised in a way he found endearing. "Now, your story first. My story second."

*

Once upon a time, only they were there in the room he now occupied, two of them. The king he killed was on the throne that day — calm as usual, but his eyes were bloodshot, his cheeks wet. How many hours has it been since the funeral? How many hours has it been since they both bid their farewells to the Crown Jewel? They were both burning inside with the same fire.

Though one intended to burn everything with it.

"I did your bidding." His venomous voice had molten everything it touched. Ashketyirlen the ones down below dubbed him, The Destroyer. He served the name justice, but it wasn't his name. He had a name here once, one that was known by everyone, one that he would hear from the sweetest of mouths. "I became your blade, I became your gun, I became your bullet. I did your bidding, Sylen."

"You ungrateful little bastard," Sylen scoffed. "I gave you your revenge! I gave you a kingdom in return!"

"I never asked for a kingdom! I asked for a prince, healthy and alive, right next to me! I was to die before him, not the other way!"

"Then you should have!"

"You have left us no choice!"

He took offence to that. "Do you think I'm not upset? Do you think I'm not in pain?"

"You have no right to be in pain!" His throat had felt like it was torn apart. "You could have saved him!" Chin up, breathing loud and fast. His hands were curled in fists he had wished to land upon the god in front of him. "You should've been the one in the ground, not him." He spat on the marble floors. "I intend to send you there."

This was the moment he dreamed of, this was the thing he always wanted to do. Let me, he begged more than once. A dutiful son, his Crown Jewel was, so he never let him. Now you're dead, and we're here. You would hate me. I hate myself for both of us already. You should've let me come with you.

"Will that be enough, Antenyr?" Sylen had asked, not moving an inch from where he sat. He was not afraid of dying, of course, he never was. Then why did you let him die in your stead? "Will just killing me satisfy you? You're quenched for blood, boy, you're just splatting blood on his name by bursting in here, asking for my head!"

"That's not my name," Antenyr had opposed. "I'm Thyren, I always was, I always will be." He called me Thyren, always, he thought. Remembering his voice wrenched his heart. "You will not call me Antenyr."

"Whatever you call yourself," the defiance was dismissed, as if it was just an annoying fly buzzing around. "Do you think it will be enough? You will start a war! You will bring ruin upon us all! It's your nature!"

"No wars," he had said. "No pantheons. No universes. It all ends here, today."

He had raised his hands. It was a wave that pulsed through him, burning everything, inch by inch.

"You will destroy everything." It wasn't an accusation. It was a simple statement, a fact, uttered in awe.

"I intend to."

"All you will have be ashes," Sylen spoke. He didn't sound afraid, he didn't even sound concerned. "Eternity is a long time, boy. Might wanna go ahead and kill yourself before you kill death as well."

"I promised him I wouldn't kill myself."

"You will be the one remaining, sitting on a throne, atop ashes and ruin."

"After I see you dead."

And he had burned everything to the ground, from the top, and each flame fanned the next higher. He stood there, in the room, watched the man in front of him die, scream, along with the rest of the universe they stood in, the time, the existence, everything screamed at the top of their lungs. He watched the sky burn, he watched the ground shrivel, trees fall one after the other. It is loud, for there's always someone to hear them fall. He watched everything coming to a halt under the ever eternal flame that illuminated his sky.

Then it was over. Faster than it started.

He had tried dying, after that of course. He tried to hang himself, though no rope left was strong enough to support his weight. He tried to cut himself, but none of the blades were strong enough, so he forged a sword out of nothing, fuelled it with his own power and tried. He tried to break his own neck, he tried to starve himself, he tried drowning, he tried suffocating himself. In each and every one, he would lose consciousness, and wake up completely healed, as if he did nothing.

There was no death to accept him, as predicted.

He built his own open prison, in which he walked freely and alone. He forgot his own voice, he forgot his own appearance, and he lost the concept of time. Even the concept of his own identity started to escape him.

He remained, as everything else continued to crumble.

Chapter 6

"Thyren," Damien said, after he finished. "It's a beautiful name."

"It was my own," he replied. "I chose it. I carved it out of every name they tried to give me... And you know those other names. How?"

"I met you as Anthyren once. Sylen's leytian, his holy blade. A miserable man with scars for days. You asked me what would happen to Haylen, knowing everything else was dying. I met you as Antenyr once. A happy prince, crumbled at seeing his love's death." Damien tilted his head to left. "You've always loved him."

"I couldn't save him. I failed at my other lives as well, it seems."

"Failure falls on me. It was my duty to save the universe from death and destruction." He looked around. "Though it seems like I've never had a chance here. Haylen died, but the universe followed after, by your hand."

"Axel, or Haylen as you call him, killed himself." Thyren muttered. "He thought he was a danger to everyone."

"Pity." Why am I here? "Did you have a Chaos here?"

"Not that I know of." A cough. "Now tell me your story."

"I am afraid I deceived you," Damien admitted. "I don't have a story worthy of telling. I keep going to places, and I keep dying... I don't even know what I'm doing here."

"Do you think anyone does?"

"Anyone but me... So, help me." He fell on his knees, he didn't even expect himself to. Everything was so tiring. "I'm losing my mind."

"If you expect sanity from me, you're at the wrong place," Thyren replied, towering over him. "For you'll see I have none left. I've never even had it to begin with."

"At least you know who you are."

"Do I?" The man laughed bitterly. "I am not any of those fresh faced kids you knew. I am not even sure if I ever was."

"You're still Thyren."

"Not anymore, kid. I haven't been that either, for a very long time. Or a very short one."

"What am I to call you then?"

"The only thing I am is destruction." The man shrugged. "Start there."

"Then help me destroy," Damien begged, still. "I'm drifting away like a leaf, and I need to know how to stand my ground."

"Standing your ground?" This earned Damien a condescending look. "You don't know how to fight?"

"Never had the chance," he admitted. "I usually die at my second day."

"But where did you begin?"

Damien had no answer to that. I didn't begin. I existed. "I don't remember," he answered the question. Do you think I'd be here if I did?

"When did you born?"

"I wasn't born."

"What wasn't born, cannot die."

"Well, here to disprove that theory, thank you very much." Damien threw his hands in the air, in despair. "I came to exist, one day, on my own, in a body I don't remember. The first time I remember waking up was beneath a burning sky, and stars falling on top of me."

"So, maybe here," the man who was no longer anyone chuckled bitterly. "I burnt the sky after all."

"Maybe. Maybe not. But I died there, and then I reborn somewhere else. I learned my name, there. Someone called me Damien, and I clung to that. I died, and then I drifted somewhere else. All I had was my memories, until they started to fade." He raised his head to look the man, the Destroyer, in the eye. "Teach me how to exist. How to stand against time, as you've done for so long."

"Existing, I can help. Not against time, we don't have any of that here." He looked around, avoiding Damien's clear gaze. "This is an open grave, nothing more, nothing less."

"If you have nothing better to do than pitying yourself, teach me something, anything." It pained him to admit, but he repeated it once more. "I'm losing my mind."

The man laughed. "You provide entertainment to a skeleton," he said. "Get up, stranger, Ashren, Damien..." He got up as well. "And follow me."

Damien did as he said. They left the room through the door they came in, but this time, there was a door right on the left of them. Wait. He was tired of the wait and see game.

The Destroyer, the Destruction, the Skeleton — the man who was all of those, and none of those at the same time, opened the door and pointed towards inside. "Go in," he said, his voice still croaking, but soft. "Sleep. We have much to do, and much to learn from each other."

Damien had no choice but to do as he said.

*

"I am going to call you Thyren," Damien announced, the next day, when he woke up. "It's easier."

The man laughed. "Whatever suits you."

And he taught him. How to control how he could appear to, and to where. His guest was a quick study, for he figured out how to travel between timelines even. In return, the kid brought him food — not necessary — and other drinks. Water, whiskey, better wine, cigarettes. A mirror, even, to remind Thyren of his own face.

Gone was the shiny eyed soldier, the fresh King of the Mountain. He was only left with ashes and dust that he reigned over, and Damien calling him Thyren felt even weirder now that he knew what he looked like.

"Come with me, just once," Damien would insist. "Once—"

"I belong here, kid," he would reply, over and over. "I made my own bed and I'm lying in it, for the foreseeable eternity."

"You don't have to."

A bitter smile. "If only it was that easy."

He taught him how to fight. Thyren had to forge him knives, swords for it first but he did — with a knife, with a sword, with his fists. Damien learnt fast, and applied fast. Even bested the man for a few times, although he always had the suspicion that Thyren let him win. It didn't bother him that much.

They slept in close rooms at first. Then in the same room. Damien was there when Thyren had his nightmares, waking up shivering and wailing from them. He would wander, and Damien would listen to his return, only voice accompanying him his own heartbeat.

"It's okay," Damien said, one night. It was too much, too much, hearing him call out for dead people, his hands searching for them while his eyes were closed. "Take a deep breath." He held onto one of his hands, squeezing his fingers. He was lying through his teeth. Nothing ever was okay, nothing was never going to be. Maybe I need to save him. Not the place.

Thyren opened his eyes, pained lines on his face replaced by angry ones. It was the only time Damien was scared of him, truly. Will he kill me as well? That option didn't induce enough fear in him, no. Is he disappointed in me? And why do I care?

"Damien," he said, in a low enough voice. "I am going to tell you this once, and only once."

"Yes?"

"Don't ever help me again."

"I didn't—"

"I know." Damien realised he was still holding his hand, and let go in that instant. Thyren rose in his bed, his head hanging low. "I know. But, don't. Okay?"

"Okay." He paused, taking a deep breath.

But the next day Damien told him about his dreams, dreams about when everything was fresh, anew, when there were still flowers, or water, or the sky was sapphire blue. He was not himself but a girl back then, she had long, blonde hair that she was so proud of. Madison, he realised with a bitter smile. He was her in his dreams, loving, beloved, afraid, feared. He would whisper names from her lips, in the dark of the night, shards of purple diamonds all around her. She would beg, she would curse, but she wasn't strong enough to get rid of them altogether.

"What happened to her?"

"Sylen killed her."

"Sylen in, his life, killed a lot of people."

Thyren told him about himself a little bit more. How a lifetime spent after ideals, how he stood against Sylen and everything he ever was, only to be a pawn always at his disposal. He wasn't proud of it. He didn't feel anything, really. Eventually he had become an empty shell, a gun to serve a master, an arrow going wherever he was aimed.

He told Damien about how one thing made it all bearable, welcoming him into his open arms and soft sheets in the nights. The one thing, the one person who tended to his wounds with kisses and whispered sweet nothings into his ears. It was the closest thing he could ever be to love. I love you more than yourself. The Crown Jewel, the Golden Flower, Haylen, Axel.

They shared wine, in memory of all the versions of themselves that died, all the good things they killed. They raised their glass for all the good things they've watched slip away from their hands. They danced to the songs they themselves sang, under the orange skies, and achingly, Damien realised this was the life he wanted. More specifically, he wanted a life not spent after chasing probabilities and possibilities.

A companion wasn't something Thyren wanted, though. Not exactly. He was having fun, and it was wrong — punishments wouldn't lead to fun, or anything good coming out. *This is my open grave.* His nightmares were getting rare, and he was actually sleeping — which was just wrong.

"Have you ever thought," Damien mused, when Thyren shared those worries with him. "Maybe that this is the universe's way of saying I forgive you?"

"What do you mean?"

"Why did I end up here? I didn't replace any version of myself, I'm here simply as myself. Something that only happened in my very first existence."

Thyren remained silent as he looked at the sky. For a tiny, insane second, he believed he saw some blue in there. *I'm going insane. Even more so.* But the boy next to him made even insanity sound so plausible and so refreshing. *I shouldn't be feeling like this. I have no right to be happy after what I've done.*

"An eternity," Damien held his hand, so cold, against his own burning skin. "You've punished yourself for an eternity."

"Or for a year. A month. A day. Time has no reign here."

"All the more reason to believe it's an eternity. Don't you think you've suffered enough?"

"No," he replied, simply. "Not enough. It'll never be enough. I killed everyone. I killed everything."

"Shhh... Breathe," the boy murmured in his ear. "Just, close your eyes and breathe."

Something in his chest lunged with each breath. Some fire within him started to subside. *I was in pain.* He thought he could never feel it, but it was just the constant existence of it that made him think so. With each breath, he felt himself getting colder.

"Open your eyes."

He did. The bright blue of the sky hurt his eyes.

"You were punishing yourself," the boy continued in the same calm voice. "Let it go... You have suffered enough."

"Do you really believe it so?"

"I do," Damien replied. "Maybe that's why I'm here — to show you, to tell you that it's time."

"Time for what?"

"Forgiveness?"

"I cannot forgive myself."

"You did what your nature called you to do." Is it really that simple? "It's time everything started anew." Maybe it is.

"It's mission accomplished for you."

"I don't know. It feels like it."

"You need to go," Thyren said. It wasn't a response, not really, not one that he wanted to get. "You need to move forward. This is not the place for it."

"How do you even know that?" Damien asked, bitter. Tethers are pulling me already. He ran his fingers through Thyren's hair. Nobody has been this gentle with me since... "But I want to stay with you."

"You need to move forward." It was more definite this time. "You need to go."

"But I won't be able to forget you. Or miss you."

"You will. Eventually. And it's okay. You've given me enough already, a permanent place in your memories is not something I can ask for."

"I won't forget you," Damien insisted. "But I'm going to ask something from you."

The sky shone blue above them, and Thyren said yes. He didn't even need to hear what to say it, he would do anything, now that he could hear the weak pulse of the actual universe in his ears. Soothing, comforting. His heart skipped beats in yearning.

Damien reached and kissed him. What it lacked in passion, it made up in compassion. Thyren stopped breathing.

"Oh, you're so beautiful," he murmured. "My King, my apocalypse, Thyren... Promise me one thing."

"Anything."

"Keep the weapons you forged for me. I'll know they are here. I'll call for them in a time of need."

"Forever," Thyren nodded, all serious. "They will be kept here, as long as I live, until you need them."

Damien reached to him, and kissed him again. A silent farewell between them it was, a silent prayer, a silent promise.

"Build it from the ground," the boy said once they separated. "Build it brick by brick. I'll return here one day, and you'll be sitting on a golden throne as you deserve."

With that he disappeared.

CHAPTER 7

Carrying his body from one timeline to the next was a pleasant surprise. Not dying, not being dragged, but instead, following a hunch. Why these places? He couldn't bring himself to care at this point.

It was a lively world, and he made sure he stayed as far as he could from the gods above or below. I am done with that shit. The universe could go and fuck itself for all he cared, for he was tired with it all. I've saved one from the brink of extinction. That should count. He didn't know who assigned him this still, but he felt successful for once. He was going to cherish it.

"Hey," he asked a random passerby. "What city is this?"

"Hysseren, Gardens District," the man replied. "Rough night?"

"Been on a bender," Damien laughed. "Thanks, man."

He had been in Hysseren, different versions of it, granted, but still the same city. Most probably, districts with the best food and drinks were the same. At least he hoped so.

He felt the strain in his chest, no mistake there. All the cogs, all the systems behind this universe were straining, grinding hard, but he didn't care. He couldn't. He didn't have any strength left.

He saw a little cafe, and walked in there. The door opened with a tiny bell, and a waiter asked how if he was on his own or if any friends would be joining.

"Alone," he said, absentmindedly. "On my own, sorry."

Waiter didn't seem to care. He just led Damien to a small table near the window, and handed him a menu. "I'll be back in a few to take your order."

"Thanks."

Garden District wasn't active at that hour in the morning. He watched a biker fell off his bike, and two people helping him out. He turned his head from the fine moment of humanity to his rusted watch, only to see it was perfectly fine and shining, working perfectly. He softly touched the face of the watch to make sure it was correct. Ten in the morning, at weekend. It was satisfactory.

"Are you ready to order?"

"Yeah, I'll have the pancakes and coffee, please."

"Right away."

He realised in a giddy feeling that he didn't have any money. It wasn't an issue. Almost as if every single nerve ending in his body crackled with electricity, he was filled with energy and the unshakeable belief that he could do and get and make and achieve anything, with just a snap of his own fingers.

I am Chaos, he thought, as his own confidence roared thunder within him. He was looking at the families riding their bicycles, but the only thing in his mind was the fact that he was Chaos, and the power he actually wielded. I can do anything. I can be anything.

The waiter put a coffee mug, and a plate full of pancakes in front of him.

"Anything else, sir?"

"No, thank you."

Before he started, he snapped his fingers and felt a heaviness in his pocket. Good. Money. He desperately wished Madison to be there. She would mock him for his comedic attempts at adapting, but she would also lend him an ear and guide him. I need guidance. His thoughts wandered to a certain god, almost immediately. Oh. If he couldn't find himself a guide, a father figure would work as well.

As he indulged in the delicious pancakes, a terrifying thought spread like ice in his mind, putting off any fire he had left from his unexpected burst of self-belief: It was his entirety that came here, instead of his consciousness occupying some other Damien's body. Is there another Damien here? He thought over it as he savoured the syrup. Somehow I'd feel him if he existed.

He shook his head to get rid of the thoughts. It could wait at least until after lunch.

*

Playing the tourist was quite the fun, and fun was he hadn't experienced in a while. He couldn't help but feel a comforting excitement every time he used his power for something minor, even just booking into a hotel with absolutely fake — so fake that it was real at that point — identity had him grinning like an idiot once he entered his room. I could live like this, he thought as he turned the shower on, hot water raising steams. I could live here forever and ever. I would be fine with that.

A period of inactivity after a strenuous series of running and chasing after some duty he felt imposed to do, even though he had no idea who imposed it to him. I have no past. I have no future. He didn't even know if he could continue to live after achieving the goal of saving the timeline, or if he would simply die of happiness and move on to another life trying to do the same. A never ending number of timelines and just one guy trying to save them. Poetic. Heroic. He was neither of those things.

As he submerged into the water, the hot water relaxing his clenched-more-than-they-should-have muscles, he closed his eyes. He thought of the leytian, the god, the king. He thought of the kind prince, the one that was torn up, the one that died far before. I would have nobody feeling sorry if I died. Truth was he didn't know. He didn't know about anything, about his own past, about his own life. Who was I before all these? The Damien persona he adopted felt more or less the same in everywhere he went, but it didn't feel like him. Carefree, fun, but also knowing things he didn't know. Sewing up the universe. Who would've thought? Maybe he should get some embroidery lessons as a part of his vacation, just in case.

He reached for the soap, and watched it create little bubbles between his fingers. He washed his hair, his body — he desperately wanted to wash the disappointment, the sadness, the failure off of him. Something in his chest tugged him, but he paid no attention to it. He washed, he rinsed, and he washed himself again. Just this once, I get to live.

He felt the water dripping off of him as he stepped outside. Looking at his own reflection made everything feel more real, it made him feel alive. He saw his own striking blue eyes, his own fresh face with a few wrinkles between his brows etched in there. His hair looked darker now that it was wet, but after all, he looked alive. This body wasn't mine. He carved a house for himself in that mind, memories of a far gone universe etched in. Every wall, in the house he made, was full of photos, pictures, notes, lines connecting things to other things. Shame all the notes were in a language he could not decipher. I would like to know who you are, whom did I steal this body from? Some part of him wanted to believe all the Damiens were there, in him, just waiting for the right moment to wake up, and take over. You'd finish my misery. Alas, he carried on.

He didn't even bother willing himself clothes when he laid down on the bed, and closed his eyes.

*

Damien dreamt.

Not of Madison, not of her memories. Not of the any other place he had been so far. He dreamt, and he dreamt of being free. He dreamt of cutting all the tethers and flying. He dreamt of hands so gentle as they touched him, he dreamt of being loved. He dreamt of the stars falling down, in burning brilliance, and Damien dreamt of himself watching it with pure bliss.

When he woke up it was already late. His heart ached with the absence of that true bliss, yet he grinned like an idiot as he dressed up to blend into the night life of the still-alive city. Almost out of habit he looked at the sky to see the ash raining down, or the burning stars, but neither were there. Hysseren was a normal city under stars that were barely visibly because of the city lights rivalling them — and winning for the most part, for they were closer — this timeline he was in didn't feel like it was doomed, and Damien was okay with that.

Before going out, he made sure dropping by the lobby to ask for a good bar. "Something with loud music and horrible drinks," he laughed.

"Well," the receptionist chuckled back as she produced a tourist map. "I'm sure all the options are listed here. Enjoy!"

Muttering something about intending to it, Damien took a simple glance at the map, and then decided to walk instead of appearing there. Chilly night air invading his lungs calmed something in him, and it was good to see some people, especially youngsters just like him, who were rushing to get a sip of their very short lives. Laughter filled the air as he reached to a street full of bars and restaurants, chatter and music accompanied it. There were couples, there were friends, and not one of them seemed like they were worried about tomorrow. He saw a red dressed girl running, and moved a step to let her pass, but she was cackling, as a boy in a blue suit followed her with the same cheer.

He walked into one of the bars, and as the music became loud enough to deafen him, he felt himself smiling. The strain in his chest, the missteps of his heart were replaced by the rhythm. He moved through to get something to drink, or a bottle, or anything basically, but his eyes got caught on a familiar sight: Blonde hair, sky blue eyes, gentle smile. Oh, fuck no. He wasn't going to deal with Haylen again.

He walked out of it to find some place else.

*

For the third time, his morning came with a surprise — annoying, this time. For the third time, he expected to wake up in a bed, his own maybe, but in a bed with his companion from last night, a very handsome man whose smile brightened Damien's day — but instead he opened his eyes in what he suspected to be the Garden District. I must have died last night, he thought for the first two times, but it was enough.

Just to be certain, he waved his hand to a random passerby. "Hey, what city is this?"

"Hysseren, Gardens District," the man replied, looking somewhat familiar doing so. "Rough night?"

"Been on a bender," Damien found himself saying, a cold crept through him. "Thanks, man."

Okay. It doesn't mean anything. If these are different timelines, maybe people other than gods are the same. He spotted a small cafe, and he thought of creating some money for himself before entering there. I can do it any time I want. Still, he felt secure. Playing the game right, at least.

He entered the cafe as he did before morning, the bell chimed as it did before. So far so good. The same waiter from before asked him if he was on his own or any friends would join him, Damien refrained from saying alone, this time.

"On my own," he said.

The small table he sat yesterday was empty again. "I'll be back in a few to take your order."

"Thanks."

Pancakes and coffee, just like before, he thought, raising his right wrist to look at the time. Oh good to know our taste in watches was just the same. He suspiciously touched the watch face to align it, it was beyond him why it was not working correctly, and he realised something but couldn't put his thoughts into words. Two to ten in the morning, at a weekend. He looked at the window and watched a biker falling, and two people helping him out. He frowned, but before he could form a coherent thought, the waiter cleared his throat to get his attention.

"Are you ready to order?"

"Yeah, I'll have the pancakes and coffee, please."

"Right away."

There was something wrong, but what exactly, he didn't know. He didn't want to care. For once, he wanted to remain passive and then watch the stars fall through the sky, burn everything to ashes. He savoured the pancakes like yesterday, using his bitter coffee to cleanse his palate, and thought of ordering some desserts after it. He didn't have an early in the morning concept, it was all the same, and he was dying all the same after all. Why am I dying to wake up in a copy of the same universe, though?

Garden District was calm. People in different timelines must have been acting the same after all. Or are they? What is the key difference that makes it a different timeline, then? It must have been something about the gods, he was sure. He forced himself not to care. Focus on the food, Damien. The warm and giddy excitement of yesterday left its place to cold and spiky worry, however. He raised his head in defiance, and signalled to the waiter. "Can I please get some chocolate ice cream, please?"

"Sure, it'll be a few minutes."

If I do different things, I'll survive, he thought. Gone was his confidence, it was too late. Somewhere in him wanted to go back, way back, to that desolate timeline, where Thyren was. At least I wasn't in danger there. Or maybe even further, and in time as well. He could maybe find Antenyr and Haylen, to warn them, and would stay there. He searched within himself to feel his connection, something that would point him in the right direction. He only could find a thread leading back to Thyren's place. Everything else before that felt dead. Burnt at one end.

Before the ice cream could come, he paid the bill in full with some extra to tip, and ran to the street. It was raining, just like yesterday, but Damien didn't care about it. He didn't care about people staring at him as well. A part in his mind said Look for the threads, and he did. He raised his hands and there they were, slim, gossamer threads that were shining. Everyone had lots, going through different parts of their bodies. They must be where they are connecting to other things and other people. A good discovery.

He lowered his head to see himself. He expected many threads tugging him to different directions, but there was only a thick one, frayed at some places. It was as if someone a knife and swung it through the rope, with no regards for an aim and a purpose. Burned ends, and only one going through his back. He tugged it, thinking the onlookers must be thinking how crazy he was. They will all be dead. Who cares what they think? He smelt the burned soil, and the dust. In my past, stands Thyren's timeline. Why not the other three?

"We need to talk," someone put their hand on Damien's shoulder, and they both disappeared.

CHAPTER 8

"Oh, great," Damien scoffed when they appeared inside a palace. "Flerketer. I hate this place."

"You've been here before?"

"Not this Flerketer, not with you. It's my schtick. I keep dying and reappearing in other timelines. But this doesn't feel like I'm dying and reappearing."

"Because it isn't," Haylen sat on one of the couches and leaned back. "This is a loop. You start at the same place every day, but unlike other people, you do different things."

"A loop?" Damien asked, sitting across him. "Oh, just the thing we needed. A loop. Just as a heads up, I'm not helping you save this place."

"Don't worry, I'm trying instead of everyone."

"Is your father alive?"

"He is."

"Start from him. I've been through how many timelines I have no idea, but in every one, he was at fault." He took a deep breath, groaning. "I'm afraid to ask about..." He paused. "I don't even know what he's called here. It's either Anthyren, or Antenyr, or Thyren. What happened to him?"

"You knew him?"

"Some versions. Is he okay?"

Haylen smiled, bitter. "He died a long time ago. When he found out he was a God."

"Who killed him?"

"He didn't leave that honour to anyone else... I can say it was a hard period for everyone."

Damien nodded. Damn it. Haylen's absence wasn't as shocking in the previous timeline, it was devastated anyway. But he thought it was all fine here. He somewhat expected them to see happy, just like they were when they were just two princes, courting each other.

"Who are you?" Haylen asked, leaning forward. His voice was barely audible, as if he was asking for a secret.

"I'm..." Damien paused. "I don't know. I'm supposed to be Damien, but I don't know if you know him."

"Can't say I'm familiar."

"Some people called me Ashren," he offered. "Chaos. But I really don't know. There is not a me anymore. I am not sure if there was even one to begin with."

Haylen waved his hand to make a bottle and two glasses appear. It must have been the signature of hospitality in Flerketer. Slow in his movements as he filled the glass, but the sincerity was there when he offered one to Damien. "Tell me your story," he said. Damien heard his own voice echoing, in his head. It made him smile. "And I'll tell you mine."

To his credit, Damien told his story, in full. It was a stupid story, and as he told Haylen, he realised even more and more he was just like a leaf drifting away with minimal agency. Nothing I did worked. Then why am I still running to the same goal? He wanted to scream, he wanted to fall on his knees and cry, but he was all grown up now. How old was I again? He was stronger than that, he wasn't going to break down.

Haylen listened to him very carefully. "Have you ever thought maybe your purpose isn't to save those universes, but let them perish? You're the Chaos after all."

"That doesn't make any sense," Damien replied. "How can I continue bringing the chaos if the universe I'm supposed to wreck havoc in dies? No, I should save it first. I won't be able to stop until I finally manage it."

"Like you did with your previous universe."

"I should find names for them, but yes. I didn't die there. I mean, I don't want to die here as well, but I'm tired, can you see my predicament?"

"Of course," the god nodded, ever so serious. "Though I still think you've misunderstood your goal, and I really shouldn't be the one convincing you, but that is how it feels." He paused. "Though it is weird that you almost never saw the end of them. You always died before those timelines could be eradicated."

"I'm feeling like I'm being tugged towards somewhere," Damien admitted. "There's a thread going through me. There were a lot of threads going through me. They all... got cut. I don't know if it was supposed to be like this, or something else but I'm worried to say the least." He smiled, as he finished his glass, and refilled it. "But now, it's time for your story."

Haylen waved his hand dismissively. "Oh, it's nowhere near as exciting as yours..."

*

Haylen was right about one thing. It wasn't exciting. The story he told was simply heart wrenching.

The universe was about to end, there was no question to that. Haylen knew that. He almost didn't care, he almost couldn't bring himself to care — his wound still fresh, still bleeding under bandages. He had just put a lover beneath the ground, and maybe even wished for everything to end. He was angry at everyone, and the only way he could dealt with it was hiding from them. His father, his kids, his family. He didn't want to see any of them.

But the universe was about to end, and Haylen spent enough time with a rebel leytian who cursed the gods for being selfish. He knew he was being selfish. Whatever was going on, it hurt him as well — it started with bruises, and continued with open wounds. He felt the energy filling him, but it was soon, too soon. He wanted to find a solution. Simply, there was not enough time.

"So," he concluded. "I stopped time. I couldn't halt it fully, I would-I would have to..." His voice trailed off, and he shook his head. "I forced everything to a loop, so nobody dies. Everything repeats, nothing changes. I am the only one who can act different every day — or I was, until you came along."

"Yeah, I truly regret it."

"I wouldn't blame you if you ran away," Haylen conceded. "You have already been through a lot. But you could help."

"The most help I can be to you is to kill your father." I have something else, maybe. "I can do it for you. You would understand if you've cracked it, right? If it worked?"

"I believe so."

"Then allow me to do so." What exactly am I thinking? Sylen will kill me again. "And if I fail to kill your father, that is what you need to try."

"Are you really sure?"

"If it doesn't work, he'll be back alive the next day. I've never had a chance to try it after all," he shrugged. "He killed me."

He extended, and opened his right palm, and snapped his left fingers. A knife appeared on his hand, pure black from blade to hilt. I am not in trouble, he thought. But I'll create trouble.

"What is that?" Haylen leaned forward, inspecting the knife without touching it. "Its energy feels a little familiar."

"A knife forged out of pure destruction," Damien answered.

"Thyren did it for you? In the... In the desolate place?" The yearning in his voice was tangible, it pierced Damien's heart like tiny needles.

"Yeah... I'll kill your father with it. Hopefully, I'll do it before he can kill me."

"If the risk is high—"

"Don't worry," Damien shrugged. "I'll just reappear somewhere else."

*

Sylen's throne room was the same. It was always the same to the point Damien felt like he was home when he saw it. For the most part, Sylen himself was the same as well. He played the King of Everything spiel far too well. Maybe because he was actually the king of everything, but the point where it brought him was truly depressing.

"So," Damien said, tired more than confident. "I'll cut to chase. This universe is dying. You know it, I know it, everyone knows it. It's your fault, and my theory is that your death will solve it."

Sylen greeted him with a big smile on his face. "So you're Chaos."

"In the flesh."

"Nice to meet you."

"I've met you so much times I don't remember most of it. In half, you killed me. In the remaining half, I died or the universe ended. So I'm not on that friendly terms with you."

"That's a shame."

"You've killed Madison as well, though."

"Unfortunately..." He lowered his head. "I can say your animosity towards me is justified." He waved his hand to create a chair for Damien. "Please sit down. Let's talk."

Damien did as he said, his knife in his hand.

"I'm not gonna tell my story," he said. "I've said it for too many times, and I'm tired of hearing it. Instead, you tell me. Why did you try to force an order that shouldn't have been?"

"I wasn't," Sylen replied, shrugging. "I was trying to reach to the the balance. That's my goal. But the balance means the end of the universe as we know it, and I was too successful." He looked solemn as he said that. "I didn't know it would lead to the death of my own child."

Damien stared at him. "What?"

"You didn't expect that, I presume."

"Of course I didn't."

"But it's the truth. I know he has been keeping the universe in a loop to prevent that. I have found no other way than dying, but I have yet to muster the courage. I guess you being here leaves me no other choice."

Damien let a relieved breath. "You're not going to kill me?"

"I see no reason to." Sylen smiled, gentle. "You've been through a lot, Ashren."

The young man pinched the bridge of his nose. "I have. A lot. A bad lot. There were a lot of timelines I couldn't save. A lot of timelines that just died. I watched stars burning. Who knows what else." It was hard not telling, especially knowing someone would finally understand. But he wasn't going to. My story shouldn't be about failures only. He was alive now.

"We all make sacrifices," Sylen said. He wasn't condescending, but wasn't compassionate either. "You with your many lives. I with my only one. Haylen," he sighed. "With the ones he care about so much. Did he tell you how he keeps this place in a loop?"

Damien shook his head. "He is the Universe personified, isn't he? I figured there was a way."

"There is always a way," Sylen conceded. "Some good, some bad. Some in between, but hurtful. Unfortunately for Haylen, it's the latter."

"What is it? Does he have to sacrifice a bunch of kittens in order to keep the place alive?"

"I think given the option, he would prefer the sacrifices, so no. No. He has to keep his son in a permanent coma, one that he placed the kid himself — unfortunate side effects of your son controlling the time."

Sylen made it sound so easy, no matter how upsetting, but in that moment, Damien felt so small. It was as if the walls got taller, Sylen and the room expanded, all of a sudden. I wouldn't do it, he thought. But to keep everyone alive? In a coma is better than dead. The doubt still stayed there. I couldn't sacrifice that much. I wouldn't.

"You're dead in another universe," he blurted instead. "It's all over, and you're dead."

"Expected. Did I die with the universe?"

"Yes, and no. If by the universe you mean Haylen, no. But with the actual universe, yes."

"I'm hoping it was painless."

Damien didn't know. He didn't know if Thyren there showed them any mercy and granted a painless death. He didn't think so. Maybe that's why he was punishing himself. He made everyone suffer. "Thyren killed you."

With that Sylen gave a hearty laugh. "Oh, that would win another one of my brothers a great bet."

"A bet?"

"They all bet on what Thyren would do once he found out he was a God. One brother of mine said Thyren would kill me."

"It was after and because Haylen's death," Damien shrugged. "I think nobody won that bet."

"Regardless," Sylen said. "It hurts my heart just a bit to know they loved each other in other timelines as well. It's a good hurt. Every parent dreams to see their child is loved by others as much as they are loved by them."

"I wouldn't know. I've never had parents." I've had a father. In a different timeline. He died as well. And he was not my father.

"Oh," Sylen murmured. "How did you come to be?"

"I don't know." A shrug. "I don't even remember much of my past."

They exchanged looks for a while, in silence. A silent understanding between a man with no future, and a man with an unknown one. I'm not even the master of my fate. At least he controls the time of his own death.

"Go away," said Sylen at last. "Run away. Don't look back. We'll be fine. I'll make sure of it."

Damien nodded. "I'll be back. One day. I'll be back."

"If everything goes as planned, I won't be here to see it," he laughed bitterly. "So as a parting gift, I'll give you an advice."

Damien raised from his seat the moment Sylen did, and as the King of the Universe walked to him, he felt less small. I matter, he repeated to himself. I can succeed. I can do what I'm supposed to do.

Sylen hugged him. It felt like eating something after months worth of hunger, it felt like quenching his thirst after days without water. Damien felt electric beneath his skin, felt warm, and felt in peace. I would be okay with dying here. But the addition quickly followed. Dying and never waking up again.

"You can't blame an anchor for doing what it does best," Sylen said when they finally separated. "It's job is to keep you where you are. If you want to move forward, what you need to do is either lifting it up, or getting rid of it entirely."

"If I got rid of it, I wouldn't be able to stop."

Sylen chuckled. "That's the thing about anchors, dear boy... You can always make a new one. Besides," his eyes gleamed. "Why would you want to stop? You're not a delicate flower, you're not an old tree. You can go anywhere, why would you want to stop?" He put one hand on the young man's shoulder. "Run, and never look back."

So Damien ran.

Chapter 9

When Damien ended up where he did, he was in a physically bad shape but emotionally great. None of his wounds healed after his brawls with humans, but he was too tired to care about it. I am alive. I am alive. He was bleeding, but he didn't care. I am alive. I am alive. I am alive.

He walked. It was hard with all the pain and the wounds, but he walked. Around him were trees, near him was a small river. He found solace in them, he found power. The scent of the evergreen trees became his strength to put one foot in front of the other. The river whispered its love to him, acknowledging his exhaustion. Just one more, one more step. He stopped once the river ended.

In front of him was a white palace, made of the prettiest of marbles by a very masterful hand. It looked seamless, as if carved out of a single block. The sun shone in such a way, Damien felt like he was looking at something divine, something blessed by all the gods in unison, constantly. It reeked of power, so familiar, so comfortable. It felt like home.

Nobody stopped him, so he continued in, passing the garden in what felt like a few steps. Every muscle in his body screamed at him, but he didn't stop. His heart was a bird in his chest, trapped in a cage, knowing what lied ahead — even before Damien himself did. Then he saw.

Here he was, not amidst ruin, not in desolation. Here he was, in all his glory, dressed in blackest of blacks, with a thin white band on his head. Here he was, sitting at the steps of the palace, his eyes closed, basking in the sun. Damien wanted to scream, he wanted to cry, he wanted to run to the man and wrap his arms around him, but he stopped before doing any of those. Wait, he thought. I couldn't have gone back.

As he stood there, drowning in indecision, the man took notice of him and frowned. And before he could come any closer, Damien fainted.

*

When he opened his eyes, he found a curious face staring at him, but it wasn't an angry curiosity — on the contrary, it had a lot of compassion in it. Damien's heart ached, every part of him wanted to do something different, all equally stupid, all equally afraid.

"Do you know me?" He asked instead.

"No, unfortunately," the man replied. "But you seem to know me."

"Maybe in another time, maybe in another place. Which name do you go by?"

The man smiled. "You have a lot of courage, considering you came here uninvited."

"Nobody invites me, I just appear in places," Damien replied, all exhausted. "Your name, please?"

"Thyren," the man replied. "Do you know my other names?"

"Anthyren Hyiressen, or Antenyr." The tortured leytian, and the gentle prince. "I knew of a Thyren as well."

"Oh, really?"

"The Destroyer. The King of Ashes. Sitting on a throne at a desolate palace, ruling the dust and ruin."

Thyren's lip twitched, and slightly curled into what should have been a smile. "I rule a universe here," he said, his voice clear. Both of his eyes were the blue of the sea. "So, who are you, then?"

"Damien. Ashren. God of Chaos. Or the Chaos himself." It rang hollow in his ears. He felt so small, so insignificant. He lowered his head to avoid Thyren's curious looks. "I don't know. I could never understand the difference."

"A god?" Thyren tilted his head, as if he was examining an artefact. "Who are your parents?"

"I don't know. I don't think I have any. Though in another timeline, my mother was Juventas and my father was Martyn, if that makes any sense."

Thyren let a hearty laugh. "The confusing speech must be coming from Martyn for sure." He patted Damien's head, as he got up. "I'll send someone to take care of your wounds. Go to sleep after that. Gods know you look like you need a year's rest. You're safe here."

You have no idea, Damien thought, and closed his eyes. For all he knew, he could trust yet another Thyren.

*

Thyren left the room in utmost silence, and desperately wished for someone who could nudge him in the right direction now. Things to take care of, things to learn. He signalled to one of his servants, and explained the situation to him in a hushed tone. "Make him comfortable," he added at the end. Is this a mistake? Is he dangerous? He couldn't fathom anything that could be a danger to him, and he wasn't even sure if he would care about being in danger.

Sitting on a throne at a desolate palace, ruling the dust and ruin.

The kid had said in another timeline. For all Thyren knew, there were only two person who would know about timelines, and only one of them seemed to be the kid's father, so no matter how much he hated being spoken in riddles, he saw no other choice. He headed to the doors.

In the palace, there were many doors. Most of them opened to pretty guest bedrooms, bathrooms, and Thyren was pretty sure one of them lead to a kitchen. But there were also doors that would take him wherever he wanted to go — dear brother of his would call it a speed dial for travel, but it was just convenience. Appearing in someone's living room was more polite if you could just knock a door twice beforehand.

He climbed the stairs, slowly, but surely. Ashren, he repeated to himself. Chaos. As if he needed any more chaos in his life than he already had. It had been a while since anyone called him Anthyren, it had been a longer while since anyone even remembered that name. It brought a bitter smile on his lips, one that he didn't intend to have, for with the name an influx of memories followed. He gripped the railing, the coldness of the marble brought him back to the present, but he hesitated looking back, even for a second — as if there were hands that would never lose their grip on him, if he ever lost his own.

Will you be happy?, the voice in his head asked as he reached to the top floor. The voice that he could never hush, the one that kept talking in a ghost's voice, haunting him from the day one. Do you think all your problems will be solved just here?

No, he thought, his posture straightened. I knew nothing would be fine. I knew I wouldn't be happy, not now, not ever. I lost that opportunity. The doors stood there, no different than their ordinary counterparts, aside from the places they opened to. But I needed to take my revenge, and by gods it was a belated one. I won't apologise for that.

He knocked the door before opening it, and then reached to the knob. No more riddles, he wished as he opened it. The smell of pine trees hit him in the face, refreshing, and calm. He walked in, to be greeted by a short haired woman standing right in front of him.

"He's been waiting for you in the library," she said.

"Oh, so he knew I was coming."

She smiled. "He knows everything."

Don't I know it? "Please lead the way, Valentine."

"Pleasure." She turned her back and started walking, sure that Thyren was following her. "You look awful. Not like a reanimated corpse awful but, extremely malnourished in a dungeon awful."

"Some improvement there then," Thyren admitted. "You look the same as always."

Honestly, he could never understand Martyn's relationship with his servants. They seemed to be privy to all his secrets, and for someone like Martyn, it was no small feat. All of them, but Valentine the most, had an undying loyalty to the guy — which often made Thyren curious. What did he do to earn it? What did they do to earn his?

"Here you go," she pointed towards the library entrance. "We're all very excited, I must admit."

"Excited for what?"

"The princeling, of course." She laughed. "Go on in, he'll tell you."

Thyren had always found the library in Martyn's place peaceful. There was the dusty smell of the books and the shelves that went on for days, but it was never dark and intimidating. It felt like a maze of knowledge, in all honesty, one that was entertaining to get lost in. But today was certainly not about the books, as he took the shortest path to the windows, knowing Martyn would wait him there, hopefully alcohol ready. I simply don't have the strength.

He wasn't wrong of course, as Martyn straight up pointed at the chair across him, and handed him a glass the moment he sat down. His eyes gleamed with a different light when he spoke.

"So," he started. "Damien."

"You know him?"

"Of course!" He threw his hands into the air, not being able to contain his smile. "I have been waiting for him for a long time."

"So what he says is true then?" Thyren raised his eyebrows. "He's your kid."

"Maybe in another timeline," Martyn shrugged. "But that's no reason for me to reject him here. He has suffered on his own enough."

Thyren had no objections there — the misery radiated from the kid, from his mimics, from his voice. That was pure exhaustion, pure resignation. Suffering had a pretty familiar smell, after all. Thyren had its own share of it.

"What's his deal, then?"

"He's been travelling from timeline to timeline," Martyn said. "I was only aware of it after our paths crossed in a different one. He was lost, he was desperate, and he did his best. That timeline ended."

"He's destroying the timelines?" Now that was a threat, that was danger. Of course. Chaos. It's designed to throw a wrench in everything.

"Not precisely," Martyn replied. "He's been trying to save them. Trying to keep it from reach the equilibrium. Then he died, and it was hard to get ahold of him."

That confused Thyren. "So he's the good guy?"

"One day, my dear friend, you'll understand the universe doesn't work in binaries. Neither do gods. That's not our function."

"We must preserve the mechanisms beyond our comprehension," Thyren sighed. "Yes. I've been given this speech a dozen times. What I want to know is, if he's a danger." He raised his hand. "Besides, let's not forget we had an actual bad guy until I..." He paused to find a better word than murdered, decapitated, spilled his guts all over the floor, got my revenge. "... took care of him."

"Yes, yes, but he's beside the point." Martyn leaned forward. "We're talking about Damien here, and there are no binaries when it comes to him." There was pride in his voice, loud and clear. He really sees him as his son. It tinged somewhere in him, some place that was long forgotten, a dull pain he got used to. "Damien is all about new possibilities."

Thyren was less excited. "If he's only been in places to save those timelines, maybe we're reaching to our end and he's here to stop it?"

Martyn dismissed that concern with a wave of his hand. "We should be fine."

"That's really reassuring."

"You're a big boy, Thyren, you surely don't expect my reassurance." He leaned back, with that playful twinkle in his eyes as always. "We should be fine. Besides, we are a bunch of all powerful beings. We can surely stop an apocalypse."

Thyren didn't say anything about how he wouldn't even lift his pinky finger to save this universe, as he nodded.

*

Damien didn't sleep. He couldn't.

Sure he was all patched up and in bandages, he even had a relaxing bath and it did wonders on his nerves, no doubt there. He asked for something to eat, and the servants provided. He asked for a drink, and they rushed to get it. But still, there was the inherent fear that all of this would end, or everything would begin again. The tugging in his chest was pronounced as ever.

So, he took a walk.

He was certain some servants were following him, in a respectful distance, but being trailed was still being trailed. It bothered him, and it hurt him — the clear distrust aside, it was belittling to his powers. Yeah, as if I haven't died ten times or something. He didn't say anything though. He kept walking in the big garden, taking mental notes of little places he wanted to hide away, under the trees there, behind the building here. He wanted to jump in the clear pool, the water must have been warm under the water — his bones would appreciate that. Not yet. He wasn't even certain if he wanted to stay here, right here, but he could at least enjoy it as long as he did.

He was walking in a haze, paying too much attention to little things, and very little attention to bigger ones. He blamed it on exhaustion when he crashed into someone, and knocked her on the ground. "I'm sorry," he said, extending his hand to her, she looked angry as she accepted it. He pulled her on her feet, and let a small oh, as he recognised her.

"Watch where you're going," she said, a bunch of butterflies spinning on her head. It looked like she had a crown of them there. "Who are you?"

"Damien," he said, simply. "And you are Saellin."

She didn't look surprised he knew that. "Nobody calls me that here. It's Jennifer." She frowned. "Can't say I've ever heard of you, though."

"I'm new to the scene," he admitted. "I'm the Chaos."

"Oh, good, we needed more of that." She shook her head. "By the way, do you know where the guy who's supposedly running all of these?"

"I have no idea. Why do you need him?"

"Because we're supposed to plan this huge Gathering and every-one on this forsaken Mountain keeps referring me to Thyren."

"We're not on a Mountain."

"I could not give less of a fuck about what we're on."

Damien started laughing. Jennifer frowned, even said something about how utterly disrespectful it was and how he was wasting her time, but he couldn't stop himself. It's not even funny. She was all the same, all caught up in the smaller details. Damien wanted to kiss her, right there, but instead, he offered her his arm. "Walk with me," he said. "We can spend some time as you're waiting for Thyren."

"I don't have much time to lose."

"You're a goddess, you have all eternity to lose. Come on. Let's walk together."

She seemed to consider his offer. "On one condition," she said.

"What's that?"

"You're gonna help me in the planning when I need you to."

He took an exaggerated bow. "Of course," he said. "Now, the walk?"

Reluctantly, she accepted the invitation, and they started walking together, slowly. Her sense of rush seemed to disappear.

"You look familiar," she murmured. "I can't put my finger on it."

"Maybe in another life," he replied. Maybe in another life we were together. The image of her smoking played in his mind, and he snapped his fingers. "Do you smoke?"

"Occasionally," she admitted.

"Is this one of those occasions?"

"It could be." He gave her one, and she took it. "You look really familiar. Or you remind me of someone else, and I'm confusing it with familiarity. All possible. Light?"

He snapped his fingers to light up both of their cigarettes, and they both inhaled their first breath of them. "I've been to many places," he said. "I've met you. Not you, you that stands here, but I've met other versions of you."

That information didn't surprise her. "Did I like you?"

"Let's say we both had a mutual understanding about many things. Feelings were beside that point."

And that was true. Damien didn't have much time to develop feelings for anyone, even in the timelines he stayed the longest. He felt detached from the emotions the poor souls in the bodies he occupied had. He knew Jennifer, of course he had, of course their paths had crossed. But they never looked at each other as anything other than some plaything they'd spend some time with.

She raised a doubtful eyebrow at that. "So, what are you doing here?"

I don't know. I never did. "Convalescence," he shrugged.

Before she could make the snarky comment he'd seen coming in her face, a loud voice said there you are, so their attentions were diverted to there immediately.

"Oh, just the man I was looking for," Jennifer said. "Your entire Court has been pointing at you for the Gathering plans."

"You should've gone to my assistants, instead of my Court — that's your mistake," Thyren said. "They are running things regarding that gathering. I'm just saying yes to whatever they suggest."

"Wonderful." She turned to Damien. "Thank you for the walk," she said. "See you in the Gathering."

With that she disappeared, leaving Thyren and Damien on their own.

"She's a handful," Thyren admitted. "I'd say Gerard and Juventas are spoiling her too much."

"Juventas," Damien frowned. "My mother, right?" Were we siblings in the timeline we met? The thought alone made his stomach clench.

"Not in this timeline, as much as I could gather." He smiled in a way that reminded Damien of the King of Ashes, which hurt his heart. That desolate place was maybe the only place he ever felt in peace. "Martyn wants to see you, though."

"Now?" He didn't want to sound afraid. He did sound afraid.

"I asked for a while, on your behalf. You were in a pretty bad shape when you came here." A gentle giant, Thyren was, no matter where he was, under what circumstances. Holy blade, architect of ruination, proud prince — all the same. All the same man under a different shell. Damien wanted to cry.

"Thanks," he said instead. "Last time I found myself in a running universe, there was a Gathering as well."

"It normally happens every twenty five years," Thyren said apologetically. "But the recent circumstances and the developments required it — more as a peace treaty."

"Was there a war?"

"We could say that." Thyren's lip twitched. "But don't tire yourself with these details — the Gathering will be fun, we all will get drunk for seven days straight, and it should be enough."

"So, we're actually on Earth?"

"Yes. Never been here?"

"No. I was strictly limited to Liffelen before, all types of it. Is Sylen alive?"

"Alexei?" Thyren shook his head. "No. He's the reason we're having the peace treaty."

"Oh, thank the sky above and ground below," Damien murmured. "One less thing to worry about."

"You were worried about him?"

"He usually runs the universe to the ground," he shrugged. "That's so good news. How did Haylen take it?"

"Why are you using their formal names?"

"Those are the only names I know of them." Damien shrugged. "It's hard keeping track of all of it."

Thyren nodded. "In that case... Haylen died before Sylen did."

Fuck. "Oh... I—I am sorry."

"Don't be." He shrugged. "It takes getting used to, but we get used to everything."

"You loved him."

"Always." He sounded sincere as he said that. "Were we happy in other timelines?"

"All the other timelines had horrible ends. You don't wanna know the answer to your question."

By now, they long circled back to the palace. "You're bleeding," Thyren pointed at Damien's waist.

"I had a bandage there," Damien lifted his shirt to check it, no surprise it was soaked with blood. "I have no idea why it's not healing."

There was no reply to his unasked question. "Let's take care of that."

*

Thyren had none of Damien's objections, as he instructed him to lay down on the bed.

"Seriously," said Damien once again. "Thanks, really, but I can take care of it."

"Do I look like someone who argues about things?" Thyren finally said. "Lay down and take off your shirt. We'll clean the wounds first."

Damien did as he said, and stared at the ceiling until Thyren returned from the adjacent bathroom with a towel and some water in a porcelain dish.

"Does it hurt?" He asked as he peeled away the bandage.

"No," Damien replied through gritted teeth. "I'm just cold."

"Oh, you big baby," Thyren chastised him with a laugh. "How did all these happen?"

"Stumbled my way through many different timelines. Not everyone was as friendly as you."

It took all his strength not to shudder when he felt the touch of the wet cloth, but he managed it. Think of something else, he ordered himself, fixing his eyes on the ceiling. He wanted to look at Thyren, he wanted to stare at his eyes. He doesn't know who I am. But he looked the same, aside from a very significant few scars, he looked exactly the same. The way he carried himself, the way he talked to Damien — it was all the same. It was all different.

Once he cleaned the wound, Thyren moved on to apply some lotion, it burned as it made contact with the open wound, but Damien was grateful for the distraction. It was hard being near him, it was hard not being able to say everything he wanted to say. It was hard not imagining himself between those arms. He is not the same man, he reminded himself. But he wasn't very convincing.

Bandage came over the lotion, and Thyren was gentle, so very gentle. Tears started rolling down from his eyes, wetting the pillow.

"Sorry," the man murmured. "It'll all be over in a second." Damien didn't bother correcting him on why he was crying.

Once the one on his waist was closed, Thyren moved to the one on his collarbone, and Damien was sure he couldn't take this one. He wanted to scream get away from me. He wanted to beg him to get closer. A weak stream of blood surfaced each time his heart pulsed, and as Thyren's fingers touched there, his heart decided to demand an outing. Kiss me, he begged in his mind. Kill me. Or I will lose my mind. He didn't say anything. His jaw screamed in pain, his teeth felt like they were cracking, they had to be just because of the sheer amount of pressure he put on them, but he remained silent.

"They were so cruel," Thyren muttered, more to himself. "Why would anyone be this cruel?"

An easy question this was, easy to ask, easy to answer. They wanted the power. They wanted the capabilities. Everything was already dying, and they wanted someone to fix it. They were killing each other already. Damien was just one more casualty for them, someone nobody would look for. I've never had someone look for me when I was gone. I left places without even looking back. I had nobody taking care of me.

But right now, here he was, once again, on the verge of insanity. I am losing my mind, he wanted to scream. Can you help with that too? His mind was a tornado of memories, his heart was a horse rushing to the finish line. Can you put me back together and make me whole again? Can I be whole just once?

Thyren was so close. He was so far away.

Damien's entire body was shaking with sobs he was trying to swallow, and he could see it was worrying Thyren so he wanted to stop, he wanted to stop feeling, but he couldn't. Get it together, he ordered himself, over and over and over again. But damned if he wasn't so tired, of everything, of nothing. Maybe I should die already. I cannot handle this.

"Are you really that cold," Thyren interrupted his chaotic train of thought. "Or do you want to talk?"

I want to die a real and final death. "There's nothing I could say." You wouldn't believe me if I told you. You wouldn't listen. You are not him after all. "It's just... I'm so tired." and lonely. "It's been a while since..." Since what, Damien?

"Since?"

Don't say it, don't say it— "Since anyone's taken care of me."

In silence, Thyren put the bandage, and nodded. "You can wear your shirt now," he said.

I fucked it up. Damien did as he said. What is he going to say now? Will he send me away? Maybe he'll kill me himself and end this misery. He sat inside the bed, looking at the man. What now?

"Are you hungry?" Thyren asked.

"Am I— what?"

"Are you hungry?"

"I think so… I've had something to eat before walking in the garden but—"

"Great, I'll ask them to prepare the dining room." He smiled, and pushed Damien back to the laying down position. "Sleep until if you can. Refrain from walks for a while."

"Where are—"

"I'm around. You need to rest. I'll come pick you up when it's time for the food."

Damien watched him leave the room, and once the door closed behind him, he reached to a pillow. He buried his face in it, screaming his lungs out.

*

Thyren came face to face with Jennifer, almost at the same exact moment he left Damien's room.

"Oh, hey Jenny," he said, walking. He knew she would follow him. "Why don't you invite yourself in?"

"Ha ha, very funny," she rolled her eyes. "There is not a single locked door in this place, I assumed it's open invitation."

"I kind of assumed people would be hesitant to enter the actual destruction's house, but now I see my assumption was baseless." He saw her rolling her eyes again. "How can I be of any assistance?"

"What's the deal with Damien?"

"Really?"

"Of course. Is he a relative?"

"Of mine, or of yours?"

"Surprise me."

"It's either." Thyren shrugged. "He's confused. Or suffering from a selective memory loss. An objective mess, if you ask me. So, I'm gonna ask you refrain from pestering him."

"Me? Pestering? Oh how dare you?" She shook her head, though she didn't seem offended. "God of Chaos, though."

"Yeah, but Martyn says he's a-ok, and I think they are related, beyond me."

Jennifer skipped steps to get in front of him, and put her hand on his chest to stop him. "Will he be at the Gathering?"

"Is there a reason he shouldn't be?"

"No," she said. "I just want to be catering to all of our guests, and I have one guest that I know nothing about."

"Jenny, you know I don't care about the Gathering."

She sighed. "I know. I'm worried, that's all."

"We're all going to be there — bunch of gods with almost unlimited power, and you're worried of this one very tired, almost sickly kid?"

"He has an edge," Jennifer said. "Something I can't quite understand. It's like he knows all of us, but we know nothing of him."

"He's been through many different timelines," Thyren shrugged. "There must have been versions of us in those places. I see no reason to worry."

"Doesn't it really worry you? How long has it been since Uncle Alexei died? When finally everything's falling into place, Chaos appears on your door?" She folded her arms. "How do you even run a universe on your own?"

"By not caring about it." It was his turn at rolling his eyes. "Seriously, relax. If all of us could survive Alexei's death, we can survive the God of Chaos as well."

She didn't look like she believed it, but she refrained from arguing further. "How are you holding up?" She asked instead.

"Just fine," Thyren replied. It's like a fresh wound I cannot stop touching. "It takes getting used to still, but fine."

Jennifer nodded. "If you want to talk... I mean, I know we didn't get along that well, but feeling alone is hard."

"Thanks," he said, thinking of what Damien had said mere minutes ago. It's been a while since anyone's taken care of me. "I really appreciate it. And if you want to talk, I'm here as well."

She nodded. "Thanks. Anyways, I have to be going. There are things I need to take care of on the other side."

"Send your mother and father my best." He gave a small bow of his head. "Take care, Jenny."

"You too."

She disappeared, leaving a handful of butterflies in her wake. Thyren tilted his head back, with a sigh. I hate being a king. He raised his hand, and one of his servant came rushing.

"Sir?"

"Prepare the dining room," he said. "For two. Small table."

"Anything special you require, sir?"

He shrugged. "Just, plenty of food. And plenty of drinks. I'm sure we have some left from the last supply I got from Dionysus."

The servant looked unsure. "I might need to check, sir." It must have been the politest way of saying you have drank the entire stock, and it almost made Thyren laugh. "But we'll have plenty for the lunch, you can be assured."

He dismissed the man, and sighed once more. I hate living this life. What was the alternative? King of Ashes, Damien's voice replied. He made a note to himself to get the details from the kid.

He agreed with Jennifer on one thing. It was strange that Chaos appeared one day, just when everyone thought they could move forward. They would bury their hatchets, they would move on, they would get their new lives. It never stops. He desperately wished Axel to be here. He would get guidance, he would get counsel, he would find solace. I miss you so much. A part of him ached with that dull, usual pain.

It had been a year since the funerals. That was what he was calling it. A year since he started a near war on Liffelen, a year since he killed Alexei. Only a year, he had spent with nightmares, night terrors, sleepless nights. It felt like an eternity. And there was some part of him, a small part, still believed this was all a dream that he would wake up from. He would wake up and Axel would call him a sleepyhead, they would get along with their day. But every day he woke up to his own bed, on his own, loneliness crushing him every day, just a tiny bit more. He knew what being on your own did to one.

And now here it was, a young man of maybe twenty in front of him. Trying to pick up the crumbles, trying to pick up the pieces, he

ran without knowing where to go. Thyren recognised that look —
it was something he had seen every morning in the mirror. It was
exhaustion.

One of the servants rushed to him. "It's all ready, sir. Should we
alert your guest as well?"

"Thanks," Thyren replied, shaking his head as if he was waking
from a slumber. "I'll go to him myself."

*

Damien, unsure of what to do, sat in the chair and looked at his
surroundings. He had been in Flerketer, and seen enough lavish, of
course — that didn't surprise him. What surprised him was the man
in front of him, and Damien preferred looking at the decorations
instead of him. It's not him, he reminded himself again and again.
He was desperate to disagree with himself, still. He doesn't know
you. You don't know him. But he felt like he did.

"They are not poisonous," Thyren chuckled, seeing Damien not
eating anything. "You can eat them safely."

"That's not what I'm worried about. I don't die."

"Oh, really?"

Damien shrugged. "I just reappear in another timeline. I've already died many times."

"Death has this weird side effect," Thyren commented. "It keeps
you yearning for it once you return from it."

"I cannot say if I've ever returned from it. I remember my final
moments, some of them at least, then opening my eyes in a new
one. In a new body. This body is stolen."

"I'm pretty sure its owner wouldn't mind."

"Another Damien, in another timeline. Maybe he wouldn't mind.
Maybe he would."

Thyren filled his glass with wine, and leaned back. "Tell me about the King of Ashes."

Damien felt his stomach drop.

"Is it a touchy subject?"

"Yes, but not bad touchy." More like I missed him and I should have never left him bad. "He's someone I hold very dear."

"I could tell." Thyren hid his smile behind his glass, then took a bite from his food. "So. Would you want to tell?"

"I think what you want to know is how he ended up there." Damien tilted his head to left. You want to know so you can avoid being like him. "He started like you did. He lost Haylen. He killed Sylen. But while killing Sylen, he destroyed everything else along."

"With his powers."

"With his powers." Damien finished his glass. The wine was strong, not much to his taste. "So, you should be fine. If you haven't done so far, you're safe." He felt the bitterness of his own voice, and it wasn't intentional — but it was there. It's not a cautionary tale. My life isn't a cautionary tale.

"I know I'm safe," Thyren said, rather nonchalant. "He just felt closest to me among all the others you mentioned."

Damien looked at him, mouth agape. It's not him.

"You loved him," Thyren continued. "Didn't you?"

"We could say that."

"It must be hard for you. Can't you go back there?"

He didn't want me to stay. "I haven't tried." He tried taking a bite from his food, but his mouth felt too dry. His hands were shaking when he reached to the glass of water. "I mean—" He wanted me to go away.

"I don't blame you," Thyren held his hand. Don't do this. Don't do this to me, I can't handle it. It's too much. "It's fine, take a deep breath."

"I have to go—" Damien took his hand back, stumbling as he hurried away from the table. "I'm sorry, I have to go—"

"Sure. It's okay." Thyren didn't even move an inch. "To where, though?"

"Amongst humans, somewhere far — I need to think and —" Away from you away from you away from you away from you away from you—

"Damien," Thyren said, finally getting up. "Can you please take a deep breath?"

He didn't know why he was feeling like this. He never thought love was something he was capable of feeling. He didn't know that he felt for a different version of the man in front of him was love. He just wanted to be near him, wanted to be under his wings again, to feel safe, secure, with no feeling of duty on his mind, no tugging at his chest.

He slowly fell on his knees, and the tears were rolling down. There was something tearing his chest apart, shattering every single one of his ribs, his heart trying to escape it by fluttering inside. I wasn't like this, he thought to himself between the earthquake that was his emotional breakdown. I wasn't like this in the previous places.

But how many places has he travelled through? Maybe even died and didn't remember? Maybe I died after I ran. Maybe that's why I'm like this. Nothing was okay, he himself the least. Deep breaths were impossible, there was no place his lungs could expand. He felt small again, so small, as if the entire room expanded around him.

Thyren watched him from afar at the beginning. Then he came closer. In a swift movement, he picked Damien in his arms, carrying him through corridors and doors. He hated that he felt secure. They are not the same person.

They eventually reached Damien's room, and Thyren gently placed him on the bed. "Stay here," he said. "I'll have someone check up on you. Once you feel better, you can go anywhere you like. Okay?"

Damien nodded. Tears hadn't stopped. "I'm sorry," he said.

"It's not your fault, don't blame yourself," came the reply. "We all crumble." Thyren turned and walked to the door.

"Did you?" Damien blurted. "Did you crumble?"

The man's hand was on the door knob, his smile was bitter as he turned to Damien.

"I crumble every day," he said. "I'm used to it."

*

Martyn and one of his rather terrifying servants arrived the next morning. To be fair to himself, Thyren lacked a certain prerequisite to be terrified, which was the ability to feel fear, but still. Valentine was dangerous, for sure, but she wore the cute mask so well, it integrated into her face. This one, whom Martyn introduced as Ferran, had no qualms about looking as anything other than stoic — which was at the very best eerie.

"He's still sleeping as far as I know," he said instead of voicing his thought, the moment they were led to the dining room. "Breakfast?"

"The hospitality at work," Martyn laughed. "I'm not gonna say no. Ferran?"

"No, thanks," Ferran replied, sounding bored. "Can I walk around the perimeter until it's time to go?"

"Sure, go ahead." Martyn shrugged, and turned to Thyren with a smile. "They are like teenage kids sometimes."

"I don't understand what's their deal, honestly. Even Valentine, I get. But this one is weird."

"Now you're being hurtful." He spread butter over his toast. "All of them are unique and helpful in their own way. Ferran is an excellent strategist."

"He looks like he was brainwashed."

"I am not Alexei." Martyn's tone turned grim all of a sudden. The tone change was reflected in his eyes then. "How is Damien?"

"Had a breakdown at lunch yesterday, and been sleeping ever since. I'm having the guys here check up on him every hour."

"Oh that poor thing..." He filled a porcelain cup with tea. "It must be hard to get adjusted to a different timeline."

Thyren wished he could read minds, just so he could understand Martyn's angle in all these. He trusted him, no doubt there, but under all the trust, there was a certain caution as well. He wanted to ask what do you want from him? Instead, he sighed. "If he chooses to have breakfast, could you at least allow him to eat before you fry his mind with all the riddles?"

"He would understand my riddles," Martyn replied, but didn't argue further. "Is he really that bad?"

"He is on the brink of collapse."

"Is there anything anyone can do, do you think?"

But before he could answer, a bleary eyed Damien walked in with apologies falling from his lips, two servants of the house trailing him. "I would hate to intrude," he said, when he was done apologising. "But I'm famished, and I'm told there's food here."

Thyren couldn't help but laugh. "You look better."

"That's a start." He sat on the chair furthest from Thyren still, but his voice was normal. "I'm not interrupting anything, right?"

Thyren saw Martyn opening his mouth, but before he could say anything, "Of course not," he said. "We were just making small talk. Martyn is an old friend."

Damien didn't look entirely convinced, but that wasn't the goal anyway. He just wanted to set the tone for the breakfast. "Weather looks always the same," the kid said. "Doesn't it get boring after a while?"

"It does," Thyren agreed. "That's why I sometimes arrange holidays on Earth. Brother dear there knows the best places for it."

"You mean Anthony," Damien said. Thyren was aware the way Martyn watched them too, but he paid no conscious attention to it. "He's around then?"

"The Court is not his thing, but he is around. So you've met him as well?"

"During a breakfast," Damien murmured, shovelling food into his mouth. He swallowed everything with a big gulp of water, and then raised his head. "He was a good man."

"He is one of the best." And he's going to kill me once he finds out I'm harbouring the actual Chaos without telling him. "You seem to get your appetite back. It's a good sign."

"I've managed to get some sleep. It helps tremendously. Still, inter-timeline travel is something I advise strongly against."

"How many of them have you been in?" Martyn asked, as innocently as possible. Thyren wanted to kick him just for the audacity.

"I don't know," Damien shrugged. "It's hard to keep track of how many times you die and run to, you know."

He's progressed to apathy fast, Thyren thought, his heart tinged with jealousy. Apathy sounded a lot better than the mess of emotions he was in. Almost unconsciously he scratched his right wrist with his left hand, to get rid of an itch beneath his skin, and put the butter knife a little further than he needed to, once he was done.

Martyn was now talking about his Kingdom. Oh, good. He found himself getting great delight at watching Damien look alive. That's the deal, kid. We fall apart, and we pick up the pieces. Do it enough times, you'll be stellar. He wanted to teach him that. He wanted to tell him the truth. You will never be alright. You'll just get real good at pretending to be.

"... isn't that right, Thyren?"

"Huh?" Thyren shook his head, he didn't even realise he was phased out of the conversation. Martyn must have noticed that. "I missed, what were we talking about?"

"I was telling our guest here that the Gathering two weeks later will all be about reconciliation and celebration."

Thyren nodded. "Oh, yeah. My great apology to Liffelians for killing their king. They seemed really upset about it."

Martyn let a loud laugh. "Alexei wasn't universally beloved, I'll give you that. But his death wasn't that dignified, which usually is the breeding ground of contempt for his killer."

"Please," Thyren raised his hand, and took a bite out of his toast. The bread was far too cold by now. "They are extremely welcome to walk in here and finish me. I'd be the most thankful. That's why I've forgone the locks on the doors."

"As you see," Martyn returned to Damien. "We all enjoy making light of our own deaths. I'm pretty sure it'll rub on you soon enough."

"Death, as a concept, just means restart for me," Damien replied. "I wish for a true end, one that I know will never come."

"Don't be so certain about that," Martyn murmured in response. "Death has the habit of touching those who are surely untouchable."

"Such heartwarming stories for the breakfast table," Thyren sighed. "If you're gonna continue like this, I'm gonna replace the tea with whiskey."

"Apologies for disrespecting the breakfast," Martyn chuckled. "Please, warm our hearts."

"The only reason I allow guests into this place is to have them entertain me," he replied. "And I don't intend to change it otherwise." He ordered a new round of toast for himself.

"Then I should host you in my place. Damien, you could join us there as well."

Princeling, said Valentine's voice in Thyren's head. He really intends to give him a kingdom. Why does he trust him this much?

But then, it was also a question for himself.

"If not Liffelen, and if not here," Damien said. "Where do you live?"

"Many years ago, I've built a pocket dimension for myself. A place away from all the politics, peaceful, and calm."

Damien raised one eyebrow. "That was you, then." A wide smile brightened his face up as he leaned forward. "You were the one who built up a new place for her!"

Martyn's face faltered. "You know the story?"

"She told me once," the young man replied. "Ashren. Guided me, as a ghost. She would speak very fondly of someone, insane enough to hand her her own universe. Never named him though. It must be you."

"Was she happy?"

"I've never met a happy person in my life, so I wouldn't know." Then his expression softened. "But she was, I think. To a degree."

Thyren felt the need to speak. "Who are you talking about?"

"Chaos before me," Damien replied, before Martyn could. "Unfortunately, Sylen killed her. Long before anything existed." He sighed. "A short life must come with the powers."

"How old are you?"

"I don't know." He reached for the porcelain teapot, and one of the servants rushed before he could to fill his glass for him. "I don't even actually know if my name was Damien. A lot of unknowns, that's what my life is."

Thyren could sense Martyn's impatience.

"If you're all finished," he said. "I would suggest moving to a more comfortable room."

*

Damien didn't feel ready for any conversation he could have with anyone, about his past or his non-existing future. Present was all he had, concrete, solid, rememberable. Another familiar face. He didn't try to convince himself that they didn't know each other — Martyn obviously had some idea about who he was, and Damien had already met a version. Maybe it'll go better than it was with Thyren.

Thyren, being the good host he was, followed them into the large living room. Windows were wide open, and the breeze brought all the good smells of the grass and the trees from outside. Despite the golden painted frames of some of the portraits on the wall, the room was awfully light on tones — whites, light greys and blues. It was staring at shiny marble under the sun, or ice. Look at me, complaining about interior design.

Once they took their places in the comfortable armchairs and couches, Martyn leaned forward.

"You were following a path," he said. "I don't know how that path is determined."

"The threads," Damien muttered, waving his hand. The glistening threads appear all over the room, making everything look like they were connected to one another. A tangled mess to an untrained eye. "This was my fate."

"You could say that. Can you follow back to the timelines where you died?"

Another hand wave, and the threads disappeared. "No. They have frayed ends. I can't keep track of them, nor my memories there." He sighed. "I always assumed I was doing the right things, followed my intuition. They didn't end up good, until..." His voice trailed off. He could feel the dry air on his skin, he could almost see the orange sky above. I survived there. I didn't die. That place will be fine.

"Until?" Martyn pressed.

"Until I went somewhere that was already dead. I arrived late. I don't know why or what happened. I shouldn't have been there. There was no me, there. I don't know."

"And you didn't die."

"And I didn't die."

That would have to be enough for it to count as not bad.

"In another timeline, you were my son."

Damien nodded. "I was a lot of things, in a lot of timelines."

"They don't matter to me," Martyn said. "You were my son." Damien wanted to believe the pride in his voice was a figment of his imagination. "I would be proud to call you that."

"Really?" He couldn't manage his tone, so expectant, so surprised. "Would you?"

"Why not?"

"I am nothing," Damien said. "I accomplished nothing, I know nothing, I have no importance. I have nothing to be proud of. I've just tried things and they never ended good. I don't even have a real identity."

Martyn reached, and held his hand. "The man I see in front of me is real enough," he said, his voice calm. You're wrong. I'm not real. I'll disappear eventually. "And you've accomplished something very important. You survived."

"That's nothing," Damien chuckled, bitter. "I didn't even actively work for it."

"Ask any of us," Martyn dismissed his objection. "Surviving no matter what is the biggest accomplishment. You were swimming against the current, and you survived." His smile was genuine enough. "I would be proud if I was ever your father. I would be grateful to call myself your father."

"You mean it."

"If you want to." Martyn walked next to him, and wrapped his arm around Damien's shoulders. "If you want to, that'd be my pleasure. To help you, to guide you whenever I can, to be here for you."

"I... I would love that actually." It pained him to admit that. I should've been strong enough on my own. Without depending anyone. What will you do when I die?

"Then it's great!" Martyn clapped his hands, and Damien saw Thyren shaking his head with a smile. "I'll be having the palace there prepared, and we can have a dinner this evening, if that works for you."

"That would be wonderful."

"Then it's settled! Ferran—"A tall redhead appeared immediately and took a bow. "Let's go."

They disappeared, and Thyren and Damien looked at each other, for a long and silent while.

"Still want to go somewhere?" Thyren broke the silence.

"Not sure," Damien said. "I'll be going for the dinner, of course." He couldn't help but smile.

"But now?"

"Not now. Why, what do you have in mind?"

Thyren looked unsure. "Usually I find some physical activities usual in taking the edge off if I'm feeling bad."

"What kind of physical activities are they?"

"If I'm on my own, archery. But if you join me, and if you're feeling up for it, we can do some fending I think."

Damien laughed. "How do you know I know about fending?"

"I could teach you if you don't know. That still counts as activity."

Damn it. "Lead the way, then. But I won't play the worthy opponent, because my wounds are still not entirely closed."

"Oh-" Thyren opened his eyes wide, and Damien wanted to get drunk his surprised expression. He's not the man you know. But then, his heart had an objection to that. But the one I'm getting to know is pretty good. "You don't have to—"

"I'm bored, and besides—" Damien decided to go full on the offensive. "You can always patch me back up."

*

It was afternoon when they finished their exercise, and despite the chilly morning weather and constant breeze in the garden, Damien was soaked with sweat once Thyren declared it was the end. He didn't even pretend he had enough strength to move, straight up laying down on the grass. The sun, finally up in the air with its full power, burned his face, but he didn't care. He closed his eyes to listen to the trees whistling. He didn't even realise Thyren had done the same, until the man spoke with a hushed tone, like his voice could shatter Damien into pieces.

"Are you alright?"

"Just tired, but normal tired." He didn't open his eyes. He was going to give this to himself, a chance to pretend he was back, he was under the orange sky again. The ground was softer, and it smelled amazingly fresh, but the voice in his ear made it easy to imagine. "How do you feel?"

"Really good," came the reply. "It's been a while I was challenged this much."

"Nobody good wants to fence with you, I take it?"

"They are hesitant." Damien could hear the hurt in his voice. "I think I'm a nightmare material for some." A pause. "I'm not gonna ask where you learned how to fight like that."

"I wouldn't expect any less."

"I must have trusted you very much," Thyren continued. Damien knew he was looking at him. He felt it in his bones. He kept his eyes closed, still. "Handing you a sword and teaching you enough to challenge me."

"He did trust me." You are not him. Anger bubbled inside him. "And I trusted him." He saved me from insanity.

"What makes you think we're that different?"

Damien blanked at that question. "What do you mean?"

"Your King of Ashes, and me. What makes you think we're so very different from each other?"

For all honesty, Damien didn't know the answer. There were few obvious things, of course. But for all his knowledge of the King of Ashes, he didn't know the King of the Mountain here.

"Your universe still stands," he pointed out.

"A momentary madness is all that separates us?"

"Would you rather me saying you're the same?"

"It's not about what I would rather, actually." Thyren replied, curiosity all over his tone. "I'm trying to understand why you think there's that hard of a distinction. Or why you need it to be so."

"Aside from the fact that I was in love with him?"

"Love can make us stupid things, I am not going to lie. I've done my fair share of those things." He sighed. "That feels like beside the point, though."

Damien finally opened his eyes, rolling to his side to look directly into Thyren's eyes. "At the very end," he said. "He loved me too. At least I believed so."

Thyren looked at him, calm, collected. "What makes you think I can't love you, too?"

"Do you want to? You don't even know me."

"I want to know you, but I feel like you don't let down your guard enough to allow me."

"It's been a day since we've met. How do you even trust me to want to know me?"

Thyren rolled his eyes. "Do you want me to hate you or something?"

"I'm just trying to understand."

"There's something about you," Thyren said. "Something I see in my reflection, every morning, on the mirror. I believe we can be friends. But I feel you don't want to be."

"I'll eventually die and leave this timeline behind, without a way back, Thyren. It would be a waste of time for you."

"So all the connections we form are meaningless, once one side of them are lost?"

Wrong words, Damien, he chastised himself. "It's not about you, actually. It's about how I would feel, remembering you, remembering my connection with you, but with no way to get it back. It's hard enough with a way to get it back. Death is finite. What I go through is not."

"At least allow me the chance?"

"Do you really want to be friends?"

"I don't treat everyone's wounds."

Maybe you are the same. "Let's be friends, then."

Thyren smiled, his eyes twinkling with a happy light. "Let's be friends."

*

The dinner at Martyn's palace promised to be interesting when Damien was welcomed by everyone, slightly bowing at each step. It was a long walk, for he chose to appear in the garden, not to intrude. The man he saw at Thyren's place, Ferran, was right next to him, leading him on the way.

"Can everyone stop bowing to me?"

"Not enjoying the attention, princeling?"

"Can't say it's something I thoroughly enjoy." He cleared his throat. "Princeling, though? For real?"

"Aren't you?"

"I'm not even a prince."

Ferran made a disbelieving sound, without speaking further.

They entered the main building together, and the bowing continued, non-stop. "Really?" Damien asked. "Really?"

"Martyn hyped you a lot."

"Did he even have the time?"

"We have been waiting for you for a while."

Damien stopped at his tracks, so suddenly, it took Ferran a few steps further to realise it and stop as well.

"What?"

"How long do you mean by a while?"

Ferran shrugged. "Martyn has been aware of you. We've all heard the stories."

"My life is not some fairytale." He was surprised he sounded hurt.

"You think being a prince in this place is a fairytale?"

"What are you doing here if it's that bad?"

Ferran laughed. "Oh, dear. If this is anything like a fairytale, most of us at Martyn's service, we would be the monsters not the heroes."

"What does that make me?"

"That makes you," Ferran walked back, grabbed Damien by the shoulder and semi-dragged him, motioning him to walk. "Either a princeling who fell into the wrong story, or someone who will eventually get his hands dirty. Or you're both. It's hard to tell with Martyn." As they reached to the dining room door, Ferran smiled. "He is a deep romantic, but he has an edge to him. So," he pushed him through it. "Enjoy your dinner."

With a deep breath, he walked in.

"Welcome home," Martyn opened his arms wide, his smile as wide. "It makes me so happy we finally have a chance to talk."

Damien narrowed his eyes. "For how long you've been waiting for me?"

"Ever since we've met."

"That would be... How many years? How many months? How many days?" He continued staring once he took his place in the ridiculously prepared table. "Also, thank you but for the love of everything, I am just one person."

The host started laughing. "I wasn't sure what you would like, so I had everything prepared just in case. People here aren't used to guests, so it's a fun change for them."

"You haven't answered my question."

"I would say at least six months. I can't fully put my finger on the date I became aware of you."

Damien closed his eyes. "I see," he said simply. He didn't see it. I've spent six months. Only six months. How many of them were with him?

"It made me so happy to find out that I've had a son. A brilliant one like you, especially."

"You purposefully miss the part where you weren't my father in the many timelines I've been."

"That bothers you?"

"I don't want you to have buyer's remorse."

"Please," Martyn scoffed. "Eat, please."

As Damien started to fill his table, short haired young woman appeared on the door. She hid her laughter rather clumsily — her eyes betrayed her, her eyes that were drifting to Damien every other second. Great. They must think I'm a joke.

"Yes, Valentine?" Martyn asked.

"You have another guest." She said, eyebrows raised in a question. "Flerl'en Ligenca?"

"Oh, what a lovely surprise." He clapped his hands. "Please bring her in, my dear, and inform the staff we're gonna need another serving on the table."

She disappeared so fast Damien thought if she was a magician, or if she had the ability to appear-and-disappear, but he thought it would be rude to point and ask. Unlike them who think pointing and laughing is fine.

The name Ligenca itself rang a bell, with no face attached to it. It was going to be good to see the person behind the name. Ligenca. Intelligence. Whoever they were, the name was always mentioned in a respectful manner — unlike Sylen's, for example, the fear always coming in default.

When Valentine entered and took one step aside, Damien finally had a chance to see her. Her long black hair reaching to her waist, her dress in a beautiful dark blue that complemented her eyes. She took one glance at Damien, then her attention was diverted to Martyn. Her red lips curved into a big smile as he got up from the table and opened his arms wide.

"Juventas," he said. "My dear friend."

Damien choked on his wine.

"Is he alright, whoever he is?" She asked, and Martyn dismissed her worry with a hand wave as he pulled a chair back for her. "He's alright, aren't you Damien?"

Damien muttered a pitiful sure, but he was not okay as he stared at the people who were his parents sometime, somewhere. He had a family. He had a father, who guided him. He had a mother, who taught him. Which one was the strict parent? Would he get in a lot of trouble with them? Whom would he run to if he was hurt? If he needed help but no judgement? On whose knees would he cry himself to sleep?

What would a life with a family look like?

And as they joked between themselves, old friends catching up, Damien focused his eyes and movement to the food, but with no actual conscious effort to it. Fill the spoon. Eat the soup. Drink wine. Take some salad to your plate. Drink wine. Just get drunk, really. His heart ached with the yearning, yearning for something he himself never had — never had the opportunity to have.

Martyn eventually turned his attention to Damien, and it was the end of a short period of time where he enjoyed the full brunt of his feelings with no one paying attention to him.

"Have you met Juventas in your travels?" He asked.

"Just heard the name," Damien muttered. "Never had the opportunity to meet in person." You were my mother. "I've seen you once though," he turned to her. "In Sylen's Court. We weren't introduced, however."

"He had a Court?" Juventas laughed. "Oh dear. Wonder how he got us on board."

"No idea." Are we any similar? "I didn't have any chance to spend much longer there."

"What happened?"

"Well, Sylen killed me, for starters." This time it was his turn to laugh. I died. Isn't it funny? "My expeditions usually didn't last long."

Juventas refrained from making a comment on the obvious meanings of those words. Instead, she narrowed her eyes as she spoke.

"Jennifer spoke very favourable of you."

He couldn't help but smile this time, genuine. "That's out of her kind heart, I'm sure."

She shook her head. "She never talks favourably about anyone after the first meeting. Unfortunately, I can't blame her father on this one. That would make you an exception though."

"It is a good exception, then."

"So you are the Chaos."

Now we're talking. "Yes," he replied, aware that Martyn was watching his every mimic, every word. "I am."

"Do you know the Chaos before you?"

It earned her a solemn nod. "Madison," he said. "We've met, once upon a time."

Juventas raised one eyebrow. "You met?"

"She was a ghost. I was lost. She guided me back into a path, but I've treaded less carefully than I should have."

Martyn cleared his throat. "My dear Juve," he said. "Damien has had a tough couple of days. I think we can discuss all these over whiskey, instead of food and wine."

"Oh, sorry." She started filling her plate as well. "It all looks delicious, Martyn."

"All for the new addition to my small family." He raised his glass towards Damien.

"The Gentlemen's Club and their adopted sons, for everything's sake," she rolled her eyes, but her tone was playful. "Gerard's got his leytian, Geoff has Thyren, now you have Damien. I don't know what you guys find in bringing astray kids home."

"Isn't it obvious?" He laughed. "We enjoy being too much on the nose."

Damien wanted to ask them if they could stop talking to him as if he wasn't around, but listening to him and focusing on the food seemed easier. Besides, for all Martyn's quirkiness, Damien didn't think they could hold a conversation about anything other than the timelines and the threads. This was a lot more preferable anyway.

He wanted to tell her. A part of him wanted to tell her. You were my mother. But what good would it be? Was he hoping his parents, here, together, would protect him from whatever was coming at him at full force? From his destiny, maybe? Did he expect them to shield him from his main responsibility that he had no idea why he had in the first place? Save the universe, one timeline at a time. They weren't even his parents, after all, no matter what Martyn said.

He stole them like he stole this body, like he stole the memories — without the intention, but with great success.

Princeling, Ferran had called him. It had a nice ring to it. Something to define myself with. Better than Chaos. Or lost. It had been only two days since he was in this timeline, at least with this timeline's standards, yet he felt like he belonged. Again. But this time, he felt like he belonged with the living. Maybe I could stay here forever. Maybe I could have a family.

However, the tugging at his chest disagreed.

He focused on the food again, this time with conscious effort. If he wasn't gonna stay here long, at the very least he could enjoy the good feelings, and the amazing food.

*

When Damien appeared on the balcony door, Thyren was already on his second bottle of wine, gazing at the stars above. He didn't need his guest to announce himself, he didn't need him to speak, but it was a welcome difference in the dead quiet of the night when he did.

"Am I interrupting something?"

"Other than my daily self-pity session, no. Help yourself a bottle if that's your poison."

Damien didn't reach for the bottles as he sat down.

"Can I?" He said, instead, pointing to his cigarette.

Thyren shrugged. "Fine by me."

They stood there, right next to each other, eyes on the sky, minds somewhere unreachable. Thyren didn't know what the kid thought of, maybe the past love, maybe the uncertainty of the future. He himself thought of Axel, once again. His mind drowned him in memories, all of them equally beautiful, all of them equally sad now when looking back.

"How was the dinner?" He asked eventually.

"Fine," Damien replied, simply. His voice was too controlled. "I've met my mother." He paused. "Not in this timeline, of course."

"Juventas," Thyren murmured. "She's a bit scary."

"Terrifying," Damien added. "But fine I guess."

They continued staring at the sky, in silence. Thyren, against his own better judgement, wanted to turn his head and look at the young man sitting next to him. To analyse him. To understand. To say I know it's torture and I've been there as well. I am still there. Finally someone who could admit going through it. The withdrawal. The wound that you couldn't stop touching.

He talked about it with everyone, of course. All the people around him had a session. They were understanding. They respected his pain. But most of them had also the get over it already, there is a bigger fish to fry undertone, which made the whole deal unbearable. Anthony, being the sanest, offered therapy. He knew many good professionals, it would be helpful.

What am I going to say to them, Anthony? He had asked. That my boyfriend, who was supposed to be immortal, died, and in retribution I killed his father who had put me in years and years worth of misery in my childhood?

But right here was someone with a fresh wound. Someone who wouldn't carry that undertone. Someone who wouldn't think he was weak for still suffering, still reaching, still bleeding internally. It took a great strength not drawing his knife and bleed under the stars. Not to join the dead.

"They called me princeling," Damien murmured, breaking the silence. Thyren shook his head as if to place his thoughts in the right places. "At Martyn's palace, I mean."

"It's cute," Thyren chuckled softly. "Suits you."

"Makes me sound like I'm a fairytale character. I feel like it at least." He sounded bitter. "I am not one."

"What's so bad about being a fairytale character?"

"Nothing. But for starters, I'm sure I won't have a happily ever after."

With that, Thyren turned his head to Damien.

"What makes you so sure?"

"It's..." He sighed, and lowered his head. "There's this thing I have to follow. Webs of fate, my divine path, whatever you call it. It's a thread. It pulls me. I'll eventually go after it."

"And you are sure there is no happiness for wherever it pulls you to."

"Anytime I followed it, I died. Except for the time I was too late. And it pulls me. I feel like I'm entangled now, went out of the course a lot."

"Can't you cut it off?"

Damien shook his head. "I'd rather not risk it."

"Oh." Thyren leaned back a bit, taking a sip from his drink. It burned his throat, a matching sensation to the one in his heart. "Still, you would make a good fairytale hero."

"Now you're messing with me," Damien chuckled. He sounded so done with everything, so tired. It's just been a few days, kid, or a few months. It's a long way to go. "Are you serious?"

"Absolutely. You're just in the period of suffering before the actual reward comes through."

"You believe there's a reward after this suffering?"

"No. There is no reward big enough to justify it anyway."

Thyren turned back to the stars, blinking there, unaware of everything — of the shattering pain that rose inside him, of the brink of collapse he was at. The universe goes on. It's just not here with me. That had to be enough, that had to be consoling. It wasn't. It never would be.

"How did he die?" Damien asked, breaking the silence once more.

"In his sleep," Thyren sighed, trying very hard not to remember how it was all fine, how he was the one who got up early and he did his best not to wake Axel up, and once he got out of the shower, he couldn't wake him up either way. "Peaceful as it gets."

"Sorry about that," the kid murmured.

"It's fine." It was not fine, and Thyren wondered if it ever would be fine. "It's just…" He stopped, trying to find the right words to tell of the black tar that covered everything inside him. "It's just like he's gone and he took all the colour with him. All the light. All the brightness."

"So, you killed Sylen."

"I had to. I had to do something, or I was going to go mad." And Axel made me promise not to kill myself if anything happened to him. And I promised like an idiot. "He assured us everything would be alright."

"And it wasn't."

"And it wasn't." He turned to Damien again, surprised that he was looking at him too. "Do you think this universe will end?"

"You would want that, wouldn't you?"

"I'm just trying to figure out if knowing everything, including me, will end and not doing anything constitutes as killing myself."

Damien laughed at that, and it was a genuine laughter. Thyren started laughing too. It felt foreign to him, hearing his own laughter, but he did, and it was exhilarating, to see he was able to do it. It felt comfortably human. It felt comfortably alive.

When their laughters finally subsided, Damien spoke softly.

"I think it would," he said. "But would it really matter after everything ends?"

Thyren had no answer to that.

*

Jennifer, of course, enlisted Damien's help with the planning of the gathering.

"We need a lot of things, and we need them fast," she said, checking her butterfly patterned notebook. "I am assuming you can perform..." She snapped her fingers. "Other things than lighting up cigarettes?"

"Pretty much anything I wish for," Damien nodded. "What do you need?"

Despite Thyren insisting that it would be absolutely fine if he didn't want to help, and how there were a lot of people who would take his place — some gladly — Damien thought it was a great distraction. Jennifer was a figure he remembered well with no great attachment, and spending time with her would had the potential to be entertaining in multiple ways.

And in his favour, Damien also had the capability to do whatever she asked of him in mere seconds, which would eventually leave more time to talk and maybe to drink.

It was the food first, then the variety of the drinks. Damien begged for the whiskey, which was accepted quickly. Anything that will get me black out drunk. He guessed he could seek out Thyren's assistants and get something heavier. Jennifer was also quite worried about the theme, so naturally they had to congregate and discuss as the small committee.

"So," she said, once they all gathered in the ballroom. "I'm thinking gold for the theme. Or maybe white?"

Jennifer then turned to Damien. "Could you please..." She mimicked an explosion. "Something?"

Damien snapped his fingers without giving too much thought, for all honesty he wasn't sure how artistic he was — but the end result with white fabrics and flowers and some breeze that brought beautiful smells, along with the entire room seeming brighter, Jennifer muttered her approval. "What do you think?" She asked the other two.

"Personally," Damien shrugged. "I am sure nobody will care as long as there's enough wine."

"I need it to be perfect," Jennifer said, her shoulders lowered. "It's been so hard this past year, I just want a clean slate with everything being perfect, and running smoothly and..." Her voice trailed off. She didn't need to finish it, Damien knew exactly what she meant.

Deep down, he wondered if it was to teach all of them a lesson, the pain, the suffering. They did things to distract themselves, but with the immortality, came a great hollowness that chased them into shattering despair, and it was a struggle to stay afloat. They would suffer, they would try to be better for it. We didn't ask for this. I didn't ask for this. Oh, how he wished to be dead, sleeping, resting.

The tugging at his chest announced itself once again, as if he just let it go and followed it, the yearning would end. It's not going to. Just another universe I'll watch the destruction of, unable to stop it. The desperation made everything even worse with all the power at his fingertips.

"You're quiet," Jennifer said all of a sudden.

"I don't want to echo myself, but I want to get so drunk I can't even recognise my face in the mirror and hope that gods can die of alcohol poisoning."

"If that were possible, one of the benevolent rulers here would be below ground," she replied. "And I know he's your patron here, but I've made fun of his alcoholism to his face as well so it should be fine."

"We're all hurting in someway," Damien shrugged. "What would you suggest to stop the pain?"

He tried his best not to sound hostile, and he thought he managed it, until Jennifer spoke again in a very solemn tone.

"Loss of a loved one is hard," she agreed, and Damien had to remind himself Axel and Alexei were related to her. "I meant no harm."

"I'm sorry," he said. "All the deaths and resurrections made me a bit jaded. It'll all turn out great and we'll have a lot of fun, trust me."

*

When they found themselves tangled under the sheets, neither were drunk — although Damien desperately wished to be. She was pretty, she always was, but she was never gentle. In the back of his mind, Damien found it extremely relieving that somethings stayed the same. For so long it had been a different game, same players, different roles. Not always different.

He enjoyed her breath on his skin, her calling his name with no expectations from him aside from his very existence. He enjoyed feeling alive, and feeling glad to be alive.

"Oh, gods," she exhaled. "If I knew it was going to be this fun, I'd suggest this the moment I saw you."

"It's easy when you know which buttons to push," he laughed.

"Oh, so I'm not unique," she rose on her elbows, with a laugh. "Lesson to be learned, you never make a girl feel just like the others."

"But the only person who is like you is you," he replied, not being able to help but grin like an idiot. "Would that count? You are so amazing, no matter what the timeline, you're always the same."

She looked like she was considering it for a second, then she laid on her back again. "Okay, I'm letting you off the hook this once."

They continued loudly breathing in silence, and it was Damien who broke the silence this time.

"If you could have anything you wanted," he asked. "What would you want first?"

"Hard hitting questions, huh?"

"It's a question I'm asking myself often. Figured it would be good to hear someone else's answer."

"What are yours?"

Dead. Happy. "I would want to stay."

"Are you going somewhere?"

"Not yet. But eventually. I could never stay."

"Why not?" She asked, it sounded so simple. "You're the Chaos. Nobody can force you to do anything."

He wanted to tell her. He wanted to make her understand. He wanted someone to finally scream at others for a solution, so that he could stop being a whipping boy for the fate, for the universe. He wanted someone to pity him, he wanted someone to have mercy on him.

She was a good candidate for all of those.

But instead, when he spoke, it was far from what he wanted to say.

"I'm duty bound."

She made a dismissing sound. "That's what cowards say to themselves instead of standing up against whatever they are running from."

"Maybe we are just exhausted."

"Of what?"

"For me personally? Failure. I'm tired of dying and restarting. I want to rest. I want to stay. I want to open my eyes into the day and not be afraid of being somewhere else." He paused. "I want sanity."

Damien closed his eyes, tight enough that colours exploded beneath his eyelids. He felt Jennifer's head on his chest, a welcome heaviness, her hair everywhere. She could listen to his heartbeat, he thought, in that moment. She could hear the worried, the chased, the running beat of his weary heart. Were you really alive if there was nobody there to hear it?

"I would want my own family," she spoke, her words making tiny vibrations in his ribcage. "A child, maybe a partner who would love me, as I loved them. We would live in a pretty house, the child would chase butterflies in the garden. We would watch the kid from afar, laughing at the antics." Her voice took a dreamy tone, and he could actually imagine the scene she was talking about.

"I'm not saying this for a partner but," he murmured. "You could have a kid, you know that, right?"

"But does it really matter if you are all alone raising a kid?"

"Why wouldn't it?"

"Do you have parents, Damien?"

He smiled. "Not that I know of. I just came to be."

"Well, I have. For most of my childhood, my dad was locked up in his own world — quite literally — with his dead lover — also literally. It leaves a dent in your heart, I can tell you that."

"It's because you've known the absence of it," he pointed out. "You were grown accustomed to the existence, and the absence bothered you. I didn't know I wanted a family until I woke up in a timeline where I had one."

"Who would you suggest to father this poor child, then?"

"I don't know many people here," Damien admitted. "I've never had enough time to know everyone. But any god would do. Any human would do. Fuck, any leytian would do. You have so many options... Give yourself at least some of what you want, Jennifer."

She raised her head and kissed him. "Oh shut up," she hissed. "This was supposed to be an emotions-free arrangement."

He tackled her, and got on top of her, kissing her back. "I've never promised that."

*

When the Gathering finally started, Thyren found it really hard to connect with most people. There were absences, surely. He couldn't blame them. He would skip the entire thing, too, if he had the chance.

The infamous Gentlemen's Club was there, of course, huddled in a small corner in the large ballroom, sitting on comfortable couches, and chatting away. Thyren admired them, really, how they seemed to be unaffected by everything. Deaths, near-wars, heavy losses — nothing seemed to chip away from their cheer.

When Anthony did his round in the room, he found his way to Thyren, his expression calmer and more sympathetic than

Thyren's. They stood side by side, nursing their drinks, until Anthony decided to break the silence.

"You're avoiding everyone."

"Is it surprising?"

"No, it's not. But it's noticeable."

Thyren let a laugh. "I'm still in mourning and they know that."

"Yeah, I wonder how you convinced them to don the blacks."

"My threats seem to carry a lot more weight now that I've successfully killed a patriarch," he shrugged. "Have you met Damien?"

"Briefly but yes. I was going to ask you about hosting an unknown deity with no regards to safety and security." His tone turned into the scolding big brother's, and Thyren wanted to laugh. Somethings never changed. "He's the Chaos?"

"Appears so."

"And it's safe?"

"What can he do? Kill me?"

"Ha ha."

"I'm serious." Thyren finished his wine, and signalled to one of the waiters for a refill. "He's not violent or anything. Just..." He paused, trying to say the right word — so many of them there were, some more heartbreaking than others. But Anthony, on the other hand, seemed so nonchalant about it.

"Broken?" He completed.

"We could say that." Is that how I am as well? Broken? In pieces? "He's been through a lot."

"Who in this room hasn't?"

"Martyn trusts him."

"Do you trust Martyn?"

It was a sigh. "What do you want from me, Anthony?"

"I am just trying to make sure you have thought this through, and not flinging yourself at something with the hopes of getting destroyed in the end."

Thyren stared at him as he got another glass from the waiter, and blinked a few times, slowly.

"I can't tell," he started, as calm as he could. "If I should find that endearing that you care about me, or concerning that you think I'm an idiot."

"You're not an idiot, you're suicidal," Anthony objected. "There's a big difference."

"The first year is over. It should only get better after this, right?"

"Are you better?"

"No." He didn't see any reason to lie. Anthony would see right through him anyway. "I am not better. I don't think I will ever be. And if you make the he wouldn't want this speech, I am storming out of here."

"I wasn't gonna say that," Anthony replied. "For we all know it doesn't matter what the dead want. They are not the ones dealing with the aftermath."

"That's what I've been telling everyone."

"But you need to open yourself back up again. An eternity is a long time to spend on your own."

This time he started to laugh. "Oh gods," he said. "Do you suggest I should take a lover?"

"I was gonna say make friends but if that works for you, why not?" He laughed as well. "I mean, I promise I won't object if it's Damien."

"I've known the kid for three weeks at most," Thyren shook his head. "I am not a moth to get drawn at the first fire I see."

Anthony nodded, all serious. "Of course. Sometimes a bit of spontaneity is good, though, if it's going to drag you out of the mud you're in. Even though it has the potential to end in a strong combustion."

"I cannot believe I'm discussing my love life with you."

"I am not discussing anything with you. I'm telling you to finally get a life and stop moping around."

"A year is nothing for us immortals, though."

"A year is a lot of things for everyone. I don't want to turn this into an intervention, but Thyren, literally the entire pantheon is talking about you depleting the liquor stocks."

"Oh, for fuck's sake, I am the King now, aren't I? Can't I abuse some resources of my kingdom without being judged for it?"

"Nope, not how that works." Anthony sighed and gently nudged him in the direction of a balcony. Thyren obliged. "You're grieving. Okay. Grieve. How long do you think it'll take?"

"I don't know! Why does everyone act like it's so simple?"

"Everyone in this room had someone they loved died, Thyren. They're speaking from a point of experience."

The cold air suddenly hit them once they stepped to the balcony. Thyren only then realised his cheeks were burning. With anger, or with shame — he didn't know. He wasn't sure. Just why can't they leave me alone? "I am tired," he spoke. "I'm just tired."

"Of...?"

"Everything. People trying to fix me, to guide me. I'm tired of living. I miss him so much." Tears pooled in the corners of his eyes, but he swiftly wiped them away. He wasn't going to have a breakdown, not now, not right now. "There are days I wake up and think it was all a dream. There are nights I see him in my dreams and I don't even want to wake up. And then everyone is like but it has been a year. Who gives a fuck?"

He finished his wine, and threw the empty glass out of the balcony, aware that Anthony was watching him with concerned eyes. Stop being concerned about me. I'll be fine. I'll survive. "What?" He asked, more hostile than he wanted it to be.

"Have you ever told anyone these?"

"Why would I even bother? Telling, hah, when did it ever solve anything?"

"You can't go on bottling it up forever. You need to scream, you need to cry, you need to break everything apart if you have to. This isn't healthy, you cannot go on like this."

"Not everyone grieves like you do. We all have different ways."

"Your way so far has been getting drunk every day, ignoring everything, and trying to go all apathetic and failing at it. Change your ways."

"I straight up killed Alexei, doesn't that count as breaking everything apart?"

"Oh, fuck off, we all knew you'd kill Alexei in a heartbeat if Axel let you years ago."

Thyren took a deep breath. "There was a timeline, apparently," he spoke, softer this time. "That I killed Alexei. And everything with him. All the places, all the gods, all the people gone. Except for me, of course. All alone on a deserted place."

Anthony didn't say anything.

"And I wonder why I haven't done that here. What stopped me? I remember that anger, flowing in my veins. I remember the misery, the desperation, the need to burn down everything. But I didn't. Is it because in that timeline I loved him more? Is it because in here

I knew he wouldn't want that? I was capable of it, then why didn't I?"

"Would you prefer to?"

"I don't know. Alone for an eternity sounds like a horrible punishment."

"You're punishing yourself the same way, though."

"I'm not alone. I have bunch of people pestering me."

"Nobody is pestering you. We're merely trying to remind you that life, unfortunately, goes on, and you are not alone. Not even in this misery."

"Oh, I'm pretty much alone in this misery."

"Thyren..."

"Seriously. It doesn't matter if I'm physically alone or not. I feel lonely without him regardless."

"Why are you punishing yourself?"

Thyren opened his mouth, but closed it without a sound. I'm not punishing myself. That was a lie. I stayed alive after him. Because he promised. I couldn't save him. That didn't sound like the answer either.

"I don't know how to live without him," he said finally. "And I'm struggling."

"You—"

"I don't. I was supposed to be dead years ago, Alexei wasn't supposed to call my bluff. Axel took me as his leytian. I had to learn how to live without planning my death, and I could only do it with him. Now I have no idea what to do. How to survive. How not to reach for him when I need someone."

"Oh, dear," Anthony wrapped his arm around Thyren's shoulder. "You find a new person, a new thing to reach to. Like we all do."

*

Damien, after his twelfth glass, found Thyren chain-drinking wine in a balcony, away from everyone.

"Long live the King," he announced his entrance, raising his glass. The man in front of him, albeit looking tired and miserable, smiled nonetheless. "I see you're taking the avoid everyone road."

"Not everyone, apparently."

"I could leave, but I'd rather not."

"Feel free to join me and dwell in a misery of your own," Thyren raised his glass back at him. "Enjoying the festivities?"

"I am cautiously observing. Not many great things happened at the last Gathering I attended to."

"Oh, really?" Thyren chuckled. "Hope we can provide a better experience."

They went quiet, and stared at the sky for a while. Both looking for different stars, longing for what they could never reach.

"You were a prince," Damien broke the silence. "You were raised here I think, with Anthony. Twins, never separated. You were so gentle, so different."

"Breaks my heart right there." He didn't seem heartbroken. "Do you mean to imply I'm not so gentle?"

"Oh, of course not," Damien laughed. "It's just — you were always so rough in all the other places I saw you. You are rough. But in there, still in love with Haylen, it was sweet." Less broken. Unlike you and I are. "That timeline literally burnt to the ground, though."

"They never give us a break, do they?"

Damien watched him, his heart racing as if it had a place to be. The false familiarity caused his insides to clench. I don't know you. The reminders to himself stopped working. Every part of his being screamed he's here, he's right here. Damien didn't know why he was trying to talk himself out of it.

"Jennifer wants to have a kid with me," he said instead, an attempt to change his internal subject. "And I told her this is insanity, but she seems quite adamant."

"Oh, you two are a thing?"

Damien hoped to dream the disappointment in the man's voice. "Let's say we filled some empty spaces in each other's life," he said. "But that doesn't matter. She knows me for three weeks. It's a huge responsibility."

"Do you want a kid?"

"I never imagined having one. Did you ever?"

Thyren sighed, turning his head to the sky. "We would discuss it with Axel sometimes. I was never sure of kind of father I would be to a child."

"I think you would be wonderful."

"You must be thinking of the prince from that other timeline, kid," Thyren laughed. "But appreciate the vote of confidence."

"But did you want a child?"

"Eventually maybe. But now, I don't think I can pull myself together enough to care for such a fragile being."

"That's what I'm thinking about," Damien murmured. "But it won't even matter — because I'll eventually go away. Die, and reappear in my next destination. I think that's why she picked me."

"Oh," Thyren turned to him fully. "Do you intend to do all that?"

"I feel like have to," Damien admitted. "Wherever it is, it's pulling me. I should've been there ages ago."

"So you will die, how?"

"Suicide? For the first time it will be on my hands to determine the time and place. I'll come up with the painless way, and then voila."

"Oh..." Thyren seemed unsure of how to respond to that. "I got used to you being here."

"I got used to being here as well." I got used to you too. I got used to the idea maybe you really are similar to him. "I'll try my best to return here."

"Will you?"

"Be able to? I don't know. But I'll try anything to do it."

"I kind of thought you'd go back to your King of Ashes."

Damien laughed. His heart felt lighter. "I might not be able to, but I intend to try at least."

"Do you have a timeframe in mind?"

"At the end of the Gathering, making it a tradition. Who knows?"

Their hands brushed on the balcony rail. Nothing more. Nothing less.

"Come back here," Thyren said, his head away from him, eyes up in the sky. "It is less lonely with you."

*

He was in a forest. The ground was cold, but also soft and forgiving. Compassionate. Damien didn't care about the worms and slugs or anything. He wanted to be away, he wanted to be alone — for the first time ever.

It was raining as he aligned his knife made out of pure energy over his heart. He closed his eyes, felt the rain and —

Chapter 10

The sun was ever so gently shining into the room through the open windows, bringing a cool morning breeze with it.

Damien slowly opened his eyes in his room, and smiled at his own reflection in the mirror above his bed. Jenny always considered this to be a vanity thing, but he found it grounding. That he was more than just an entity, but some living, breathing thing that walked around to be pain in other people's asses.

But right now, all he thought was how he was starving.

He got out of his bed, singing a happy tune, to take a shower first, dress then, and bother his servants to prepare him a large breakfast. Not that he would eat all of them, but for sure he would have guests, as he always did.

*

When Jenny dropped by, the first thing she commented on was how horrible he looked.

"Very kind of you," Damien replied, buttering his toast. Right next to him, Ferran was sipping his tea as he was reading some newspaper from who knew which city or country. Either it was the most interesting thing, or Ferran was sending the please release me from the agony of watching you two banter message. Damien absolutely was not going to release him from the agony.

"No, but seriously," she said, taking a seat at the table and waving her finger aggressively at the butler for a service. "Eyes bloodshot, dark circles underneath, skin as pale as a ghost — Ferran, don't you agree?"

"I've been telling him that ever since we've moved here, Saellin," Ferran replied, his face still hidden by the newspaper. "He does not listen to me."

"Oh, fuck off," Damien leaned back just so they could meet eyes. "I'm at my prime and handsome as ever."

"Whatever you say, princeling."

Damien shook his head. "Tea?"

"No, thanks," Jenny replied, reaching for the coffee pot instead. "Any plans today?"

"Relaxing and some sunbathing here. If I'm really ghostly pale, I could use some sun. How about you?"

She shrugged. "Family dinner in the evening, you're invited as well. Until then, I think I'll stay here. Sunbathing sounds amazing."

"Great then." His eyes lit up, and Jenny laughed at that. "I'll get dressed upstairs. Jenny, do you need to change as well?"

She nodded. They didn't even bother taking the stairs.

*

"There's a crack," Damien murmured, as Jenny threw herself on to the bed, panting. "Can you see that?"

"Where?" She asked, but she wasn't even looking. "In the mirror?"

"Yeah," Damien raised his head. "It wasn't there this morning."

If one could hear the sound of eyes being rolled, this would be as loud as a fire engine. "For the millionth time, why do you even have a mirror right above your bed?"

Damien turned to her. "I enjoy watching myself."

"Oh, for fucks' sake."

"Really. I enjoy my body way too much to only confine it to stupid vertical mirrors."

"You're weird."

He turned towards her and rose above his elbows. "Yet you like me."

"I use you for my own pleasure, there is a difference," she pointed out. "My feelings for you are more on a neutral ground."

"I take it as a compliment." He laughed, and her laughter followed. "What dinner, though? Why are we having a dinner? What happened?"

"I don't know either. Though, everyone's being strange lately. Everyone. My mom, your mom, my dad, your dad... Did you notice anything?"

Damien forced his mind to keep track of the last few days, but strangely enough, found close to nothing there — as if everything restarted this morning, and he was out of it for a while. "I think I was too drunk to notice something," he said. "Or high. Can't tell."

"Man, you're experimenting with crazy things if they can give you a blackout."

"Alleviates the pain of existence." He reached to the nightstand to get a cigarette. "Want one?"

"No, thanks," she replied. "Do you really have to? The smell is nauseating."

"Really? Didn't know you feel so." He lit it up either way, inhaling it deeply. "Nothing like breathing a bit of poison to start a day."

"I tell you every single time. Also, it's not like it can kill you — is it really poison if it's harmless?"

"We're not invulnerable, we're immortal," Damien shook his head. Ashes scattered on the floor as he carelessly swung his hand to the other side of the bed. "It's a very important distinction. I'm after the harm. It's death I'm not chasing." He exhaled. "I don't want to think, for some reason."

She turned her head towards him. "What do you mean?"

"I am not sure. I think I cracked the mirror, but I don't know how. When. Why."

"You can wave your hand and fix it."

He shook his head. "That's not my point."

"Your point is confusing and stupid. Please do what we're here to do, Damien."

Damien put out his cigarette and pulled her to himself, kissing her. "You mean this?"

She laughed. He thought it was a nice thing that he didn't have to think on too hard.

*

Swimming in the sea wasn't exactly Damien's favourite activity, and a pool was actually not that different. Even the most tranquil moments floating would suddenly turn into him finding himself in the depths no matter how shallow, and struggling immensely to breathe. The aching relief of his lungs, that was the only thing came to mind when he thought of .

But as he found himself underwater this time, he didn't feel panic. He was okay with it. Water burnt his throat, he was feeling lightheaded, and in desperate need of oxygen but he was calm. When he reached to the surface, though, it wasn't the sun burning his skin, or the breeze caressing it. No, what he saw was a bed, an arm wrapped around his chest — and it was so realistic, he could feel the weight of it.

He thrashed in the water, swallowing a lot, but eventually he settled. He was floating, calm, tranquil, but every part of his body ached as if he just ran a marathon. What was that? Who was that? Jenny yelled something from the sidelines that how he could not know how to swim, though Damien couldn't even acknowledge what exactly she was saying.

He swam to the side of the pool and got out of it in an instant, looking at the water as if it was some monster that trapped him, but the water itself looked as innocuous as possible.

"Are you okay?" Jenny asked, finally realising there was some-thing wrong.

"I'm gonna get dressed," Damien replied absentmindedly. "You can stay here."

"Hey," she grabbed his wrist, pulling him to sit him down. "Look at me."

"I'm fine," Damien tried to get out of her grip, but failed to do so. Black spots swam in his vision, the whole world swaying. What is wrong with me? "I just need some rest-"

"No, what you need is someone to look at you and take care of you." She raised her head, yelling for Ferran, who appeared immediately. "Will you please accompany this idiot to his room and wait for me until I get back with his mother?"

"That won't be necessary," Damien tried to speak, but at the same time, someone in his ear was talking about families and how important they were. He couldn't differentiate between anything.

Ferran helped him on his feet, and stopped him from falling when he wobbled. "I think I'm not okay," he whispered, words having great difficulty getting out of his mouth.

"You think?" Ferran asked, as they appeared in Damien's room. Sarcasm was not able to cover up his concern. "I told you to take it easy, princeling."

"Don't call me that," Damien said as he laid down on his bed. "I told you, I'm not some fairytale character."

"You have never told me this before," Ferran frowned. "I think we need your father here, not your mother."

"He would worry too much." Would he? Who is he anyway?

"You need to be worried about."

"Ferran..." The room swayed again, he was sure Ferran was speaking in his ear, sarcasm apparent, but the man in front of him didn't seem to be moving his lips. "The mirror's cracked."

The crack was there, alright. It had gotten larger in his absence, looking like a spiderweb. Branches upon branches, but still confined to a corner, Damien frowned. "Who cracks it?"

"I have no idea," Ferran said. "Look, kid, I know nobody wants to talk about it but, you haven't been well since—"

The door swung open, and a very worried Madison entered, along with Martyn. Wait, hold on, Damien thought, raising in the bed to greet them. She isn't dead? "I worried you, didn't I?" He asked.

They both nodded, hurrying to his side, Madison looking straight into his eyes. "What happened?" She asked, not sounding accusatory.

"I probably got too high with neutralisers, that's all," Damien replied. "They make me hallucinate as they leave my system, it's nothing to be worried about."

He noticed Ferran and Martyn looking at each other, the former shrugging in defeat. It's not his fault, though. But Damien, despite his cool explanation, knew it wasn't his fault either. I don't even remember getting high.

"You need to dial down on it," Martyn said, eventually.

"I know, father, but the nightmares and the pain..." What pain? What dreams? What am I talking about?

"What do you dream about?" Madison asked.

Damien froze. First thing came to mind was a sky on fire, raining stars. It was a deserted, destroyed palace with a rusted throne. When did I have that nightmare?

"I don't remember," he said, choking on the words. An idiot could've told he was lying, but neither of his parents pressed him about it. "I'm fine, really, Jenny got too scared, that's all."

Martyn nodded, and Madison placed a kiss on his forehead.

"Rest until dinner tonight," she said. "Juventas can take a look at you after dinner, just to be on the safe side."

"Yeah," Damien said, laying back. His eyes drifted to the crack inadvertently. "Don't worry about me."

But he was worried about himself, worried of going mad.

*

The dinner was fun enough, but Damien felt no power in him to speak or laugh. He monopolised the wine bottle, and nobody made any objections, so he nodded along, smiled when he felt appropriate and that was the extent of his addition for the most of it.

Everyone seemed... extremely gentle towards him. They all had this weird way of talking to him as if he was made of glass and their words could've broken him if spoken too loud. They made sure they patted him on the back as they talked, which made him feel like a child. Which was all the more reason to stay quiet.

But he wasn't alone in that. Axel was sitting right next to him, his hand bruised — it seemed like it was going along his arm, but his sleeve covered it. He, too, was quiet, until he turned his head towards Damien.

"Do you feel different?" He asked, quiet, eyes drifting to others as if they shouldn't have heard this. "Weird?"

"I always feel like that," Damien replied, emptying the bottle in his glass. "Why?"

Axel pointed at his hand. "I think there's something wrong. In general."

"Well, if you ever burst open and spill light, I'm your guy to sew you back up," Damien murmured. "But bruises, I'm lost."

He stopped. Burst open and sewn back up? What am I talking about? But Axel didn't seem surprised. If anything, there was interest in his eyes.

"Do you have nightmares?"

"Did you talk to my mom?"

"No," Axel frowned. "What do you see?"

Damien couldn't stop the words. "Stars raining upon us. A rusty throne in the middle of a ruined palace, Uncle Alexei's palace, I think. I don't remember much of it. What about you?"

"Pretty much the same, except for the ruined palace. That's interesting."

"It's just weird." Damien shook his head, reaching to a new bottle. "Do you think there's something wrong?"

"Oh, I know it is. I just don't know what."

A icy feeling pierced through Damien's heart. It was paralysing, sending shivers down his spine. "Will we be alright?" He asked, feeling too young for all these.

"I should hope so," Axel sighed, finishing his own glass of wine. "We're here to ensure it, aren't we?"

"Are we?"

"We have responsibilities, Damien," Axel tilted his head. "We don't exist just for existing's sake."

The young god wanted to ask what if they existed just for existing's sake, what if they were just meant to be happy -- but deep down he knew, he knew there had to be a purpose to his existence. Was saving the universe that purpose, though? He was the Chaos after all.

"Maybe we're better off leaving everything to itself," he muttered. "Maybe that's our responsibility. Making sure nobody fucks it up trying to fix it."

"Nonsense," Axel waved his hand. "If that was the case, we wouldn't be here in the first place. We would have no use."

"Do we have one?"

"What's gotten into you?" Axel's eyes narrowed. "Of course we do. We are gods, we are needed to make sure everything goes as smooth as possible."

"I am Chaos," Damien said, though he sounded unsure. "It's not my job to make things smooth. We have my mom, and your dad for those."

"Rumours were true," Axel sighed. "You have something wrong with you."

But Damien didn't feel like he was in the wrong, rather everyone else was being weird.

"I have to go," he said, pushing his chair and getting up. All of his cousins showed signs of distress at that, only ones that stood indifferent were Jennifer and Axel, but he paid no attention to that. He walked towards Juventas, which felt strange as well, and bid her a good night.

He had to find Ferran.

*

It wasn't hard to find Ferran as he was chilling outside of Juventas' palace.

"Oh," he said once he saw Damien outside. "Is the dinner over?"

"For me, yes," muttered Damien, lighting up his cigarette. "You need to tell me something."

"Sure. What do you have in mind?"

The young god paused, exhaling a large cloud of smoke. "I haven't been well," he started. "I haven't been well since when?"

Ferran froze. "What do you mean?"

"Before my parents came you were saying something. You haven't been well since— since when?"

"Look—"

"Everyone's been treating me like I could disappear any second. What happened?"

"You seriously don't remember?"

"Do I look like it?"

The man sighed, his shoulders dropping. "You killed yourself, Damien."

An icy feeling took over Damien in that second, as if there was ice water running in his veins instead of warm blood. It made sense, it made so much sense, but it also meant he had a huge, gaping hole in his memory which was frightening. The wording, also. You killed yourself. Not tried, or attempted. What did I do?

"What else don't I remember?"

"Nothing that I know of."

"How am I alive?"

Ferran sighed again. "I don't know the intricacies, but Thyren and Anthony handled it, under Axel's supervision."

Thyren and Anthony. Somewhere in his mind, it meant something else. He couldn't put a name to it, he couldn't bring up the context. Why don't I remember the moment I woke up? Why don't I remember how I did it?"

"Did it have something to do with my mirror?"

"Aside from it exploding into sand, not much."

"Why did it explode?"

"I don't know, kiddo, what do you want from me?"

Damien stopped. "You know, what? Forget it." He said. "Let's get wasted."

*

Lanenketer always offered the best drinks and places to get wasted, and Damien would never argue about it. Sure, there were a lot of good bars on Earth as well, but none of them compared, especially to Hysserian bars.

"Huh," he said once they found themselves in the Garden District of Hysseren. "It's not raining ash."

Ferran raised one eyebrow. "Should it?"

"I guess not." Damien shook his head. "Let's go."

Once they made their way to one of the better bars of the city, the god didn't waste any seconds to find himself a secluded spot and ordering a few bottles of the strongest things they had.

"Just... strongest?" The waiter asked.

"Yeah, straight up look at your stock, get me a few bottles of whatever has the highest amount of alcohol. You can replenish it as they are emptied."

"You're really going for it," Ferran commented, once the waiter nodded and turned away, disappearing in the crowd. "Are you sure?"

Damien nodded. "It can't make it any worse."

Before he could reach to his first bottle to fill his glass, his mind swirled in colours. The sounds reached to his ears, but it was all distorted and meaningless.

*

He wasn't there, he was in a lonely house decorated in a wide spectrum of black and white. He was staring at the ceiling and the ceiling was a mirror — everything was red in the bed, slowly covering everything. His fingers were clasped around the cold hilt of a kitchen knife — nothing ceremonious.

He felt his own blood trickling down, oxygen slowly leaving his brain as his vision got darker and darker. It wasn't a gentle tether or a sharp hook, but peaceful slumber of non-existence, and he figured he could live with that —

*

He was there, a glass of wine in his hand, a heavy mask on his face, enjoying the hereditary hospitality. There were others dancing, or making out, or disappearing into the night, but Damien preferred playing the observer just for a little while more.

Masks didn't mean much once you knew the mannerisms, after all.

No, though — observer wasn't the right word, especially given he was in no condition to observe anything. The entire room blurred in front of his eyes, same voices from different conversations, different contexts blocked his ears, as he held onto the table until his fingers turned white.

"Come on, Damien," He hardly managed to bring his focus to the woman now talking to him. Butterflies spun around her head. "Are you really that light weight? It's your second wine."

"I'm high on life itself."

"You cannot be serious."

"I'm unhinged," Damien laughed, he didn't know to whom he was answering. "I think I need to play it safe, tonight."

"Don't deny yourself the pleasures of debauchery at its finest."

"With whom?"

"Anyone." She shrugged. "It's your choice, really."

"You mean, you?"

Before she could say anything, Damien pushed the table, got up, with a visible sway in his actions. "I need to —"

*

He was in a bed, under a soft blanket. It was warm, and he wasn't alone. He turned to his side to see blanket failing to protect the back of his companion — so many scars, so many, lines, cuts, burn marks.

His companion turned towards him and Damien's breath hitched in his throat.

"Good morning sleepyhead." Blue eyes, softened with a touch of fresh green at the centre. A small scar was going through his left eyebrow, Damien wanted to heal it, he wanted to erase all of the scars —

*

"It's not killing, it's saving. Like how you would cut the dead branches of a tree - are you listening to me?"

Damien realised he wasn't. Or maybe he was but he wasn't. It was weird. "I know I'm actually not killing..." He couldn't bring himself to finish the sentence. "But the existence in the universe. Humans, animals, plants, even rocks and water and everything."

"It happened once. It can happen again. It should happen again." He raised his arms, both covered in dark bruises. "It will happen anyway. It's de—

*

"Are you alright?"

Ferran's voice was coming from very far away, but Damien managed to hear it, to give it meaning. He tried to move his mouth, but his muscles weren't too keen on cooperating. Instead, he shook his head, as his vision came back to him.

"I am not," he said finally, as calm as he could. His heart was beating so fast, he was sure it was visible from outside. "I'm remembering things that couldn't have happened."

"Are you hallucinating?"

"No — I am sure they are memories." He filled his glass as he intended. "This is not about me. There's something wrong in general."

Wrong. That was a word.

How would one describe feeling wrong?

You'd look at a puzzle, and there would be a piece forcefully stuck one of the parts — it would leave you with an unease, something wouldn't settle in your mind, you'd want to go and fix it immediately. Damien felt like he himself was that piece, that he shouldn't have been where he has been. Wherever that was. Not somewhere familiar for sure.

With a tremor overcoming his body, he opened his eyes to come face to face with a terror stricken Ferran.

"What is wrong with you?"

Damien blanked at the question. "Where are we?"

"Hysseren. Again, what is wrong with you? Describe it to me, so I can figure out how I can help you."

"I'm drifting."

He sounded like he knew what he was saying. He didn't.

"Okay," Ferran got up, signalling to the waiter to bring the check. "I'm taking you back to your aunt, so that she can look at your head and see what's wrong."

"I don't remember what I should remember," Damien mumbled as Ferran took care of everything else. I saw myself staring at myself through the mirror. But it didn't feel like his memory.

"I am scared," he said once they were in fresh air.

"Me too, princeling," Ferran murmured, a hand on Damien's shoulder. "But it will be fine."

For some reason, Damien couldn't be certain of it.

*

Juventas was surprised to see Damien and Ferran at her doorstep, so soon after they left, but she bit all the questions about the circumstances once she saw the look on Damien's face.

"What's wrong?" She asked, and honestly, he wondered why everyone expected him to have answers.

"I don't know, you tell me," he said, walking inside. "Apparently I killed myself, but aside from remembering things I've never lived through, I don't remember anything about it."

They stared at each other, both of them resembling Madison in their own way. They didn't need words, or so it seemed. Exchanged looks were telling everything they wanted to.

Ferran felt like an outsider, but he stayed — stayed for Damien's sake, because for all the gods above and below, someone had to take care of this kid before he went insane.

"Let's go to my study," she nodded. "And talk about it."

"There's nothing to talk about," Damien said, his voice was shaking. "Help me remember. You need to help me remember."

"Yes, we're going to talk about that," she gently pushed him towards the door of her study, and he obliged.

Once inside, she had him sit down and she sat across him. "You cannot possibly remember anything about the time you were dead."

"Why, is it forbidden?"

"No, it's literally impossible." Juventas sighed. "Maybe Gerard would be a more appropriate person to discuss this, but it's impossible."

"But I do! I am not making them up, or I am not hallucinating. I don't remember how I killed myself. Or why. But I remember stars raining on me, and..." His voice hitched in his throat. I remember someone who took care of my wounds. "Help me."

She seemed unsure but she nodded regardless. "Okay, we can try something."

"Really?"

"Really. Now, look into my eyes," she said. "And don't blink."

"No matter what?"

"No matter what," she put her fingertips on his forehead. There was a smile on her face. "This can hurt you. Raise your hand if you want to stop, okay?"

"Okay," he muttered.

"On three..." She said. "One... Two..."

Pain. Immense, chest tightening, heart stopping pain.

His vision swayed once more, colours mixing into each other. When they stopped and settled, Damien recognised the room he was in, and smiled slowly as he made his way to the bed in the middle of the room.

Everything was screaming. The whole world, the whole universe was burning in his mind, but at the same time, it was silent, it was calm, it was cold even. His own reflection smiled back at him from the mirror on the ceiling. He was spent, eyes sunken deep, face full of never-before-existed lines, but still. He was there.

Sharp side of the knife in his hand was merciful, as it didn't feel like a cut but like a lover's whisper on his neck.

*

"The universe as we know it ending would be the merciful ending." He shook his head with a weak smile. "You say you've been there, at the beginning. You should know that."

"This is your universe, though. First to die, your wake up call, is your son."

"Don't I know it..." Alexei sighed once again. "One at a time. So first..." He raised his sword, a menacing gleam overshadowed all the light his eyes carried. "First, I'll deal with you."

Terror took a hold of Damien's heart, as he stood tall in the familiar territory of helplessness. He closed his eyes and held his breath—

*

As everyone tried to find something to fix it, he simply walked to the bar. He, too of course, noticed the sky above. Everything felt a lot hotter, second by second. His face was slick with sweat, his skin already feeling hotter. He ran a hand through his hair as he looked through the endless bottles in front of him, trying to pick an appropriate one for the end of life as he knew it.

Yet when he found the one, he paused before opening it. He needed to toast to something. Nothing came to mind until he looked through the windows to see the stars on fire. "To the stars!" His own body felt like it was boiling up from inside. "It was a pleasant—"

*

No, Damien thought, or said, as he felt his mouth moving. He was dead, he was alive, he died again, and again, and again. Stop it.

The feelings came, following the visions of catastrophe: Stars raining, the universe bursting, he himself exploding and taking everything with him. But it wasn't all bad. He saw Jennifer there, laughing with him, he saw good camaraderie, friendships, ro-mances, he saw—

*

"How do you even know that?" Damien asked, bitter. Tethers are pulling me already. He ran his fingers through Thyren's hair. Nobody has been this gentle with me since… "But I want to stay with you."

"You need to move forward." It was more definite this time.

"But I won't be able to forget you. Or miss you."

"You will. Eventually. And it's okay. You've given me enough already, a permanent place in your memories is not something I can ask for."

"I won't forget you," Damien insisted. "But I'm going to ask something from you."

The sky shone blue above them, and Thyren said yes. He didn't even need to hear what to say it, he would do anything, now that he could hear the weak pulse of the actual universe in his ears. Soothing, comforting. His heart skipped beats in yearning.

Damien reached and kissed him. What it lacked in passion, it made up in compassion. Thyren stopped breathing.

*

"You can't blame an anchor for doing what it does best," Alexei said when they finally separated from their hug. "It's job is to keep you where you are. If you want to move forward, what you need to do is either lifting it up, or getting rid of it entirely."

"If I got rid of it, I wouldn't be able to stop."

Alexei chuckled. "You can always make a new one. Besides," his eyes gleamed. "Why would you want to stop? You're not a delicate flower, you're not an old tree. You can go anywhere, why would you want to stop?" He put one hand on Damien's shoulder. "Run, and never look back."

*

He ran. He ran until he had no breath left. His lungs were aching with the effort, his legs shook — they felt less like meat and bones but like water. He wanted to stop, to sleep, to die in a corner. Maybe he did. It was blurry.

Humans were everywhere, hunger stricken, dying humans. They reached to him with fingers that almost had no skin on them. Their touch bruised him, their hands turned into claws — they wanted him, almost like zombies who found fresh meat. He ran. He kicked, he scratched, he ran.

*

He was in a forest. The ground was cold, but also soft and forgiving. Compassionate. Damien didn't care about the worms and slugs or anything. He wanted to be away, he wanted to be alone — for the first time ever.

It was raining as he aligned his knife made out of pure energy over his heart. He closed his eyes, felt the rain and —

*

He opened his eyes. Thyren was there, as was Axel. They didn't say anything, and left the room. He fell asleep.

Then he woke up again.

He saw his mother that was not his mother, but also was his own flesh and blood. He saw Ferran through the corner of his eye, Martyn's dutiful soldier that followed him — his own angel, and a total stranger.

Damien stood up. He felt nauseated. His ears were ringing with a high pitched screech, his eyes were blocked with tons of flying black spots. Someone — had to be Ferran — held him tightly as if to say fall. I'm here for you.

Falling was easy. Getting over the nausea and talking was not.

"The universe is about to end," he managed to say, though. His jaw felt like it was bound by steel wires. He was sure blood would pour out of his mouth with each word, and was surprised when it didn't. "We need to—" he was panting, his chest wasn't rising fast enough to catch up with his need for air. "We need to—"

"You're confused, it's normal," Juventas said, pushing Damien's hair, wet with sweat. "Take slow breaths."

"I'm not confused." Damien shook his head. He did try to take slow breaths though, as much as he could. He was dizzy, but he gripped Ferran's arm with strength he didn't think he could muster. "I've died- I've died so many times and —"

"We can deal with it tomorrow."

"We don't have the time," he got up again — he didn't even remember when he sat down. "I need to..." He remembered the man sitting on the rusty throne, one eye scarred and white, being so gentle with him. He remembered a balcony, and brush of two hands. An urge to throw up rose from his stomach, but he managed to swallow it. "We need to..."

His body couldn't take it. He passed out.

*

When he woke up, he found not only Ferran, but his parents along with his aunt at the end of his bed. Please give me some time. Let me understand.

"You scared us all, princeling," Ferran murmured, handing him a large glass of water.

"I scared myself as well," Damien replied. His eyes drifted to Madison and Martyn, looking paler than ever. "I am sorry," he said to both of them.

"For what?" asked Martyn, though he sounded like someone was strangling him. "If anything, we should be the ones to apologise."

They walked towards him, and sat on the bed — on left there was his father, on right his mother. Damien felt desperately unworthy of the attention they were paying to him.

You wondered what it was like to have parents, a scrutinising voice spoke inside his head. This is how it feels.

"I killed myself," he started. "I was in pain, and I was afraid I was going to ruin everything. I thought everyone was better off without me."

"Which was wrong," Martyn said, as Madison nodded. "We would've found a way, Damien."

"You couldn't have," Damien shook his head. Now I know why I did what I did. "Not to this. This place is doomed. It's the end times, and it wasn't because of me. We're reaching to the balance state."

Both of his parents gave each other uneasy looks. Oh, he lost his mind, Damien was sure they were thinking. We need to get rid of him.

But when Martyn spoke, it wasn't anything like that. He simply said, "Okay," and took a deep breath. "Let's take this one step at a time. Juve mentioned something about you remembering all the lives you lived when you were dead."

"Yes. I don't know why but I went through so many timelines, and most of them died, I did my best, dad, but I couldn't save them-"

"It's okay... I have a working theory about the reason, but that's for later. Now you're saying the same is going to happen to us as well?"

Damien nodded.

"So, how can we stop this from happening?"

"I don't know the exact mechanism behind it. But I think I need to speak to Axel and Thyren first." He stopped. "But in short, I think we need to kill Alexei."

*

"This universe is about to end. We need to fix it."

Damien pulled no punches back.

"That much Madison told me before I came here," Axel said. "What makes you think that?"

"I've been through a lot. I've seen a lot. Those bruises? They aren't good news, and I think, deep down, you know it as much as I do."

Thyren looked at the kid. He remembered how he was laying in a dried pool of his own blood, eyes open, staring without seeing at a ceiling right above his own bed. There wasn't a note. Not even a goodbye letter. Just shards after shards of glass and so, so much blood.

But now, here he was, standing on his own two feet, staring at the two of them with eyes that were washed with madness. Not the scary kind, the angry, the burning. It was more out of doubt and ruin. Returning from the dead must be tough, he thought. After everything.

"You're right," Axel spoke, his voice calm as ever. Thyren, without even thinking, pulled him closer to himself. "This place is doomed. What do we need to do?"

"Well, killing your dad is a start."

Axel and Thyren shared a look. "You're serious?" Axel asked.

"Yeah. I can't do it, because I never could. I always failed."

"You may have failed then but I'm sure you won't this time. After all, even if you failed -- you helped us tremendously. Bought us so much time."

"What do you mean?" Damien asked, but Thyren could see the realisation dawning in his face. "What help?"

"When you killed yourself, there was no way of bringing you back to life without breaking things that shouldn't have been broken. But then we figured a way to balance it all out."

"And what did you do?"

"Let's say we tied your path to some other timelines that desperately needed your help." Axel smiled. "And you've been tremendously successful."

Damien raised one eyebrow, in a way that made him look exactly like Madison. Like mother, like son. "Most of those timelines died."

"Died?" Thyren didn't know if the question came out of him or Axel.

"They died, they burned, they crashed, exploded on themselves, or sometimes I died before they could."

"You remember?"

"I do," Damien said after a pause.

"I see." Axel sighed. Thyren felt the same disappointment. "Well, this is a bit unsettling. I didn't want to believe when Juventas told me about it."

"Believe in what?"

"You weren't supposed to remember anything. But you do."

"Supposed to?"

"It would've been easier for you. None of us had any experience in such a thing, of course, but we anticipated some outcomes. Sad to see we were wrong."

"You're focusing on the wrong thing. I saw the death of many timelines. I couldn't save them."

"That's okay. They weren't supposed to be saved, anyway."

The silence was deafening. Damien visibly froze, all blood from his face withdrawing.

"What do you mean by they weren't supposed to be saved?"

"You were there to ensure they didn't survive."

"What?"

"Everything ends, eventually," Thyren spoke. "You're the Chaos, you should know that better than everyone."

"I thought... I was supposed to save them."

He sounded so very broken.

"That was the issue," Axel said, as gently as he could. "You thought. You shouldn't have. You should have followed the path we carved for you. I don't know what happened, or how you came to carry your memories through timelines after you died, but anyway. The result is mostly good, so well done!"

"Well done?"

"You gave us so much time to fix our problem here. Because you knew the end was coming. The balance was about to be reached before it should. That's what drove you mad."

Damien laughed. "Oh, really?"

"I don't expect you to understand. But you still have one last thing to do."

"Oh, fuck no. Get fucked," the kid replied, getting up. "I will be enjoying when it rains stars on us."

"There's nowhere to go from here, Damien. This is the last stop."

"No loss there. I was dead anyway," Damien shrugged. "Like I said, get fucked both of you. I'm out of here."

Thyren rolled his eyes. "You're not going anywhere, kid."

It was madness, but the scary kind, angry, vengeful, burning. Damien's eyes shone red. "Do you really want to test me?"

"You're not going anywhere until we let you go."

"Oh, fuck off." Bitterness seeped through his words. "What do you want me to do? Kill Sylen? Kill him yourself, I'm sure you want to anyway."

"Why would I?" Thyren leaned back, one eyebrow raised, daring him.

"Well, it's either him or your darling prince here. Before all of these, I would gladly do it to keep you two lovebirds together. Right now? You both can die and I wouldn't shed a single tear."

"You tried to save other timelines, didn't you?" Axel leaned forward. "Why not here?"

Damien frowned. "Let me see," he said, in a mocking tone. Thyren wanted to crush his head. "A good motivation is that you saw a suicidal person, and wanted to exploit his misfortune. You've sent me through timelines that were destined to be doomed and had me killed hundreds of times, in hundreds of different ways. You don't even seem to regret that." He shook his head. "I felt sorry for you two. When you tried doing everything in the right way to keep your timelines alive. When you killed them. When you had to get other people suffer to keep everything alive."

"Survival is not selfish," Thyren said. "You cannot blame us for that."

"It's not survival I'm blaming you for," Damien spat. "I'm blaming you for never regretting making me suffer. I'm not fighting your battle for you. Kill Sylen yourselves."

"It has to be you," Axel said. Thyren admired his calmness.

"It doesn't. It never had to be me, yet you made it to be."

"It was necessary."

"Was it really? All those timelines, they could've been saved if we killed Sylen. It was the same here, from the beginning."

"I didn't want to kill my father. I just wanted some more time until we figured out a different solution. That's why we did what we did to you."

"Bad news then. It's still either him, or you."

"I know."

"And he'll most definitely kill me." Damien pointed out, in a mundane way. As if he was saying there were stars in the sky.

"That's a sacrifice I'm willing to make," Axel shrugged. You said it yourself, you were dead anyway."

The kid stared at both of them, his eyes lost all the light to them. Now, he seemed a lot more dangerous. "I'm giving you a chance to walk back on that sentence."

"I am not going to," Axel stayed perfectly still, shoulders straight. "We all have responsibilities towards the universe. This is yours."

"My life means nothing to you?"

"You said it yourself, kid. You killed yourself, and then you died hundreds of times. Once more won't hurt. You'll go back to square one."

Damien started laughing. "Oh, so very clever. What happens to you when he kills me though? Will you find yet another pawn then? Maybe a different version of me, from a different timeline, huh?" He leaned forward, staring directly into Axel's eyes. "Why do you need it to be me?"

Axel shrugged. "It's what you're destined to do."

"You don't have the power to dictate a destiny to me."

With that, he disappeared out of the room. Axel sighed wearily.

"Well," Thyren muttered, pulling him closer to himself. "That went about as good as it could be."

"This is not over," Axel replied.

*

Ferran had all the signs of extreme worry when Damien sat next to him.

"Relax," Damien said. "I'm fine. I don't intend to kill myself again."

"That's not what I was worried about."

"What was it?"

"What you could've done to those two, for example."

The young god laughed. "Do you know what they did to me?"

"Your father mentioned some stuff about tying knots upon knots on some threads," Ferran shrugged. "I didn't understand it, so I am assuming something bad."

"Something cruel, rather," Damien murmured. "Bad, good, they don't exist, do they?"

Ferran remained silent. Damien took it as a sign to continue, so he did as he made a slight move with his head and getting up. He felt like he couldn't be contained, right now, pure anger was running in his veins.

"You see someone suffering, right? You look at him, and feel what? You feel sorry, gone before his time, etcetera, etcetera. They looked at someone suffering, and thought, why shouldn't we use it to our own advantage?"

"What did they do to you?"

Something in Ferran's voice vibrated in a dangerous way. Damien had to laugh, remembering all the Ferrans he ever met. Somehow, there were certain things that didn't change.

"I died hundreds of times. I watched the universe as I knew it die hundreds of times, I watched myself getting killed by Alexei, and turns out, it was all his plan. I want to tear this timeline apart with my own hands."

"Does..." Ferran cleared his throat. "Does your father know about this?"

"I don't think so. The thing is, how am I gonna tell him?" Damien sighed, walking with no aim. "He is going to kill everyone here — especially considering what happened with Madison."

"Your mother?"

This earned a frown from Damien. "Oh," he said. "I guess that couldn't have been here. I am talking of a Madison who wasn't my mother in another timeline. She was a nice lady, the chaos before me. Their Alexei killed her."

"Oh..."

"I think my dad loved him. At least in other timelines. It's hard to understand what I already knew and what I lived through."

Ferran, without a word, pulled him to a hug. "I'm not gonna let them kill you, princeling," he said. "I won't let them harm you."

Damien smiled, and muttered a silent thanks. They already hurt me enough, he thought. And they want to hurt me more.

Yet, there was something in his mind. A last resort. Last resistance.

*

Of course, they returned inside. Axel and Thyren were gone, luckily, because at the mention of their names Ferran flexed his fingers, and Damien could not bear the thought of him getting killed attacking the two. They would. Just to spite me at this point.

A terrifying thought followed it. Then I would kill them, simple as that.

He looked at his parents, with worry etched onto their faces. I am alive, though. I am alive. There were so many things running through his head at the same, exact time, he had to close his eyes.

"I have lived hundreds of lives," he began, before they could say anything. "It sounds like an exaggeration, but it isn't, and I remember them all, and it hurts."

"You asked Juve to help you remember," Madison said, arms crossed.

"I am not saying it's her fault, mother." It isn't. It's not her fault, it's nobody's but his anyway. "I am stating the facts." His eyes drifted to his father, who looked almost stoic. Almost. "There was a Madison in the other places. Chaos. Ashren. She was chaos, not order — not like you, mother, though you looked the same. Who was the Chaos before me here?"

"How do you know about him?"

"It happened here as well? Alexei killed him? It happened?"

"How do you—"

"That Madison told me. In another timeline, she was a ghost. In there, she tried to help me. She told me her story, and it happened here, too?"

"What happened after she told you that?"

"Alexei killed me, too. Because I told him he had to die to save the universe."

All three of them stared at each other.

"This universe is about to reach its destination," Damien sighed. "I am sorry. I am really sorry about it, but there's nothing I can do. I can't do what Axel is asking of me."

"What is he asking of you?" asked Martyn.

"Killing of his father. Which I tried. Not here, but I tried. I failed. I don't want to try and fail yet again."

Madison and Martyn exchanged worried looks.

"What do you plan to do?" Martyn asked, his jaw was clenched so hard, Damien was surprised at how he could talk. He expected to hear his teeth cracking.

"I don't know," Damien shrugged. A last resort. "All I know is, I cannot kill Uncle Alexei."

"That'd be my advice as well," Martyn said, and closed his eyes. Then, as if he found the solution, he smiled and opened his eyes, leaning back in the armchair.

"I can kill him. I could even get others to join me in it."

"Oh, no," Damien shook his head. "No, no, no. This is on Axel. If he wants to save his own skin, he needs to make some sacrifices. But enough of this."

He walked to them and pulled them in a hug. They didn't let him go for a long while.

*

It was a good month before Axel and Damien found themselves on the opposite sides of a very confined room.

That month wasn't easy. Damien spent most of it in his room, and any time he had to be in the same place as Axel, Axel didn't waste any time before reminding Damien of his duty, and how everything existed to serve the Universe any way. "You're no exception, Damien. No matter how you resist, you'll do what is the best for the universe. That's the destiny woven for you, for everyone."

Hence, Damien tried to avoid him.

When they met again, alone, it was per Axel's request. His father was adamant Damien could reject it, but he had no intention to. He knew he wasn't going to avoid Axel forever, and it was maybe better sooner than later.

The impending doom banged its drums even louder now. They both knew it. They both felt it. Neither of them wanted to do anything about it and they both expected what was necessary from the other.

Thyren was there, of course, as the dutiful soldier still. Even though he had incredible power at his fingertips, he still followed his love — Damien couldn't blame him. He would've done the same if he had the chance. I will do that when I have the chance.

"I am assuming," Axel started, leaning back, comfortable. "You have decided to do the right thing."

Damien nodded. "That depends," he replied, upon seeing the relief on Axel's face. I would rather kill you. Maybe I'll do just that. "On what you define as the right thing, though."

"Right and wrong aren't subject to subjectivity."

"They are. They most certainly are."

Damien was no fool. He could see the smile on Axel's face going tense and sharp, he could notice Thyren flexing his fingers. They meant business, no doubt. Luckily, so did Damien.

"I am not going to deny how terrible I have been feeling over the whole ordeal," he stated, staring at those two, staring right into their eyes. I am not scared of you. "Also conflicted. I once, twice, a hundred times loved you. I tried to save you. I failed. Over and over again. And now, I have the definite answer, yet, I can't bring myself to lift a finger."

"So you know what's the right thing," Axel said. "You just don't want to do it."

"I have no intention to help those who put me through that ordeal. I should've stayed dead."

"You can still be dead."

"If I'm dead, it means your plan failed. If you believe that'll be the end result, stop pushing for it."

Axel opened his mouth, then closed it. "What's your proposal?"

"What should've happened. Your boyfriend over there goes ahead and kills your dad, and we all live happily ever after."

"Why would I do that?" Thyren spoke for the first time.

"To save your boyfriend? Oh, don't you love him enough for that?"

Before Thyren could say anything, Axel put a calming hand on his knee. "Oh baby," he said then, looking at Damien. "You think you can manipulate us?"

"It's working on your boyfriend. Hundreds of timelines, and he starts the same. Sharp, but brittle. I love that. I always did."

"You don't know me," Thyren said through gritted teeth.

"I do know you. I know a hundred versions of you. I've fallen in love with some of them even. There was one who destroyed the entire universe just because Axel died. Do you think you can do that?"

"You don't know what I'm capable of."

"I do know it. I know everything. Thank your boyfriend for that. Do you think those timelines are that different from each other?"

"Shut him up," Thyren said to Axel, eyes still trained on Damien. "Or I'll kill him before Alexei can."

"I'm pretty sure you can," Damien replied. For a flash second he saw the King of Ashes there, that edge, that danger. "I would suggest you not to."

"Give me one good reason if you're not gonna do what you're supposed to do, then." Thyren leaned forward. "I can end it for you, once and for all. Like you wanted."

I would love to die at your hands. Not yours. But yours.

"I don't have a reason," he said instead. "Because I can't kill Alexei. Sorry, that was never my destiny. It was always yours. Either after Axel dies, or before. Up to you. Because I won't be able to kill Alexei even if I want to. That means your boyfriend is doomed." It was wrong, but Damien wanted to twist the knife a bit more. "That is, of course, if you care enough about him to do something about it."

There were missing pictures after that. Damien found himself on the ground, Thyren pressing on his trachea with enough of a grip to leave him breathless. They stared at each other.

But Damien wasn't looking at him.

His vision blurred, possibly because he didn't have enough air in his lungs. His brain, splitting into two with a pain that had nothing to do with being slammed on the ground, decided to punish him for the action that brought him here. It was the same face, after all.

I don't treat anyone's wounds, the man in his head — the man who stood in front of him, but also was so so far away said. Damien could feel the pain beneath his bandages, he could feel another Thyren's, the King of the Mountain's, fingers working on the wound.

He started crying, as he gasped for air.

The Thyren in front of him released his grip, just a bit., only to retighten it — even more so. Something in his eyes seemed feral, he seemed like he was taking delight in this show of power. I've seen bigger power than yours. Your powers, at their peak. But in his mind, the man in front of him was the one who told him to come back.

It's less lonely with you here.

"Oh, you sweet child," Axel leaned to Damien's ear, and Damien realised he had lost the concept of time and place for a moment. "Do you think you have a say in this? Do you think you're making your own decisions?"

Damien pried his eyes away from Thyren, and turned to Axel. His eyes were still full of water, but now at least his own mind wasn't working against him. "What do you mean?" He choked on the words.

"I've woven your threads, I've picked every single step you were going to take — no matter what you do, no matter how you think you rebel, you're doing my bidding."

"No," Damien said. It made no sense. But it also felt too real. "That's not true."

"It's not? You're sure?" Axel laughed. "Then why did you come back here?"

The young man closed his eyes. Total darkness. His throat hurt, but he could breathe — better than nothing. He thought of the reason of his return. The tethers. Something was pulling me.

"So," Axel continued. "Do all you want. There's no way out of this duty."

"Maybe," Damien replied, raising his hand. He felt the power at the tip of his fingers, so comforting, so disgusting at the same time.

He waved his hand once, and they both stood up, walking back ten steps away from him.

The confusion on their faces was almost too delightful, and he cursed his luck for being blinded by his own tears and choking too much to enjoy it.

Without saying a word, Damien waved his hand again. The entire room was filled with gossamer threads in an instance, glistening slightly as it connected all of them.

"You see it," Axel spoke.

"Shh," Damien stood up and made a closing motion with his hand. Axel stared at him with wide eyes. "I am thinking."

He snapped his fingers. A long, black sword appeared out of nowhere.

"Tethers, you say," he murmured. "Knots you tied, right? Well, about them..."

He swung the sword right in front of him. And disappeared in that very second.

Chapter 11

Damien was dancing with a beautiful girl who had a dress made out of live butterflies. Her laughter sounded like it was made of pure sunshine.

"Oh," she said, throwing her head back. Her long hair flowed like water. Tears pooled in the corners of her ocean blue eyes. "You entertain me so much."

"I exist to serve," Damien heard himself reply. The music was all muffled, as if nothing else but her mattered. "And to please."

"You do both of them really good," she said.

And the tune changed, so they started dancing once more, despite the fact that Damien found it really hard to follow the notes, or the rhythm. He was just following her lead. A few golden butterflies were circling them from above. He turned his head to look for some waiter walking around with a plate full of wine glasses, but there didn't seem to be any waiters. Or any people.

"Isn't it weird?" He said, as he turned his head towards her. But it wasn't her there — nor he was holding her. Now, some strong hands were handling him, and there were no music coming.

"Who takes care of you?" The owner of the strong hands asked. He was watching Damien with great interest, even though one of his eyes didn't seem like it was seeing anything. A scar was going through it. "After all the battles, who picks you up from the ground?"

"Nobody," Damien replied. "I take care of myself."

"Shame," the man's face got solemn. "Close your eyes, Damien."

"Do you know me?" Do I know you?

"Close your eyes, Damien."

He did. There was a thumping sound, he didn't know if it was his heart or war drums or something else entirely. He closed his eyes, believing somewhere deep inside that he was safe and sound, as he was in the arms of that man, and they danced to a song Damien couldn't hear. His heart ached with a yearning he couldn't name what for.

"This won't last forever," he said, his eyes still closed.

"It won't," the man agreed. "Eventually, you'll wake up."

"Am I sleeping?"

There was no answer until they did a few more turns.

"You are resting," came the answer. "Who cleans your wounds?"

"Nobody," Damien echoed himself. "I let them bleed out."

"Shame," the man said again, but there was something different in his voice. Damien opened his eyes, to see it was the same man but with less scars on his face. The most prominent one went through his eyebrow, and stopped above his eye. "I would take care of them for you."

"You would?"

"Come back to me, Damien."

"Where, when you're already here?"

His words echoed from empty walls. There was nobody, he was alone, staring at a mirror. He saw himself, or at least he thought he saw himself. The reflection in the mirror looked a lot like him, but distorted somehow. The reflection's eyes were sunken, almost shadowy. Every line that separated him from his surroundings was blurred, as if he wasn't a separate entity but an extension of it.

The reflection smiled.

"You see the hands wrapped around your throat, don't you princeling?" It, he, said. "Tying tiny, cute little knots around your joints. He'll be excitedly pulling them to make you do whatever he wants."

It was still the same mirror, but Damien no longer saw the creepy reflection -- instead, it was him, bruised and beaten but him undoubtedly. Slender, pale fingers were busy tying gossamer threads to his throat, his arms, his legs. The puppeteer, Damien thought of him, I am at his mercy.

"You are mine," a voice whispered in his ear. "You are mine to do as I please. You only exist to do whatever I make you do. In death, in life."

"No," Damien said, and immediately the thread around his throat got tighter. "No," he said, struggling. Tears pooled in the corner of his eyes. Thread got even tighter. He tried to slid his fingers between it and his windpipe, but his hands didn't budge.

"You're not here to think. You're not here to speak. You are only here to do whatever I want you to do."

"I'm not your toy."

"That's where you're wrong," the Puppeteer said, coming towards the light. Damien knew him, of course he did, they met in so many universes. The gentle prince, the crown jewel, the golden flower.

He was holding the ends of the threads tightly. His smile wasn't cruel, nor his voice. He spoke so very softly, and so very simply.

Damien wanted to gauge his eyes out.

"You exist to serve me. You exist to please me, like everything is. And you are good at both of them."

"No," Damien replied once again. "I am not here to serve you. It's not my nature." It was hard speaking, but he did. "If you want to kill me for that, do it."

"If it comes to that, I will do it."

"Then don't wait. I am very tired, and I could use the rest."

Despite the tug of all the threads at once, he raised his hands to his throats, grasping the thread on his throat. It cut his fingers like glass, but he didn't budge. The pain tore his mind apart, but there was no going back.

Once he managed to tear the thread itself, he felt the blood trickling down to his chest, but he paid no attention to it. He looked at his tormenter, straight in the eye.

"I was here before all," he said. Was I really? "You're eventually going to return to me." Will he really?

"Well, not exactly you," the reflection's voice echoed from the walls. "But, good enough, eh?"

Shadowy fingers were untying the rest of the threads. Damien closed his eyes once more. The rhythm of the drums got louder.

*

It didn't surprise him to find out the drums were beating in his head, in sync with his heartbeat, when he opened his eyes.

He was in a comfortable bed, in a dimly lit room. He was thankful — honestly, his eyes didn't feel like they could handle any more light than of a couple of candles.

There was someone sitting next to him, though, a woman with very long hair. She had a book in her hand, a finger casually between the pages, she was sleeping on the chair. He hoped she wasn't there for him.

He closed his eyes, taking calm and big breaths to silence the pulse beating in his head. It didn't help, honestly, closing his eyes made it even worse — everything, every memory he had ever lived through, started flashing. It was very hard to distinguish between where he was and what he was doing at the moment and what his mind thought he was doing.

He instead decided to stare at the ceiling, continuing with the big breaths. His lungs appreciated that action, and rewarded him with some relief of sorts. He was gonna take it.

When he heard something, he turned his head to look at the woman, seeing her shifting uncomfortably in her sleep. The book slipped from her fingers, and hit the ground before Damien could reach to it. She, too, woke up.

He stayed silent as she regained her composure, and her eyes drifted to him eventually.

"You're awake," she said, in flawless Hysserian dialect. Somehow, the thought of being on Lanenketer comforted him. Well, as long as it didn't rain ash upon them.

"I am," he said. "And I must have been a terrible burden to you-"

"Nonsense," she replied, waving her hand to light up several more candles. Damien had to close his eyes for a second. "You're soaking wet."

"I'm sorry."

"It's okay, I was expecting it. The physicians said the fever was the way to burn the poison, and sweat was to get it out of your system." Damien opened his eyes, and found her towering over him. Her big blue eyes were on him with intense interest. "I will call one of them here, and will inform an interested party. Then I'll be back."

That alerted Damien. "Interested party?"

"We could call him my patron, as well. I didn't take you in out of the kindness of my heart, Ashren." Her eyes held a joyful gaze. "I am not exactly known for that, to be perfectly frank."

I couldn't care less about your fame, Damien thought, his throat achingly dry. Who are you serving to?

Then another thought interrupted his thought train. "Wait. Poison?"

"The physicians thought you were poisoned. When you appeared in my garden, you were feverish, unconscious, but speaking — telling things nobody could comprehend."

"I am not poisoned." Or was I? Did Haylen poison me before having that discussion with me? Maybe he did and I don't remember it — "Who are you?"

She smiled, too condescendingly understanding, and raised her head only very subtly. "Erihnam Nelesten-Hyiressen-Sylanen," she said. "Queen of the Central Lands."

Wait. Did I just appear to Lanenketer? "Hysseren? We're in Hysseren, then?"

"I see you're no stranger to our lands. Though I shouldn't have been surprised."

Damien actually he had a lot of questions, but also, he was utterly confused. In his mind, he was having this conversation with a Sylanen Prince with golden hair. He was also being dragged on the ground, and also drinking a cup of tea with Sylen. Nausea rose from his throat. He tried to focus on the woman in front of him.

"Who is this interested party?" He managed to ask.

"Don't concern yourself with that," she said, her voice colder. "You'll find out, maybe sooner than later."

"Well, if it's Haylen — don't bother."

"Why is that?"

"I'll rather kill myself again."

She nodded. "I'll keep that in mind. Do you want to back to sleep?"

"I don't think I can sleep."

She waved her hand again, and all the candles dimmed. "I'll ask the servants to fetch you fresh clothes, and then the physicians will check you. If you want a bath, you'll need to wait for the morning."

"Thank... you?"

"No need. I'm doing what I'm ordered to do. If you're not going to fall asleep, I might bring you a guest."

She walked out of the room, and Damien dragged his eyes to the ceiling. They hurt, every part of his body hurt, yet his brain was disturbingly alert.

Two young male servants entered the room with fresh clothes. Damien considered begging them to leave him alone, but then decided having a bit of dignity was better no matter what.

With great effort he lifted himself off the bed.

*

In the lower quarters of the Hysseren Palace, and in the city, many people didn't exactly like Erihnam Nelesten. She was estimated to be thousands and thousands of years old, with no heirs and no intention of leaving the throne to someone else.

And, not because she was a tyrant, but because the day she was crowned and proclaimed as the Messenger of the Gods, she announced that all the gods they knew were dead, and there was now only one God who was everything.

It was hard to erase all the memories of Gods of Old from people. Not that she didn't try, but even she wasn't able to be in every city, every town, every house and every room. People whispered to each other, and they kept whispering for thousands and thousands of years. They silently branded her a heretic, called her with less colourful and kind names, and kept praying to their old gods in secret.

She knew it. Neither her, nor her God cared about it.

Her servants bowed as she made her way to her room, all the candle flames on the walls standing even taller. There was only one thing in her mind, and nothing else was going to distract her.

Two guards opened the heavy wooden doors to her room, and as she walked in, she already knew who was there. Erihnam smiled to herself.

"He looks a lot like you," she said, as she took off her crown.

"Oh, I am unique, and you know that," replied her guest from the bed. "Is he alright?"

"Awake, confused, and dare I say a bit scared? He wanted to know if you were Haylen."

Erihnam heard the bed croaking with the man's weight, but she kept purposefully looking away from him, as if her jewellery box was much more interesting. "He'd rather die again, apparently."

"Did he tell you why?"

"No," Erihnam finally turned to her God, shadows surrounding him startling her as always. The skeletal figure of the God never failed to send shivers down his spine, no matter how many years it had been. "My physicians keep telling me he was poisoned."

"Your physicians are morons," he said. "He wasn't poisoned. He was exhausted."

"So it wasn't the antidotes they were hell bent on administering that worked?"

"I think it took me only a few seconds to replace those with neutralisers."

He motioned her to come to bed. She pointed out the full attire on herself. "I have many things to attend to, and I'd rather not get dressed out."

He made an unsatisfied sound. "I am the only thing you should attend to."

"I think you should attend to your guest, first," Erihnam replied, with a smirk. "We'll have an eternity after you solve that puzzle."

"It's not a puzzle, darling," the God leapt out of the bed, stretching his arms. "There is some bad blood between him and Haylen, and I'm only doing the kid a favour."

Erihnam frowned with this. "Haylen is alive?"

"Not here. Don't tire your beautiful head with these, though, my queen."

"Seth-"

Seth, the Skeletal God of Everything, leaned to Erihnam and kissed her. "I'll tell you everything. Be patient."

With that, he disappeared.

*

The physician handed Damien a small glass, full of a purple liquid.

"Drink this, please," the man said, putting his tools in his bag. "It will help you purge the remainder of the poison in your system."

Damien was ninety-nine percent sure it wasn't antidote, but straight up neutralisers — still he finished the glass in one big swallow. The physician kept talking about how he needed to take easy and similar stuff, but Damien was focused more on the immediate relief: The drumming in his head silenced, memories no more clashing, and his vision cleared. It was heaven.

"Please let us know immediately if you feel worse," the physician concluded.

"I will, thank you," Damien lowered his head.

The guy got out of the room, and Damien collapsed on the bed again. He felt calm, so calm he could've fallen asleep right at that moment.

The shadows in his room elongated, got darker and thicker, as if they were tangible. He briefly considered reaching to them, but then decided against it — if what he consumed was truly neutralisers, he would have no powers to defend himself. He didn't have any will to do it, either.

"It's so good to finally see you coherent," a familiar voice spoke.

"What?" Damien asked.

In the corner of the room, right next to the door, there was a tall man, with a wide smile on his face. His eyes were sunken, his figure skeletal. The man didn't look like he was walking when he moved to the middle of the room, but more like he was hovering, carried by his shadow.

It was the man from his dream.

Damien was looking at himself.

"You're... You're real."

"I am, very much," Seth smiled again, a smile so sharp it felt like someone etched it onto his face. "As are you."

"Where am I then?"

"My domain, to which I welcome you heartily, Damien."

Damien was unsure of what he should say. "Thank you?"

"You're welcome. I am sorry for what you've been through."

"You know what I've been through?"

"Unfortunately. Axel had never found enjoyment in being gentle."

A shiver went down Damien's spine. "You know him?"

"Of course. I guess we can say it is my fault that he put you through this. He had to be banking on you being like me."

Damien's heart was pounding in his chest now. I need to get out of here. I need to run away. His eyes drifted from one corner of the room to the other, trying to find an exit that wasn't blocked by his shadowy twin. The only option seemed to be the window, which - by the looks of the sky - was too high from the ground.

"Calm down. Nobody is going to hurt you. He can't reach you here."

"Who are you?"

"Oh, very rude of me. My name is Seth, and I happen to be the God of Everything around here."

"So this is another timeline where..." His voice trailed off. God of Everything? Where is everyone else?

"I used to be the God of Chaos as well," Seth answered his unasked question. "Just like you. Then a lot of things happened, and now we're here."

Damien let a very shaky breath. "Is that timeline... Is that timeline dead?"

"No, no of course not." Seth smiled, raising one hand in a calming manner. "I took care of that. You can relax. It should've been me all along, but well..."

Now, sense and logic were slowly replacing the sheer panic in Damien's head. There was a bigger story here, there had to be, but a corner of his head whispered to be careful. What if you're doing what Haylen already planned you to do? What if everything he's saying is a lie?

A cold, pure sense of fear gripped his heart. What if none of this is happening?

Seth must have understood his hesitancy. "Let me tell you the story," he said. "Then you can have a bit more context, huh?"

*

Once upon a time, there were a lot of timelines that began when the universe as a whole came to existence. There were gods, there were goddesses — there were many of them, in many different timelines. Under different names, under different guises — they all worked for the universe as a whole.

In some of those, there was balance, whose only task was to make his timeline reach a point of balance. It would take a long time, granted, and nobody would understand him for the point of balance meant certain death for everyone. Immortality, after all, was just a fancy word for living as long as the universe lived. Humans named him Sylen.

In some of those, there was also chaos. In most of that some, chaos was a beautiful blonde lady named Madison. In some, she lived. In some, she killed Sylen. In some, she was killed by Sylen. It went on. Humans named her Ashren.

And in one timeline, humans continued calling chaos Ashren - but this time, Ashren was a skinny kid with dark hair named Seth. He was there at the beginning, and he was not a shining example of logic and reasoning. He wanted to solve problems quickly. Power at his fingertips was too big for him, but it didn't scare him as much as it scared others.

Then came Haylen, Sylen's precious little baby.

Seth had no care for him, he was out there, doing his own thing, messing with humans, messing with leytiannen. He didn't want to stay amongst the gods who despised him for no reason, and nobody called him back anyway.

One day, many many years after Haylen's arrival, Seth met a man named Axel while he was amongst humans and knew right away that he wanted him. He wanted to protect him, he wanted to make him happy, he wanted to give his own leashes to him and be at his disposal. He would set everything on fire, just to make Axel smile, and he would do it without a moment's hesitation.

No question there, Axel liked him as well. They spent so much time amongst humans, each oblivious to the true nature of their respective existences, they shared a bed — at nights, and only at nights. Seth enjoyed giving up whatever control he had, he enjoyed being pinned to the bed by Axel's strong but gentle hands, having to implore for whatever he wanted — more, just please, I need more.

Axel would give him more. He would go rougher, he would go faster, he would hold back more. His teeth would always find that one spot on his neck that made Seth whimper like a kitten, and he would speak just the right words to keep him on the edge.

Eventually, they understood who they truly were — Ashren, and Haylen. It didn't stop them. If anything, they went in harder. Seth enjoyed being Axel's little toy, and Axel enjoyed having one of the most powerful beings in the whole universe as his little pet. You exist for me, just like everything else.

Their relationship quickly expanded to include daytime, and places other than their beds. Seth returned to his place amongst gods, but everyone knew he wore an invisible collar around his neck, that he was a slave to the universe they were all supposed to serve. That didn't make him less scary. He didn't want to be.

Then, after many years that humans kept measuring and calculating incorrectly, everything started going downhill when bruises and scars started to appear on Axel's body.

Seth blamed himself for it. Surely, he must have done something wrong, and he needed to fix it. He stepped away from Axel, even though with his entire being, he ached for him. He returned to his fun amongst humans, spent his nights and days acting like one of them. Occasionally, he would gamble — just so he could use his powers, in a less harming way, because he believed he was the source of Axel's misery.

That was until Axel found him.

Seth stopped running away, and Axel told him about the solution. It will be fine. Trust me.

It was fine. Until it wasn't, until Seth lost his mind with pain and power, and until a lot of things.

*

Seth knew he had to take responsibility this time. Axel believed it was he himself who unleashed the monster that was Seth upon Flerketer, but in reality, they were both the monsters mothers warned their children against in the nights.

Seth never hid it. Axel, on the other hand, was always so very successful at acting as civil as possible.

"Once upon a time," Seth, sitting on the throne sideways, spoke, looking at the blonde man in front of him. In his hand, he was twirling an old sword with dented edges. "I was in this exact same place. In the same exact position. I used this sword back then, do you remember?"

Axel doubted his own memories as he looked at him. I remember how you killed my father at my behest. But that Seth looked a lot more humanly. The man here, even though the piercing blue eyes and raven black hair were the same — he was more skeleton than a living body. Shadows in the room seemed to elongate his features that distorted his proportions, but he didn't look sick. He was just less human, that was all.

"The sword is clean now," Axel said, after a period of silence.

"Oh, because I didn't use it this time." He threw the sword away, it fell onto the ground with a loud clank that echoed in the room. "I didn't need to."

"How—"

"Is this how you greet an old friend?" Seth almost jumped, and stood up in front of Axel. He was moving in a smoke-like fashion, fast, seamless. "Tsk tsk tsk... Are you always like this, or is this just your display of animosity towards me?"

"How are you here?"

"Baby, you really didn't think you are the only one who can cross through timelines, did you?" He sighed, so loud, so annoying. "I solved your problem. I bought you a lot of time. Where's my thanks for it?"

"I never asked you to."

"You might not have this time," the man agreed. "But still — what are old friends for?"

"Seth," Axel said, raising his head. "What are you doing here?"

The man took great delight in hearing his name from Axel. His face brightened up with a smile that made him look even less humanly, he looked like a skeleton even more. His hollow eyes shone with a light that carried no warmth, but they were happily bright nonetheless. Axel couldn't help but shudder.

"I wasn't actually going to intervene," he admitted. "I thought, why do I care? I already gave him a universe, pristine, clean, with so much time, and he threw it away." He was walking around Axel in a circle, looking at him from every angle possible. He stopped all of a sudden, his voice colder when he spoke. "Then I saw the kid."

"Damien."

"That would be him. Looks exactly like me, except more humanly and more naive. Oh, it was then I realised you haven't changed at all. For fuck's sake, you should've straight up asked me."

"I did what was necessary."

"You mean you did what was necessary to traumatise him," Seth completed the sentence. Axel felt like he was being judged, by the insanest of the judges. "I am not surprised. You were always a selfish creature. That's why I loved you." He sighed again, but this time it was filled with sorrow. "You knew, Axel. You had to know.

Killing Alexei would drive him insane. Someone else killing Alexei while he was here would also drive him insane. He didn't deserve that."

"And?"

"So, I waited until he was gone, and in a safe distance."

Axel narrowed his eyes. "You screwed up my plans, didn't you?"

"Of course. It didn't take too much, I undid one knot, and tied it to another place — where he would survive, he would not die, and he would be cared for. But I knew he was going to come here. Eventually."

He put his arm around Axel's shoulders, and it took all the strength in Axel's body not to fight him, not to wrap his own hands around Seth's neck and break it like a twig. I can turn this around. I can be done with it.

"I knew where you were, obviously," Seth continued, this time in a whisper. "The moment you came here I knew where you were — I have to admit, you leaving was something I truly needed for my self actualisation."

"What do you mean?"

"I have a universe at my fingertips now, Axel," Seth laughed, giddy, excited. "Everyone else is gone."

"You cannot sustain it for long," Axel said, distant. "You don't have the powers for it."

"Oh, but I do."

Axel knew he shouldn't have asked. He knew he should've said oh, fine, congratulations and left the palace — or maybe he should've called Thyren in, and they would rid of this mess together.

But his curiosity got the better of him.

"What did you do?"

"I did," Seth said, with a huge grin on his face. "whatever I wanted to do. What you were so afraid of me doing."

Axel closed his eyes for a second. "Did you really have to kill them?"

Seth shrugged. "It was bound to happen. Besides—" he raised his hand to silence Axel's obvious argument. "Why do you care? You left them all behind."

"What other choice did I have?"

"Oh, come on. We all knew you did it because you were scared, that was it. You had me right in your palm. You were the only one I would stop for."

"Didn't you say that me leaving was actually good for you?"

"Eventually, yes. Eventually, I killed everyone, and took their powers to myself. The one and only god, as the humans call me. I have to admit, I still have a few screws loose, and there are days I wail in pain — but other than that, I'm fine."

"So, stop haunting me, then."

"Never," Seth clenched his jaw. "You played with me like a toy, and screw the end result, I'm gonna do the same to you. Not now maybe, because you're disgustingly happy with that boyfriend of yours, and I still love you enough to avoid disrupting your happiness. Not enough to stop haunting you."

"Will you stay?"

"Oh, no. But you will live with the knowledge that I can pop right back into your life, anytime I want. You will hear a whisper and wonder if it's coming from me. It will be fun enough until I actually come back."

"I can stop you even setting foot in this timeline."

"You don't have the power, Axel. You might be the universe, but I am literally everything now."

He flicked invisible dust off of his shoulder, and started walking to the door. "Oh," he said, turning back with an elegance Axel didn't expect from him. "A word of caution to the wise. Don't ever play with the threads again."

"Why not?"

"They are not your thing. You do too much damage."

"That was the intent."

Seth smiled, and in that moment, he resembled Damien a lot more. "Yeah. Figured. You damaged a lot of things."

"You, for example."

"Oh, don't take credit for all of it. I was already damaged when you first found me." His face stayed the same with his smile, but something there screamed agony. "I personally don't expect an apology for crimes against me."

"I wasn't going to give you one. I did whatever's necessary."

"And you hated me for doing whatever's necessary. Such hypocrisy."

Axel looked at him, through him. "I didn't hate you, Seth," he murmured.

"Oh, really?"

"I was just scared of you."

"Understandable. Still hurts, though. You could've at least said goodbye."

"You loved me, didn't you?"

"Why the past tense?" Seth grabbed his own left arm with his right and, as if all he wanted to do was wrapping his arms around

Axel, but this had to suffice. "I still do. And I know you never did. And it's okay."

"Is it really?"

"Of course it is." He smiled wider. "We all have the power to create our own destinies, Axel. I could never blame you for using yours. I only blame you for not apologising when you should have."

Against his own better judgement, Axel moved towards him. Seth didn't make a sound, he didn't move an inch as his eyes were trained on the blonde man, a childlike curiosity to understand his motives.

"Are you going to kill me?" He finally asked Axel, when the distance between them was only a few steps. It was funny how easily he could've reached him, how easily he could've pulled him to himself. He didn't do it, though. Neither him, nor Axel disrupted the status quo.

"No," Axel replied his question, silently. "I know it would be better if you were dead. But no."

"Did you do all that to Damien because he reminded you of me?"

"I did whatever's necessary to save this timeline." It sounded hollow this time. Both of them knew that.

Seth closed the distance. "I still miss you."

"You really want someone to tighten your leash when you haven't got any?"

"Or choke me if necessary." He laughed, and Axel found himself expecting it to sound sinister. It was genuine. "I miss the times when life was simpler."

"You made it more complicated."

"At your request." His voice wasn't louder than a murmur, but everything was crystal clear. "I miss you, because often times I find myself lonely."

This time, it was Axel's time to laugh. "Then you shouldn't have killed everybody."

"You, like many others, confuse being alone with loneliness, darling." Something in his tone made Axel suddenly realise that Seth was much, much older than him. Ancient. "You understood me. You understood what it means to be selfish and how it wasn't something to be ashamed of. The others? Not so much. They too were selfish, of course. Almost everyone is. Issue was, they would never admit it to themselves. We all put our own survival above everyone else's. This is what we're designed to do."

"You expect me to apologise for my own selfishness, though."

"I expect you," Seth said, with a deep breath, as if he was just a teacher to a stubborn child. "To apologise for casualties who are still alive. Not to me, of course. But apologising when you actually can shows the existence of a conscience. Selfishness and that can coexist."

As he turned once more, Axel grabbed his hand.

"Don't leave, not just yet," he said, not believing the words coming out of his own mouth. "Stay for dinner."

Seth smiled. "My dear," he said, placing a gentle kiss on Axel's hand. "You don't want that, not really. But if you really want to spend more time with me, you can always visit the hometown." He let him go, and continued his walk towards the door. "Oh," he said, before disappearing. "You can bring the boyfriend, too."

*

Of course, he didn't tell Damien about how it was a bittersweet reunion. The boy was already out of his mind scared, and telling how the man who put him through that misery was an ex lover was a terrible idea.

He stuck to the truth as much as possible, though for the past at least. However, no sentence changed the frozen in fear expression in Damien's now large as plate eyes, but at least he wasn't breathing like a wild animal trapped in a cage.

"You knew?" Damien asked, at the end. His words were bordering on unintelligible, he wasn't blinking. "Did you know what he did?"

"Yeah... Now, tell me something."

Seth leaned forward. Damien, almost involuntarily, leaned back in response.

"You were mumbling about a destroyer, when they brought you here. Must have been one of us, since you called him Ashketyirlen."

"Was I? Did I?" *Of course I called for him.*

"Yes." Seth was smiling now, which wasn't less scary. "Who is he?"

Damien felt his heart stopping. *Why do you want to know? Do you want to kill him? Is this Haylen's grand plan?*

"It's okay if you don't want to share," Seth added. "It got me curious, because you kept calling for him. Him, and a Thyren — the latter of which I can understand, because apparently those Thyrens are very appealing for the Flerketer pantheon."

"Where is the rest of the Flerketer pantheon?"

"All dead," Seth replied. "I killed them all, absorbed their powers, and now I'm the God of Everything. That's the reason Axel escaped, he was worried I'd do this."

"And he wanted to use me as his weapon then."

"He's used to that from me, I am not going to lie. I would do it again if he asked me to, and I did even though he didn't."

"You killed Sylen?"

"It was easier. Less maddening for everyone. I had to wait until there was a window for your escape, though. It was a bit haphazard, and I'm sorry for that. I crash-landed you on Lanenketer, instead of Flerketer. Though I must admit, Erihnam is a much better host than I am."

It's a lie, his mind spoke with that quiet voice. This is something Haylen planned, like he planned everything.

"Oh, he scared you so well..." It was a sigh, it was disappointment. "Damien... What did he tell you? I mean Axel. What did he tell you?"

Damien shook his head. "I... I need to rest." He was sure something moved in the corner of his eye, and a whisper echoed in his ear as if it was spoken now: Do you think you have a say in this?

Seth nodded. "Yes. Sure. Rest, sleep. We'll talk later."

He almost blended into shadows, rather than disappearing straight away. Damien couldn't shake the feeling that the shadows around him were now watching him.

*

Falling asleep, waking up, and falling asleep again had Damien lost track of time, against his better judgement.

He knew the deal. From one of his many lifetimes, he wasn't sure which or when, he knew about the neutralisers. He could almost touch the memory of him injecting a syringe full of it to himself, and coming down from the high of it. I need to stay calm. I know this.

His brain was a chorus of memories again, many things happening at the same time. But what pinned him to the bed, unable to move, was the man at the end of his bed.

Damien was pretty sure it was just a hallucination. *I am dreaming. Coming down from the high of it. He is not here.*

"Such a child," Haylen scolded him. *He's not here. He's not here. I am dreaming.* "You thought you could run away from me? And to where? You're such a child, still, Damien."

Drips of sweat on his forehead were pretty reluctant to resist gravity. Damien wiped them with his hand, it was surprisingly shaky. He didn't blink, though. He looked straight at Haylen. *Even if you're real, I'm no longer scared of you.*

"Don't be stupid, you're very scared of me. Not me, per se, but you're scared of what I can make you do for me."

He moved forward, and pushed Damien's hair away from his face. It was almost gentle, almost. There was no guarantee of those fingers not finding their way to his throat. *Is he going to kill me? Am I okay with dying?*

"You would want to shut me up, wouldn't you? Using your power to force me to shut up... Seth is always a dear, he filled you up to your eyes with neutralisers. He wouldn't want you to hurt me, such a darling. You don't have a power over me now. As it should be."

"Sylen is dead," Damien blurted, it was hard through his gritted teeth, but still. "He is dead! Why are you here? What do you want from me?"

Haylen sighed. "You've disrupted my plans, Damien. Briefly, and I must admit — cutting the threads threw me off the curve a bit. A clever move I wouldn't expect from you. I always thought of you as the..." He leaned to his ear, his hot breath breezing over Damien's wet skin. "Die when you can't find another option person."

Their eyes met again. It was pure hatred in Haylen's eyes, pure, primal, simple.

"What do you want from me?" Damien asked.

"I need you to understand, Damien. I need you to understand how no matter what you do, you're always playing to my hand."

"I am not doing anything."

"And that's by my choice. I carved every single path you walked after you died. You shouldn't blame others for taking the reins when you so willingly want to give up on them."

"I was in pain," Damien croaked. "I wanted the pain to end—"

"You were in pain, because you were in denial of your nature. It's in your nature to serve me. Just like Seth did. Just like Madison would, if she was alive. What makes you think you were so special that you could rebel against your own calling?"

Damien, in that moment, realised how the chorus of memories were silenced in his head. It was only Haylen's voice, and his face now. Every cell in his body consumed by an existential terror, likes of which he never felt before. It wasn't even fight or flight, he was stuck in freeze.

Those cursed fingers found their way to Damien's hair again, stroking them like a concerned father would streak his sick kid's hair. I wish my father was here. Or Thyren. My Thyren.

"Come back here. It's less lonely with you here."

Damien should've asked him to leave a light on, to act like his very own lighthouse, his North Star.

"Do you want to go home, Damien?"

"Home?"

"Home. Your parents are very worried about you. Don't you miss Ferran?"

Tears pooled in the corner of Damien's eyes. I don't have a home. I wanna go to the King of Ashes. I wanna go to the King of the Mountain.

"You'll never see them, how very sad..." Haylen's whisper in his ear was a lullaby now. Damien closed his eyes. "You have nothing. Nobody. Accept the truth, Damien. Be in peace with your nature."

"My nature?"

"You're doing whatever I planned you to do. I knew you were not going to accept killing Alexei, so I sent you here. Seth always has a soft spot for me. I knew he'd come to help. My help. Now, no matter what you do, you're doing exactly what I anticipated you doing." Haylen smiled, warm, genuine. "No matter how far you run, you'll always end up in—"

The door was swung open. A servant announced that Her Royal Highness, Messenger of the Gods, Queen Erihnam Hyiressen-Sylanen was coming, at the top of his lungs.

Damien tried to return back to Haylen, but he wasn't there. When Erihnam finally made her grand entrance, his eyes were still searching for Haylen.

"I doubt our walls provide that much entertainment, Ashren," she said.

"I—" Damien didn't know what to say. The chorus in his mind was gaining traction again. "Can someone bring me water?"

"Absolutely." She raised her hand, and within seconds a servant ran inside with a tall glass full of water. It was fresh, it was cold, and Damien thought he was drinking straight up life. "How do you feel today?"

"Awful. My head is pounding, and I just need to get out of here."

She nodded. "If by here you mean this room, it's the reason I am here, to ask if you wanted to accompany me in the gardens. If you mean to get out of my sight entirely, I would say that's not possible."

"Would that make me a prisoner with a slightly longer leash?"

"I would say a guest of whose safety and health we would like to be certain." She smiled wide. "You're a lot more chatty, I take this as a good sign."

Damien shrugged. "Anything to satisfy you."

"After my physicians check you, you can take a bath, and then we can enjoy our stroll in the garden."

"My schedule for the day determined, then."

Erihnam's face visibly got colder.

"I understand you've been through a lot. But I'm not going to tolerate you not appreciating our hospitality."

"I didn't mean to," Damien conceded. No need to make an enemy now. "I am sorry, your Highness."

"Eventually my patron will decide if you will be walking out of here. But for now, I'd recommend you to look at it from the good side."

"I will."

"Then it's settled. Health check, bath, garden. We'll decide the rest after that."

She turned and walked out of the room without another word.

Damien sighed. A warm bath was a good start.

*

The physician didn't say anything important. Damien complied with everything he requested, but at the end, he raised his hand to interrupt the man's monologue.

"Painkillers," he said. "I need painkillers."

"Where exactly do you have pain?"

"My head feels like it's being torn into two."

The physician seemed unsure, but nodded nevertheless. "I will have it sent here along with your food. Any other complaints? Nausea, blurred vision, maybe nightmares?"

Oh I have nightmares, alright. Waking ones. Hallucinations. "Nothing else," he said. In a corner of his mind, the memory of him taking a stroll in Hysseren's night life played. He was about to turn a corner to find Haylen, there. One of the good ones. One that didn't try to have me killed on a suicide mission.

The physician was saying something. Damien found himself nodding along without hearing a single word. In his ears, it was only the tacky music at the bar.

One of the servants came in to tell him his bath was prepared. He had no idea when the physician left.

"It is weird, isn't it?" Haylen said, appearing right next to him. "Everyone seems to be helping you, when they don't even know you."

"They know Seth apparently," Damien replied, walking to the bathroom. The hot steam caressed his face the moment he opened the door. It promised comfort.

"Seth just wants to have you plump and fat, so that when it's convenient, he can put you in the oven and eat you."

Damien took of his shirt. "Is he a cannibal now?"

"Metaphorically," Haylen conceded, laughing. "Why do you find him more trustworthy than I am? Is it because I don't bother hiding my actual intentions, or the truth from you?"

"You did the same thing to me, Haylen."

In the corner of his mind, he was still living through the day where he met the version of Haylen who had to put his own child into a coma to relive the same day, just to find a solution. I was supposed to end that timeline, too?

Haylen was now talking about something, but Damien paid no attention to him. He was standing in the middle of the bathroom, watching himself interact with another Haylen, and another Sylen. I found that place myself. Why did I go there? Did he really plan for me to land there?

In his ear, Haylen — his tormenter, his puppeteer — kept talking. "You're all on your own. I know your next step, but you don't know where those steps are taking you. Even the tiniest ones. I was very careful about the details."

"No," Damien shook his head. "This is not happening, I am hallucinating."

"This isn't a hallucination, Damien. I am here, I am here with you — with each step you take. Look into the mirror and tell me what you see."

I got there, Damien thought. After I left the King of Ashes. He just followed his intuition, closed his eyes and found himself there. Why those two consecutively? Why did I have to be there?

He still did what Haylen said, though. He walked to the mirror, and looked at himself: A shell of what he knew himself to be. He looked a lot more Seth in a way, as skeletal as he was, but on top of that — he looked exhausted. I must be starving. He didn't feel hunger.

Loss of time as a concept came to him in waves. For how long have I been here? There were way too many lines on his face than he would have expected. Am I really at the age I remember to be? How old do I think I am? He wanted to snap his fingers to make something, anything appear out of thin air, just to feel his power. He raised his hand, but then stopped.

"You don't know where those steps are taking you."

Standing behind him was Haylen, smiling with his classic, gentle smile that didn't change through timelines. His fingers were on Damien's shoulders. Damien expected to see threads, but there weren't any.

Why did I end up in that already destroyed timeline?

It made sense. It made so much sense. Haylen planned it all along, to give him the illusion of choice. Was I supposed to destroy that place as well? With him in it? Then he found himself there, in a time loop, with a Haylen who was doing something cruel to his own child. Why those two timelines were connected?

The chorus of memories in his head started again. They were loud, they were so loud, he closed his hands over his ears — futile, futile. How long has it been since I came here? Even the steam disappeared, the water must have gone cold. I should take a bath still. Or maybe drown myself in the bathtub.

He put one foot in the bathtub. The water was still lukewarm, better than ice cold, but it flooded to the floor, only a bit. Damien found somewhat of a comfort in that. I am a physical being, he laughed at himself. Not a ghost or a memory. This is real.

He couldn't bring his other foot in, though. Something slipped beneath, and everything went pitch black.

*

Damien was dancing with a beautiful girl who had a dress made out of live butterflies. Her laughter sounded like it was made of pure sunshine.

"Like I told you," she said, throwing her head back. Her long hair flowed like water. She was serious, and determined. "I want to have your kid."

"I wouldn't make a good father," Damien heard himself reply. The music was all muffled, as if nothing else but her mattered. "Poor kid, especially if they take after my insanity."

"I have dealt with insanity enough," she said. "Besides, I am not asking you to be a father."

And the tune changed, so they started dancing once more, despite the fact that Damien found it really hard to follow the notes, or the rhythm. He was just following her lead. A few golden butterflies were circling them from above. He turned his head to look for some waiter walking around with a plate full of wine glasses, but there didn't seem to be any waiters. Or any people.

"Isn't it weird?" He said, as he turned his head towards her. But it wasn't her there — nor he was holding her. Now, some strong hands were handling him, and there were no music coming.

"They didn't treat you well," The owner of the strong hands commented. He was watching Damien with great interest, even though one of his eyes didn't seem like it was seeing anything. A scar was going through it. "Why did you let that happen?"

"You speak like I had a choice," Damien replied. "You sent me away."

"You were strong enough to stand your ground," the man's face got solemn. "At least I thought so."

"Why didn't you want me with you?"

"Close your eyes, Damien."

He did. There was a thumping sound, he didn't know if it was his heart or war drums or something else entirely. He closed his eyes, believing somewhere deep inside that he was safe and sound, as he was in the arms of that man, and they danced to a song Damien couldn't hear. His heart ached with a yearning he couldn't name what for.

"You'll let me go again." he said, his eyes still closed.

"It was for your own good," the man objected. "You needed to spread your wings."

"I don't have wings. Can't you just help me?"

There was no answer until they did a few more turns.

"You need to help yourself," came the answer. "What happened to your wings?"

"I don't know, I never had them," Damien sighed. "Can't you come here and help me?"

"You're somewhere I can't follow you," the man said, but there was something different in his voice. Damien opened his eyes, to see it was the same man but with less scars on his face. The most prominent one went through his eyebrow, and stopped above his eye. "Otherwise, I'd be there in a heartbeat."

"You would?"

"Come back to me, Damien."

"I don't know where you are anymore."

His words echoed from empty walls. There was nobody, he was alone, staring at a mirror. He saw himself, or at least he thought he saw himself. The reflection in the mirror looked a lot like him, but distorted somehow. The reflection's eyes were sunken, almost shadowy. Every line that separated him from his surroundings was blurred, as if he wasn't a separate entity but an extension of it.

The reflection smiled.

"Look at yourself Damien," It, he, said. "Look at yourself, and tell me what you see."

It was still the same mirror, but Damien no longer saw the creepy reflection -- instead, it was him, tired and thinner but him undoubtedly. Long, pale fingers were busy tying gossamer threads to his throat, his arms, his legs. The puppeteer, Damien thought of him, I am at his mercy.

"Stop resisting," a voice whispered in his ear. Two voices were intertwined into one. "Accept your nature, accept your reason to exist."

"No," Damien said, and immediately the thread around his throat got tighter. "No," he said, struggling. Tears pooled in the corners of his eyes. Thread got even tighter. He tried to slid his fingers between it and his windpipe, but his hands didn't budge.

"You're not here to think. You're not here to speak. You are only here to do whatever I want you to do. You are mine."

"I am not."

"That's where you're wrong," the Puppeteer said, coming towards the light. Damien knew him, of course he did, they met in so many universes. The gentle prince, the crown jewel, the golden flower. He was holding the ends of the threads tightly. His smile wasn't cruel, nor his voice. He spoke so very softly, and so very simply, as his hand was joined by another, skeletal, shadowy hand. They both were busy with the threads.

Damien wanted to gauge his eyes out.

"You exist to serve me. You exist to please me, like everything is. And you are good at both of them."

"No," Damien replied once again. "I am not here to serve you. It's not my nature." It was hard speaking, but he did. "If you want to kill me for that, do it."

"Death is a luxury you haven't earned."

"Why do you torment me still?"

Despite the tug of all the threads at once, he raised his hands to his throats, grasping the thread on his throat. It cut his fingers like glass, but he didn't budge. The pain tore his mind apart, but there was no going back.

Once he managed to tear the thread itself, he felt the blood trickling down to his chest, but he paid no attention to it. He looked at his tormenter, straight in the eye.

"I am free," he said. Am I really? "I will do whatever I want." Will I really?

"Well, not exactly," the reflection's voice echoed from the walls. "But, illusion of choice is as good as any illusion, eh?"

Shadowy fingers were tying new threads.

"No," Damien said again, raising his hands. Everything was clear, so very clear. His hands were on fire, but he didn't care. The threads caught fire. He saw them melting, melting into each other.

"I am Chaos," he said. "I am my own destiny."

The drums were no longer beating.

*

When he opened his eyes, he found Erihnam and Seth staring at him with intense expressions in their faces. He heard Erihnam sighing in relief, but Seth was still frowning.

"Are you alright?" He asked.

"I've seen better days," Damien said, pushing all the covers and getting out of the bed. The floor swayed beneath his feet, but he stayed as still as he could. I have to get out of here. "How about you?"

"You're asking about me?" Seth asked, voice risen with disbelief. "You've fallen and hit your head, there was blood everywhere and—"

"Did you dose me up with neutralisers again?"

"Did I —" Seth paused. "What?"

"Simple enough. Did you dose me up with neutralisers again?"

"How did you know—"

"I have lived at least a few hundred lives, I've dabbled in all kinds of drugs, trust me. So, did you?"

"Of course not, you'd die."

"Oh thank all the gods above and below." Damien started moving his fingers, his power felt too unreachable. He felt as if his body wouldn't be able to handle it. "He is here, you know?"

"Who?"

Damien didn't reply. In his ear Haylen spoke nonstop. In his mind, his memories were fusing into each other, and he was constantly dying. In reality, he was pacing in the room, as Erihnam stared at him with fear in her big, blue eyes and Seth just listened to him, frozen.

Damien knew he was about to make a big mistake, but he was sure that the mistake was his.

"You're so sure I didn't want this?" Haylen asked.

"You wanted me to destroy those timelines," Damien replied, with a shrug. "I am going to do something that will not get you what you wanted."

Seth looked around. "Who are you talking to?"

"Haylen. Or Axel as you call him. He's here, right behind you, watching me with great concern in his face."

Seth, inadvertently, turned his head and looked back. "There's nobody here."

"I am not hallucinating. The high is already worn off."

"Damien," Seth grabbed him from the shoulders. "There's just me, you, and Erihnam here. I would know."

"He planned my every step, Seth," Damien laughed. "Every step. Every breath. Every cross, every turn. He knew I was going to end up here, he knew you'd help him, he knew everything." He started laughing even more. Tips of his fingers were electrified now, he could almost smell the electricity in the air.

"He does not have the power for it."

"He does." Damien shook his head. "He had me live hundreds of lives, just so I could die along with those timelines. He ensured I destroyed those timelines."

"I know. I was the one finally gave you the reins—"

"You didn't. You didn't, I kept going where he wanted me to go, doing what he wanted me to do. All those timelines ended." He took a deep breath, a gratifying one. "He knew I was going to end up here, and he is here. He is here. I was just playing to his hand all along."

"Damien," Seth said, with a patient tone, like someone would speak to a child. "You're not thinking clearly."

"But it all makes sense! All those timelines ended, I ended them." A part of his head, the part that weirdly spoke with Thyren's voice objected. Not exactly. Not all of them were you. Most of them were Sylen. "Because he wanted me to."

"But you didn't kill Alexei."

"He knew I wasn't going to do that. He knew you were going to come in and save the day."

Seth smiled bitterly. "My sweet child, Axel's foresight is not his strong suit, trust me."

"Why would I trust anyone? I can't even trust myself! Except for this one thing..."

He waved his hand, and was genuinely surprised when the threads appeared.

"Erihnam," Seth said, to the terrified queen who stayed silent through all this. "Please leave the room."

"Seth-" She started.

"Please. I will find you. Please."

She did as he said, and got out of the room. It was now the two gods, one of Chaos, one of Everything.

Seth sighed as the door closed behind Erihnam. "You're not thinking clearly, Damien," he said finally.

"I am. The screaming in my head is finally silent, even he isn't speaking now. Terrified. For once I will be breaking the cycle. Then..."

"Then what?"

"I don't know! Maybe I'll be dead, just as I intended!" Tears started rolling from his eyes, he raised his head to look at the ceiling, with the hopes he'd see a mirror there — a mirror reflecting a young man in a lot of blood, eyes open, dead, in peace. "Don't worry. I won't put you in any danger."

"I am not worried about this place. I am worried about you."

"You don't even know me."

"Are you really going to pull that on me?"

They both looked at each other, in silence.

"How many days has it been since I came here?"

"Six days since you came, and we're still in the same day that you woke up. Why?"

"I don't have a concept of time anymore," Damien shrugged. "So, I wanted to have it back. Just something to make sense out of it." I don't have anything anymore. Not a home. Not a family.

Maybe, just maybe, and it was a long shot, maybe somewhere to return to.

"Whatever you plan on doing, tell me."

"I am not going to. If I tell you, he'll know, and he'll stop me. This is my one shot at breaking his grasp of me." He paused. "I'm going to make this count."

Damien held on to two threads. He smiled at Seth. Calm down. I just need to understand. The threads started melting in his hands. It hurt, it hurt him so much but he kept smiling. His hands were burning, but he didn't care. It was entertaining seeing the realisation dawning on Seth's face. He is going to try to stop me.

He brought two threads together.

"Thanks for everything, though."

Damien disappeared, leaving nothing but a certain burnt smell behind him.

CHAPTER 12

G alen General Hospital wasn't exactly unfamiliar with unidentified people finding their way to the hospital garden with several illnesses. It was a standard procedure for them: Get the person in, scan their fingerprints, identify them, and treat them while notifying their families. Simple and clean.

So, when a Tuesday morning, a young man of maybe twenty five managed to walk in the hospital building, and collapsed right in front of the reception desk, they didn't even question. Guesses were that he was probably an addict, and lost his belongings with his ID. A fairly frequent. scenario. A quick staffer had already scanned his fingerprints into the system as they put him on a gurney.

The surprise began when the system returned nothing, and for the first time in a very long time, the hospital had a proper John Doe.

*

The word of a John Doe with literally no identification travelled fast in the hospital.

"Police are on their way," the elderly nurse, everyone's favourite Joanna, on the reception desk told one of the doctors who was rushing to the John Doe's bay. "They were very interested with our young outlaw."

A relatively easy day they expected, in all honesty. Unless a bus crashed into another bus, their day was supposed to be calm and uneventful.

"We had a person who is not registered into any systems crash into our ER instead," Ned Barrett, a third year resident, remarked.

They were waiting for the labs to come out. Everything seemed fine, no bleeding, normal oxygen levels, clear imaging — the only problem was the burn marks in the man's hands, as if he held onto something very hot, but other than that, he should've been as healthy as a horse.

"My money's on withdrawal," Kate Jenkins, the chief resident, commented. "To be honest, he doesn't strike me as an addict, but you never know."

"Traumatic stress," Ned replied. "How much do you want to bet?"

Before they could place their bets, someone put their hands on their shoulders. "Has nobody told you betting on diagnosis is wrong, kids?"

Both Ned and Kate, recognising the owner of the voice, turned back in an instant, apologies falling from their lips. January Hepburn raised his hands to stop them in their tracks. "Heard all about the carnage, and didn't want to miss out on the fun. What and who do we have here?"

"John Doe, early to mid-twenties, unconscious with no issues other than severe burns in both hands. We're waiting for the blood tests to come back," Kate explained. "I am expecting something coming up in his toxicology reports, Grasshopper here thinks it's psychological."

Hepburn scoffed. "A John Doe in this day and age?"

"Maybe his fingerprints were wiped by whatever burnt his hands," Kate commented.

"Then police would be able to ID him, and our jobs would be a lot easier," Ned replied. "And for some reason, I don't think our jobs will be as easy."

"Have you paged someone from dermatology?" Hepburn asked, slowly making his way to the trauma bay John Doe occupied. "To check his hands?"

"We handled it," Ned murmured. "Cleaned, rinsed, bandaged. His unresponsive state to that stimuli was also noted."

He thought the guy seemed so vulnerable, laying on the bed like that. So young, so helpless. He wondered what brought the guy here.

"Blood results," Kate said, raising her tablet. "Everything is within the normal range. Tox clean."

Ned hunched over to look at it himself. Hepburn, who was not interested in the actual numbers, was still staring at the patient.

"Hope someone called neuro," he said. "Let me know what comes up."

*

When Damien finally opened his eyes, he found himself surrounded, with several needles poking through his skin. Wait where am I?

The people around the bed looked genuinely excited when they noticed his awakening. What happened?

It came to him in waves, as they started talking loudly, at the same time. Hospital. This must be a hospital. How did I come here? He intended to be somewhere else. With someone else. He intended to go back.

"Can you understand us?" One of the doctors, a fresh faced woman, asked. Then, when Damien didn't answer, she tried it in a different language. It's not the language, he wanted to say. I can understand you in every language just fine.

But his issue was that he couldn't decide what to do. He knew he wasn't okay, his hands hurt immensely, but he couldn't find it in himself to even wince with the pain. Should I speak? Should I stay here? Should I get out?

Someone was pointing a strong light at his eyes. He blinked them a second too late, but at least the colours exploding beneath his eyelids were preferable to seeing curious faces of doctors. I should've been healing. Why are my hands still hurting?

A pulsing ache created static between his thoughts. His head felt like it was splitting into two, the chorus of memories was joined by doctors' chatter. Shut up. Just, shut up. Let me think.

He opened his eyes back again, as if in slow motion. He felt small, so small. His heart was a prisoner in his ribcage, pounding the bars and the walls to get out. Breathing in an out was a chore now, it was a burden. What is going on with me?

Pressure built up in his ears, and the roaring of what he assumed to be his own blood rushing through all his organs drowned all the other voices, his memories, and the doctors.

In his ear, a soft voice rose above all. He wanted to cover his ears, he wanted to put his fingers in them and scream at the top of his lungs, just to escape that voice. He knew it wouldn't do any good. He also couldn't command his muscles for any movement.

"You really thought it was your own idea? To do what you did, to come here?" A chuckle followed the words, a condescending chuckle. "I don't want you dead yet."

Time stopped. The rush of blood was inaudible now, the room was getting dark before his eyes. Even his heart stopped.

Everything went pitch black, with a steady beeping sound in the background.

*

When Damien woke up again, or at least opened his eyes, everything felt really slow. What am I on? Another, very disturbing thought followed it. How am I responding to whatever they're giving me?

The pulsing ache from before was replaced with a steady, dull, yet as loud one. He wanted to switch positions in the bed, but found it impossible. For some reasons none of his extremities wanted to obey his commands. I command timelines, he wanted to laugh. Yet I can't even lift a finger.

Somewhere, something beeped; in slow motion. The sound came from so far away, and it was so low he actually wondered if he wasn't actually hearing it. But eventually, in a time period that felt like years to him, someone entered his view. They must have set up an alarm. How very charming.

The person in his view gave him a good look, then raised her head to look at something else over his head — are there monitors? There must be. — and then left the room. Whatever she saw, she didn't look impressed by it.

After eons and eons, two other people in their white coats occupied each side of the bed he was laying on. What do you want to understand? One of them lowered her head to look at him, straight in the eyes.

"He looks like he's conscious," she remarked, raising a finger and bringing it in front of his eyes. "Follow my finger." She then repeated it in five other languages. I can understand you just fine. He followed her finger, just to get her to stop cycling through the languages.

"Oh, so you can understand me," she said. Damien blinked. Is this his plan? Putting these people in front of me, having me respond to them? He would normally find the term butterfly effect funny. Now, not so much. "Can you speak? Normally can you speak?"

He blinked again. Let's establish the setting. One for yes, two for no. He wanted to get out of here so badly.

"Not yet," came the voice of his tormenter. Is this why those drugs they gave me worked? Did they also give me neutralisers? Then where the fuck am I? "You need to get better, Damien. We will do so many things together."

He saw the movement in the left corner of the room. Almost scared, he focused his eyes there. It wasn't surprising seeing Haylen, sitting on the guest chair, comfortably. "Bingo, champion," he clapped his hands. "You've found me."

Terror took over his body and mind. The slow motion movements caught up to speed. I need to get out of here. I need to get away from him. Machinery in the room started beeping. Both doctors followed his eyes to see what he was looking at.

The polyglot one returned her attention almost immediately to Damien when the other simply left the room, yelling for people and - or - things. "Do you know where you are?"

He blinked twice. He was still not looking at her.

"Twice... Does that mean no?"

One blink. Get with the program, please.

"Great. You're in Galen General Hospital, in Eurasia. Do you have anyone we can contact about you?"

Eurasia... Eurasia... Why does the name sound familiar? He blinked twice again. How am I supposed to tell you to call for Gods for everything's sake? When they even haven't heard my pleas?

"Okay... Did you use anything that could put you into this position recently? Any substances? Alcohol?"

I don't think I had the time. Haylen also looked like he was listening to her, even more attentively than Damien did. It's my life. Why are you listening? Maybe I should do the opposite of whatever he says? What if it's also his plan?

More people barged in, all of them chiming in with ideas. I am not sick, Damien thought, he wanted to yell. Just, let me go, please.

The machines were still beeping. His eyes still were on the corner.

"Do we have anyone from Psychiatry?" One of the newcomers asked.

"Not yet," another replied. "You think he's hallucinating, Janus?"

The man, Janus, nodded. "Either that, or something we couldn't catch on the imaging. For some reason, I'm leaning more on the psychologic reasons this time."

Damien was still staring at the same corner. Why are you so quiet now, did a cat got your tongue?

Instead of Haylen, Janus was the one who talked to him. "Hey," he said. "Can you look at me?"

Such a polite request. He turned his eyes towards to the doctor, and was surprised to find him smiling. I thought my state was serious. Why the smiles?

"Awesome. I am Janus Hepburn from Internal Medicine, and with me are the best doctors in this sector. We are trying to understand how we can help you, do you think you can help us?"

He blinked once. The female doctor from before explained the basic yes and no system. Janus clapped his hands. "Great. So you're already acquainted with my incredible fellow here, Doctor Crenshaw?" he said with enthusiasm. He then turned to the room. "Who's coming from psychiatry?"

"Esher, but just got the word," Crenshaw said. "IIA is here."

"Firstly, fuck Esher, and second IIA is here?" Janus looked at her. "Yeah, no. I am not letting anyone discharge him."

Who the fuck are IIA? Damien wished he could open his mouth. What are these people going to do to me?

"That might not be up to you. Since he's admitted for unidentified neurological disorder, if neuro clears him—"

Janus nodded. "Yeah. Gotcha." He turned his attention to Damien. "Just give me a few minutes, will you?"

Damien didn't even blink as he watched Janus yelling "Find me Miller," and storming out of his room. Who the fuck is Miller?

*

Crenshaw, with a simple pen and paper, still running the yes and no game by the time same nurse made her way to Damien's room.

"So," she said. "Are you seeing someone?"

Damien blinked once.

"Are they talking as well?"

One blink once again.

Haylen laughed. "You're such a coward, Damien. Why don't you just tell them you're an entity, or a god, from some place else and you're seeing another god here with you?"

Fuck off, Damien thought. He wished he was able to communicate with his thoughts. Maybe I can do that. After all, finger snapping was just theatrics. If I can just concentrate. He closed his eyes, to reach that familiar feeling. To the warmth filling his veins, his lungs. Come on. It used to be so easy.

Crenshaw was saying something to the nurse. He didn't care. Haylen was talking about some grand and how everything was going according to it. He didn't listen. I am Chaos, he thought. I am Chaos, and I will not be controlled.

There was nothing inside him, nothing. No power, no strength. He was an empty shell of himself, of all the lives he lived, all the things he did. His hands were burning again, they were tingling with the pain. I should've stayed dead. They should've buried me and ended my misery ages ago.

There was no way out of it. No way to ignore the world around him forever. He opened his eyes, in despair.

A very familiar face was just there, in front of him.

"Princeling," he said.

Damien felt like crying.

Millions of memories played in his head. Princeling. He didn't know which timeline he was in, he didn't know who this Ferran was — but given he called him Princeling, it had to be one he knew. I am safe. I am finally safe.

A sly sound in his head spoke with Haylen's voice. Damien realised he was nowhere to be seen, even though his voice was there. "Oh, just like I planned!" It was saying now.

Shut the fuck up, Damien retorted in his mind. Even if it's your plan, let me have this.

He managed to raise his hand, trying to reach him. Tears pooled in the corners of his eyes. I am safe. I am safe. Ferran, first hesitant, met his hand half way. I am safe. Oh, I am safe. His hands hurt when he squeezed Ferran's, but he didn't care. He's real. I am real. I am safe.

"How are you, Damien?"

Speaking was still too grand of an effort. He managed to shook his head. My father is here. He has to be here. Maybe I just crashed into this side of my original timeline. A part of him was terrified by that thought. That means Haylen is still there. He can still reach me.

But no. He wasn't alone.

He wasn't alone anymore.

*

It took him several weeks until he could convince his mouth to speak. Slowly. Form the words. He was still too terrified to make conversations, or speak in long sentences. It's still his plan. I am still moving according to his plans.

Sleeping was the hard part. He kept going back to that same moment, where he was pinned to the ground and looking at Thyren's eyes, not the Thyren he knew, though, a stranger, a tormenter.

Do you think you have a say in this?

He woke up, once again, drenched in sweat in his large bed. My father's palace, he thought. Good enough. He didn't tell his father about it. Wait. Is this Martyn my father? Where am I? He didn't tell him what Haylen said. He wanted to. He wanted to tell everything and let the blood flow, and relieve himself of the burden but he couldn't.

He got out of the bed. To the kitchen. The thirst was unbearable, his throat was made out of sandpaper. I know this place. Finding the kitchen should be easy. It was the first time he experienced true disorientation.

But kitchen was near, and it had a light on, so it wasn't a big challenge to find it.

When he walked in, it didn't surprise him seeing Ferran there, drinking a tall glass of cold water as he was reading something. Ferran always had something to read when he wasn't pacing around, or guarding Damien. His presence was probably the only thing that brought a bit of peace of mind.

"Hey," he said, softly. "Couldn't sleep?"

Despite his best efforts, Ferran was startled. "Not much," he replied, closing his book. "What about you?"

"Nightmares upon nightmares."

He looked at the cabinets. There were so many glasses, so many of them, his hand remained frozen as he reached to one of them. Which one? Did he plan this as well? Am I making a premeditated choice? Will I pick the one that will break as I take a sip and cut my throat from within?

"You alright there?" Ferran interrupted his rollercoaster of thought.

"You know what," Damien said. "I am not. I am not alright, and I don't think I have been for a long time, though I am not sure how long that long time is."

Without getting a glass, he sat on the opposite side of the kitchen counter. His eyes were on the ground, as if marble floors offered something interesting.

"I have lived too many lives," he said. "Way too many lives. I died too many times as well, I am talking about hundreds of times here. Some part of my mind, even as we speak, believes that I am dying — at the hands of Sylen, or myself, or the universe exploding on us. Pick your poison. I picked mine, and they brought me back to life." He took a deep breath. "I am sure they thought it was a great gift to give me."

"One could argue life is a gift, indeed."

"Well, not for me. I was in pain, I am still in pain, and now I can't even sleep. Death was supposed to be peace for me, but they didn't let that happen."

"They?" Ferran questioned, leaning forward.

"Haylen, of course. Haylen and the Twins." He swallowed, his throat tinged in protest. "They dragged me through so many time-lines where I just died, where I just ended universes. My hands are so bloody now, and it wasn't even my choice. And I keep reliving all of them, at the same time, and I cannot even stop it."

Ferran looked white under the dimmed kitchen lights. Even his red hair seemed to lost its colour. Damien didn't seem to notice it, however. His eyes were still on the ground.

"And you know what he said to me? Do you think you have a say in this?" He chuckled, tears rolling from his eyes. He wasn't even seeing the floor anymore. "He planned my every move. My every step. Every sentence. Every breath. He planned everything."

"I feel like that shouldn't be possible."

"I thought so, too." He smiled, bitter. "But here I am! I cannot even decide which glass I should pick, because it's still a choice, and I just feel like all my choices are premeditated, and what if he made these choices as well and what good am I if I can't even trust my own mi—"

Then, and only then he raised his head, to meet Ferran's eyes. Never judging, he would never find judgement there. Ferran knew him forever, Ferran would never judge him for crying, for falling apart, for disintegrating.

Damien started sobbing. His heart was aching, his hands were aching, and every part of himself was aching. He was slowly bleeding out, but there was nobody to help him — nobody to save him from Haylen's cold voice in the nights, whispering how it's just part of the plan and how he's just a pawn. Kill me. He wanted to kneel in front of Ferran and beg him for the sweet release of death. He can kill me. I don't have my powers still.

Ferran stared at him, his face an enigma of unreadable emotions. There was no judgement, absolutely not, but an uncertainty as to what the next steps should be. Damien didn't know either. He just wanted to stop feeling.

Eventually Damien's sobs subsided. He got up, without saying one single word, and stood still for a while — until the world stayed still before his eyes. Ants were eating away his field of vision, they were crawling in from his ears — he could hear it, he could hear the ringing.

Ferran caught him before he could hit the floor, but Damien was already too gone to realise that.

*

The next morning, it was business as usual for Damien. He still found himself unable to talk, mouth just refusing to form long sentences, just short words, and one half of his body refused to cooperate with him.

He vaguely remembered walking around the night before, talking to Ferran, and everything else — but he wasn't sure if it was actually the night before, or ten lifetimes ago, or just a dream. I need to sort this memory thing out.

First difference from the days before was that Ferran basically moved himself into Damien's room now. Every single servant walking in to help Damien out was now doing it under the scary scrutiny of Ferran, and even though he could never verbally admit it, Damien felt a lot safer for it.

Second one came as a request from Martyn, when he asked him to visit the library. Damien remembered enjoying his father's library, so he showed his approval with a nod, and before he could do anything else, Ferran put him on a wheelchair.

"Relax, Princeling," he said. "Martyn just wants to help you out. Just like everyone here. He is the Master Weaver, and trust me, nobody can control him."

Master Weaver. He had never heard this epithet before.

"Remember?" Do you remember it? "Yesterday?" It happened yesterday?

"Yes," Ferran affirmed. "You broke down, then fainted. Martyn's doctors insist it's just conversion disorder, so, apparently it's all in your head."

Damien's eyes got large. "Haylen." He's in my head. He's in my head, he's still controlling me. That's why I fainted after telling—

Ferran knocked the library door, and leaned in Damien's ear. "Don't know where you think you are, kid, but trust me. Haylen is long dead here."

Martyn opened the library door himself. "I can take it from here, Ferran, thank you."

Ferran simply nodded, and gave Damien's shoulder a squeeze. "See you later, Princeling."

Martyn, now in control of the wheelchair, pushed Damien inside with relative ease. "If you want to read any books, just show me. I will even get a servant to read them for you."

Damien shook his head. What am I doing here? He wanted to ask, he wanted to speak. But he just couldn't get it out. "What?" He could ask.

"I love the library," Martyn replied. Damien wasn't sure if his question was understood correctly. "It's calm, it's quiet and nobody dare disturb me here. Once upon a time, I killed someone here. Took their heart out. Fun times."

What the fuck are you talking about? "What?" He repeated again.

"Don't worry," Martyn said. "We're here for something different."

Near the window, there was a small wooden loom on a beautiful desk. There were many colourful yarns as well. Damien turned his eyes from the desk to Martyn.

"Weaving," explained Martyn. "Once upon a time, I taught a young girl about the intricacies of basket weaving. It takes time, you see how eventually everything connects, and besides - it was fun."

Damien smiled, weakly. "Your Madison?" He asked.

"Oh, I forgot. You've met her, right?"

He nodded. Several versions of her. With different powers even. Maybe I am talking to her right now. He focused on the loom. It looked so beautiful. I am also dying.

"Now," Martyn continued. "We're going to weave some carpets together. I know you cannot use one half of your body, so you'll just watch me until you gain functionality in both sides."

"Why?"

"We deal with a lot of threads, Damien. Just not as colourful. I've found principles remain similar." He laughed. "Besides, my doctors think it might get your head off the traumatic events you've been through."

He positioned Damien somewhere he could see the process, and got behind the loom.

Damien focused his gaze on the yarns.

*

It took Damien another several weeks until he could move the remaining half of his body. He was still not talking, but at least he could write his sentences on a notebook, which was a vast improvement.

Martyn insisted on continuing the weaving lessons, which required active participation now. Damien welcomed the opportunity, at least now he had something to do despite continuous interference from Haylen in his ear. He is dead. I am either seeing a ghost, or it's a trick my mind plays. It's not real.

No matter what he couldn't convince himself.

"Pick your colours," Martyn pointed towards the rainbow coalition of yarns on the table. "Whichever you want."

Damien shook his head. I don't want to make any decisions. Not yet.

"My boy, you cannot sit in constant paralysis," Martyn said. "Eventually, you have to make decisions. Some will turn out bad, some will turn out good. Which is okay. None of us are absolved of making errors on our way."

Damien brought up his notebook, gripping his pen unnecessarily strong. His handwriting didn't satisfy him, but he wasn't going to dwell on it. "I am afraid I don't make the choices."

He thought Martyn was going to ask for clarifications. Or maybe he would even get angry. He added, after a brief pause. "I know it makes no sense."

"It makes complete sense, actually," Martyn replied. He was smiling wide, as he put an arm around Damien's shoulders. "But the thing is, my son," he said, not being able to keep pride away from his voice. "You are Chaos. Nobody can determine your actions."

He is lying, some part of him thought. He is lying to get me to relax. It has to be a part of Haylen's plans—

He shook his head, freeing himself from Martyn. You're wrong. They did it before. He got his notebook again, writing, hurried. "He did. He had me destroy timelines."

Martyn seemed unsure of what to say. The silence between them grew for a solid minute. Then, it was Martyn who broke it.

"Come to my side of the table, please."

Damien complied with his request. He didn't know what he was going to see there, or what he was going to do — but he wanted to trust Martyn. The one who's not my father. Somehow, that didn't mean anything to him.

"Do you see my colours?" Martyn asked, pointing at his own loom. "Only three of them. Light blue, purple, and white. They are the only ones there."

Damien nodded. What does that have to do with anything?

"So, first. Do you think, if I picked up the red ball of yarn there and set it ablaze, would it affect the already woven section?"

What kind of a question is this? Damien shook his head.

"What about any of the blue, purple or white?"

What are we trying to do here? He didn't have an answer.

"Let's try it," Martyn said, reaching to the closest one — white. He set ablaze the entire remaining yarn, and Damien watched, unable to blink or look away. When the fire eventually died, loom was — expectedly — unaffected.

"So, consider yourself as the woven part of our small carpet here. No tethers to the other parts, whatever happens to them, it cannot affect you."

With this Damien turned to him. He understood, and it felt like a bright summer day. I cut them all. I cut all the tethers. Myself.

"Damien," Martyn said. "Even if everything Haylen told you was true, which is impossible... You have no tethers anymore."

Relief hit Damien like a truck. He looked at his hands, to see the scarring left of the burns. I did this myself. It was my call, and I did it. It was all me.

"I really wonder what the story behind those burns is, though," Martyn added, with a chuckle.

Damien didn't try speaking, or writing. He simply hugged Martyn.

Chapter 13

"That concludes our weekly session," the elderly woman said, closing her notebook. "I would say this has been very productive."

"Oh," Thyren replied. "Time flies."

"It does indeed." She smiled. "Now, before you go, I want you to remember once again—"

"This is not the consequence of my actions, nor a punishment." Thyren sounded fed up, but once she nodded her approval, his face lightened. "Thank you Isabel."

"Good luck in your emergency meeting, Thyren."

In all honesty, Thyren never thought therapy would work for him. But when insomnia hit, Anthony accepted no objections. It was a clear order at that point, and the last thing Thyren wanted was upsetting his brother. After all, he wouldn't lose anything by speaking for two hours every week.

But Isabel Larkin, who was apparently working with Anthony for a long time, turned out to be someone beyond his imagination of what therapy was. They started from reframing Thyren's old experiences, the most impactful ones, one by one. Now they were in coping mechanisms, the healthy ones.

And he was progressing well. Very well in fact, unexpectedly well. It was weird not reaching for a knife whenever he felt like he was getting suffocated, but on the other hand, it felt like the right thing, and that alone was quite refreshing.

In his third session, Isabel had asked him what changed and brought him here. Why exactly do you want to get better for, if nothing about how you view the world changed?

"I am not here to tell you to get over it, Thyren," she had said. "I am not here to offer you sympathies, either. You wanted to help yourself. I am just a tool for you to achieve that."

"I wanted to help myself? My brother forced me here."

She hadn't bought that. "You say yourself that you killed two gods. Do you think your brother can force you to anything?"

It still took Thyren a while to come up with a good reason for himself.

"There's someone," Thyren eventually had said, in their fifth session. "We could say he crashed into my life."

"Oh," Isabel had raised her eyebrows, in a playful way. "A romantic interest?"

"No, absolutely not." It felt wrong categorising anyone in that way. "I don't think I have the ability to be romantically interested in someone anymore, anyway, but no." He had paused, giving himself a minute to put all his thoughts in an order. "He was fragile, too fragile. If opportunity arises, I want to help him."

And it wasn't a lie. Come back. It's less lonely with you here. He wanted to help Damien, as much as he could. He didn't know if they were ever going to meet again, but he wanted to be there, just in case. There, ready, and fully.

But even then, when Anthony called him one morning to tell about Damien's return, he was underprepared. He came back. It didn't sound good, nothing in life would ever be that easy — so it wasn't surprising. Martyn getting involved and taking care of the kid was also totally expected.

Surprise came when Martyn called all of them for an emergency meeting.

At least Thyren had enough of a common sense to schedule it after his therapy session.

*

Martyn walked into Thyren's house with a big grin on his face. "Are you still low on liquor stock?"

"Fuck off," Thyren retorted. "I would have you know I am now a higher functioning member of this stupid society of gods, and I'm better than almost all of you, because I'm actually going to therapy."

"Oof," Martyn chuckled. "That's something we all need, I am not going to deny that. Where's your brother?"

"Washing his hands, he should be around soon."

When Anthony joined them and saluted both of them with a hand wave, Martyn took a deep breath. "So," he said. "The reason I gathered you here is — as both of you know — Damien's return."

Anthony nodded. "Oh yeah," he said. "How's the kid? Last I saw him, he was horrible."

"Still not good, but we're getting there," Martyn replied. "And Anthony, I thank you for your help there."

"No problem. Kid picked my brother's hospital to crash into, he pretty much created his own luck there."

Thyren looked at them without saying anything.

Less lonely with you here. He had meant it. But by here, he didn't mean the same timeline, different places.

"A couple issues," Martyn said. "And, honestly Thyren, Damien was a bit averse to you in the beginning for reasons I'll explain, but for the last few weeks, I am the one not green lighting a meeting between you."

"Oh," Thyren said. "So, our universe is ending as well?"

Anthony turned his head to Thyren almost in light speed. "What?"

"No," Martyn replied, ignoring Anthony. "This isn't about us, but we have common players in the game, so it complicates things."

"Like?"

"Long story short," Martyn bit his lip before starting. "There is a timeline, where everyone is alive. Alexei, Axel, everyone."

He allowed the twins a while to comprehend the real meaning of that sentence.

"Good for them," Thyren replied eventually through gritted teeth. "That interests us how?"

"Well, apparently Axel there was… How to say this… He was more Alexei than Alexei himself. Damien insists on calling him Haylen, and I really don't know why. But to make it easier, let's adopt the same method of reference."

Anthony shook his head. "Nope. Don't believe it. I cannot fathom a universe where Axel is the bad guy."

"I didn't want to believe it, but well..." He shrugged. "The story starts with Damien's death. Insanity, suicide whole nine yards. Nothing unfamiliar if you've ever met Chaos before."

"Or Alexei," Thyren said.

"Or him," Martyn chuckled. "In the end, the kid sends himself to Frea Peases, then you, Anthony, come in."

Thyren had a bad feeling as to where this story was going. "He, I mean their Anthony, brought him back," he completed.

Martyn nodded. "Yes," he said. "But not entirely. Yes, Anthony used his powers, but Haylen did something too."

"Like...?"

"Like somehow messing with the threads and putting Damien through a lot of timelines before he could actually come back to life."

Thyren frowned. "That was the reason he couldn't die?"

"Would you rather him to?" Anthony asked.

"No, but that's not the issue. He was talking about how death meant just restart for him. It was A—Haylen's doing?"

"Unfortunately," Martyn replied. "That's not even all, by the way."

"Oh, come on."

"So, for all we know, Damien dies here. Then wakes up in his own original timeline, all well. Issue is, that timeline is also about to die, which is why Haylen orchestrated all these in the first place, and then he asks Damien to kill Sylen."

Thyren scoffed at that. "Why? A version of me wasn't around?"

It was a sigh, a very exasperated, bitter sigh. "A version of you," Martyn said, tilting his head slightly to the left. "A version that is very identical to you was indeed there, Thyren."

"And? That should've been the fucking end of it, right?"

"It wasn't. And actually, that's the reason I haven't let you two meet yet."

Anthony interjected on behalf of his brother. "Martyn... Can you please skip to the important part?"

"Well, it's a bit hard to tell. Apparently Haylen told Damien that it was all his grand plan. That he planned everything, all the timelines ending, him opposing the plan, everything."

"Oh, that's what you meant by being more Alexei than Alexei."

"He said that while that very identical version of you pinned him to the ground from his throat, Thyren."

The twins went paper white with that. Thyren looked at Martyn, jaw dropped, trying to come up with a logical reason. He couldn't form the words, he couldn't even think coherently.

"And since he got help from their Juventas to remember every-thing," Martyn continued. He looked like an executioner, getting ready to drop the blade. "His memories are mixed and merged into each other. He's terrified of a Thyren he thinks he knows, but also he doesn't know and he maybe wanted to return back to."

Come back here. It's less lonely with you here.

"I think there's a misunderstanding there," Anthony said. "I just cannot fathom any version of Thyren who doesn't have an intrinsic hate for Alexei. That's like, a volcano that spews cool water."

"That's also not it," Martyn said. "Damien somehow escaped there. That part is a bit more complicated, and unnecessary, but the thing is... He did something, that should've been also impossible."

Anthony laughed. "We've been through all these," he twirled his finger pointing at the ceiling. "And you're talking about impossi-bles?"

"He merged two timelines."

"Okay, I take back my words. He did what?"

"He merged two timelines. He says he wanted to do it to spite Haylen. That part is the reason why he doesn't want to talk to you yet, Thyren."

Thyren felt like he knew the answer. "It has something to do with his King of Ashes, right?"

"He merged his timeline, with one that he saved. In which Thyren died a long time ago, and Haylen was the only one standing."

The amount of possibilities flashed in Thyren's head. The possibility of there being an Axel, alive, well, walking, talking, laughing and happy — he just wanted to get out, and go there, and find him, and end this nightmare—

"Thyren?" Anthony asked, his voice low with concern. "Are you with us?"

"Yes," he said. "Yeah, and what happened?"

"And then he crashed here. Into a hospital. I think he was trying to come back here here, but at that point he exhausted all the energy he had."

He could've given me a life with Axel instead of him. The thought brought some glooming questions along. Why didn't he think I deserved it?

A momentary madness is all that separates us?

"But," Anthony's voice interrupted his train of thought. Thyren immediately realised Anthony was thinking of something similar in less sharp tones. "I don't get it. That's not our Axel? That's not the Axel we know and we love, and..." He sighed. "But that's not our Axel?"

Would you rather me saying you're the same?

"Maybe aside from a few timelines," Martyn said. "None of us are exactly the same as our versions in other timelines, correct."

I'm trying to understand why you think there's that hard of a distinction. Or why you need it to be so.

"That Axel," Martyn continued. "Had kids, apparently. Time, that he had to keep in a coma to prevent the universe explode on itself. A time loop. A smart move, actually, a painful one, for a father, but a smart move."

"How were they saved?"

"Alexei killed himself."

That took Thyren out of his thoughts. "Alexei? Like, Alexei? Flerl'en Sylen Alexei? He made a sacrifice?"

"Just as I told you. None of us are the exact same."

Thyren got up. "Excuse me," he said, hands raised. "I need to get some air first, and then I will schedule an extra session with my therapist."

He turned, and as he walked to the garden, Anthony yelled from behind him.

"Your therapy bills are breaking my bank, Hyiressen!"

Thyren's answer wasn't vocal, it was rather a gesture of his fingers.

"Now what?" Anthony asked Martyn, as he turned his eyes away from Thyren, with a smile.

"Now, we heal," Martyn said. "Maybe I should take Damien to your therapist as well."

"As long as you're paying," Anthony shrugged. "You seem awfully comfortable in that fatherly role, I must say."

This time, it was Martyn who smiled. "I'm a natural."

*

"Morning everyone," Damien greeted them as loud as he could when he got downstairs. Everyone was a very crowded way of saying hello to three people, of course, but the illusion of grandeur didn't bother Damien that much.

Martyn's Musketeers, he got used to calling them, with no objections so far. Damien often wondered their purpose — aside from Ferran's, because that was clearly babysitting Damien, which was more than welcome — but thought it would be rude to ask. So he never did. Deep down, he believed they liked him for that.

"Morning Princeling," Valentine said, her smile being the biggest. "How are you feeling today?"

"Better than yesterday, worse than tomorrow. Where's Martyn?"

"Off for some business," Ferran replied on behalf of Valentine. "Do you want some tea?"

The third on the table, Alya, laughed at Ferran's speed. Damien found it funny as well, no doubt there, Ferran's mother hen attitude was something he always found amusing in a flattering way — but Ferran seemed to disagree as he only cast a glance towards Alya. That was the end of her laughter there.

"Tea is fine," Damien sat without further commentary. "Do you guys really eat this much?"

"Not everyone is recovering from inter-timeline trauma," Valentine responded, looking very offended. Damien would've taken her seriously if it wasn't for the mischievous tinkle in her eyes. "So, we eat this much. You better start to as well, or Ferran will tie you down on a chair and feed you with a spoon."

"He wouldn't." Damien turned to Ferran. "You wouldn't right?"

Ferran raised one eyebrow. "Do you really want to know the answer to that?"

"That is an answer in itself already." Damien reached for the pastries, filling his plate.

"Good kid," Ferran said, all serious.

But before Damien could give an answer, someone appeared in the middle of the room. Ferran was the first one getting out of the table, holding a dagger in one hand, open enough to be threatening, but not downright hostile.

"How can we be of assistance?"

"I bring a message from Flerl'en Saellin," the man said. A leytian, Damien figured. "To Flerl'en Ashren?"

Alya, putting butter over her toast, scoffed. "I'll never get used to them calling him Ashren."

"Instills respect, I guess," Valentine responded. She didn't look like she cared the leytian being there. "What's the message, though?"

The leytian, looking honourably annoyed, fixed his eyes on Damien.

"Flerl'en Saellin wants to know if you have some time today for a tea in the afternoon. Her place of choice was your..." He paused, and the insult in that was almost tangible. "Royal garden, but of course, she wanted me to let you know she can host you in Flerketer as well."

"Sure," Damien shrugged. "I have all the time in the world. Our garden is perfectly fine, thank you."

"Then I will let her know of that. Thank you, sire."

He bowed, and then disappeared again. Alya frowned.

"Should have we invited him to breakfast?"

"Oh, that would be a bad idea, Alya," Valentine said, opening her eyes wide in mock terror. "Because the big bad guard over there," she pointed at Ferran. "Was ready to slit his throat in any given second."

Damien turned to Ferran, but Ferran didn't seem to pay attention to them.

"You're alright?"

"I should be asking that question to you," Ferran said.

"Yeah, but I'm all up for disrupting the routines. You know, with chaos and all?"

Ferran nodded. "We should let Martyn know you're quickly gaining a sense of humour."

*

For a split second, Damien wondered if he had ever danced with her, and if she really had a butterfly dress on her. He tried to remember the taste of canapés, and the champagne, he tried to remember the music playing in the room.

"Still chain smoking?" She asked, as soon as she got into Damien's earshot. "And care to share with a stranger?"

"A stranger wouldn't be the word I'd use to describe you," he said, offering one to her. "Hello, Jennifer."

She smiled wide. "It's nice to see you talking. Honestly the stories they told..." She shook her head as she got the cigarette from him. She held it between her fingers, expecting him to light it up. "Catatonic, paralysed, confused..."

"I was all three," he shrugged, handing her a lighter. "But eventually, you find ways to cope. I'm weaving carpets now."

Jennifer frowned, uncertain. "Carpets?"

"Oh yeah, colourful, tiny carpet-like things. Whenever I feel too overwhelmed, I go straight to my loom."

"I can't tell if you're being serious."

"I am being serious." He laughed. "How have you been?"

"Standard, stable," she shrugged. "You tell me, you've been on an adventure."

"If you can call it that..."

"I don't know," she said. "Can you?"

He narrowed his eyes. "I fail to see your angle here."

Jennifer leaned forward. "You're back," she whispered, conspiratorially. "You literally died here, and came back. If that's not an adventure, I don't know what is."

Damien looked at her, annoyed. "It's traumatic, that's what it is."

"We held a small funeral for you here," she continued. "A very small, you could almost say it was a family affair. Martyn, Thyren, me. Very small. Martyn's idea. I believe Anthony was also there, but he was mainly there to make sure Thyren was okay."

"Really?"

"Oh, yeah. I think Thyren still has the knife you used. He said he was going to keep it company until you came back. I honestly, didn't believe you'd be able to. Though, clearly, I was wrong. You're here."

"I had no idea."

"For us, funerals are a must have," Jennifer explained. "A way to say farewell. Makes it more tangible." She blinked her eyes rapidly. Damien didn't say anything, even though he noticed the tears. "So, how was the other side? Or wherever you went to?"

"Awful?" Damien tried to smile. "Honestly, I don't even want to remember, but it haunts me in my dreams. Such a bummer. How about you?"

She leaned back in her chair. "Nothing out of the ordinary. Trying to get on good terms with my dad, again, bringing teenage rebellion back to Flerketer, after literally too many thousands of years." She laughed, and Damien realised how much he liked her laughter. "Mom insists I'm being childish, but I look the part, so I play it."

"I wish you good luck when you have that child of yours eventually," Damien laughed back. "What do they call it? Karma?"

"I lack a certain prerequisite to be affected by karma," Jennifer said, raising her head. "That is, being a mortal."

"I don't think universal balance cares about that."

"I don't think you of all people should care about universal balance."

"Ouch." He reached to his glass of water. "You said tea, but I haven't offered you any. Would you like some?"

"Sure," Jennifer replied. "Anything that tastes bitter, please."

Damien raised his hand, and a servant just appeared out of nowhere. It had startled him when he was just getting used to the palace, but it lost its novelty on him pretty quick. "Can we get black tea here, please?"

When the servant left, Jennifer folded her arms. "Also, it's not like I am going to have a child any time soon."

"Oh. Still haven't found a viable candidate?"

She gave him the side-eye. "It's all your fault. When you introduced not being insane into my criteria list as a must-have, you basically killed my candidate pool."

"Not everyone you know can be insane."

"Spoken like someone who hasn't met any of the Pantheons," she shook her head. "I don't know how we all were in the other timelines, but in here, I don't know a single sane person. That includes me, by the way."

A small teapot and two cups were put on their table in extreme silence, as Damien and Jennifer just looked at each other.

"So," she said, once the servant went away. "I put it on hold until you came back."

"I thought you didn't believe I would be able to."

"That was the point. It was meant to be like... if the sun rises from the west. Now, in hindsight, I should've said if the sun rises from the west instead."

"You can still say that."

"It would be cheating. I dared the odds, and you've beaten them all."

Damien shook his head, chuckling. "No, you cannot pin that on me, Jennifer."

"Why is that?"

"I told you in the beginning. I don't die."

Jennifer bared her teeth. "Do you really want to put it to test?"

"Now I don't know. But back then I literally didn't die in the conventional meaning of the word."

"I want to remind you that my father is the God of Death," Jennifer said, pouring herself tea. "I would suggest you not to test me on this."

"Oh," he said. "Do you think he'd kill me if you asked him?"

"Nope."

"But if you asked really nice?" Damien leaned towards her. "Really, really nice?"

"If you know how to do that, maybe you should try it yourself."

"No, thank you. I don't know where I'll end up, and if it's back to where I started, I will go straight into a jacket."

She looked at him puzzled.

"A straitjacket?"

"Oh, fuck off, that was a terrible joke."

"Can you imagine if you had a kid with me and the kid started spouting awful puns like that?"

"You imagined what that would be like?"

Damien fell silent.

"I'm just joking," Jennifer said, waving her hand dismissively. "I am not here to persuade you. But I enjoyed our chatter when you were here, and I haven't enjoyed anyone's chatter like that in the time you were gone. You should take that as a compliment."

"I do." And he did. He knew, if he had any tethers left one would be tied to Jennifer. "I enjoy our times together so much, in almost every timeline, there was a you I spent time with."

"And I'm taking this as a compliment."

"As you should," Damien laughed. "Our relationship is always so funny to me, though."

"Why is that?"

"I think we're cousins originally. I mean, where I am originally from. Your mother, and my mother — sisters. There's one we're siblings, even."

"What?" She started coughing, Damien gently pat her on the back. She put her tea on the table, her eyes larger in shock. "We? Us? Siblings? You and me?"

"Sharing mothers," he explained. "Juventas was my mother as well."

"Ugh," Jennifer rolled her eyes. "I would be an awful older sister. I don't think you'd be as enjoyable as a little brother, either."

"How do you know you're older?"

"My mom and Martyn are pretty recent news."

"Wait, that's a thing here, too?"

She laughed, finishing her tea. "Why are you that surprised?"

"I don't know." He frowned. "Can you imagine them actually having a child here, as well?"

"Oh," Jennifer's expression changed, too. "Do you think we would have a second one of you? I'll keep my fingers crossed for a better sense of humour."

Damien considered being hurt at that, but laughing was far easier.

"But forget the old people," Jennifer disrupted the laughter. "Go back to me and you. Cousins, then. Who was your mother?"

"I don't think she exists here. Goddess of Order, Syleren." Or maybe she does. In a different way. But maybe you don't know about her.

"Oh, that is weird. I didn't even think that was possible..." She paused. "Though you're here, so it must be possible. Wait — in how many of those timelines were we a thing?"

"You're the only person who can make such light of my predicament."

"I am assuming from your non-adverse reaction to me, We've been at least fine."

"Oh, we were more than just fine," Damien said, and he meant it. "Have I told you that I had a mirror above my bed?"

"I am so glad I haven't met that version of you," she shook her head. "What an asshole..."

"To be fair, you called that me to my face often. But also you called me a bunch of other things, and I don't think I can or should disclose them in public."

"You call this public?" She pointed at their general vicinity. There was nobody around them. "Remind me to never discuss my fantasies with you."

"I am assuming at least one of Martyn's Musketeers is around us, so I would not rather risk it."

"Martyn's wha-" Realisation dawned on her. "You're a very rude guest."

"Who says I'm a guest here?" Damien laughed, finally drinking his tea. It was way too cold to be enjoyable, but it refreshed his throat nonetheless. "They all call me princeling."

She made a face. "Doesn't suit you."

"Couldn't agree more."

Jennifer, leaning back, narrowed her eyes, though. "Go back to the bunch of other things part, please."

"With pleasure. But we're still in a public place."

"Should I take that as an invitation to go to somewhere more private?"

Damien laughed. His heart felt lighter for it. "Maybe later?" He offered. "Certainly not today. I still haven't regained my powers, see?" He pulled a cigarette, and snapped his fingers to light it up. Nothing happened. "I'm just a mere mortal."

Jennifer made a disgusted face. "Then why am I spending time with you?" But her voice got serious after that. "Do you think you'll get better?"

"I am hoping eventually," he said, while snapping his fingers a few more times. Giving up, he pulled his lighter from his pocket and lit it up with that. "I am not in a hurry. My head is finally silent. There aren't any hallucinations yet. Living the dream life, that's what I call it."

She reached over the table, and put her hand over his.

"You are a terrible liar, Damien," she said.

"I am, aren't I?" His eyes got teary.

"How do you really feel?"

He shook his head. "Terribly lonely. No other words to describe it." He sighed. "Sometimes I wish that funeral was really my end."

She held his hand, intertwining their fingers. She half expected him to pull his hand away, and he would expect that from himself as well — but he didn't. He stayed still, barely breathing, and looked into her eyes, those big, beautiful, blue eyes. At least somethings never change.

"You have all of us," she said. "If nobody else, us, your funeral crew. We have your back."

Maybe take one name from that list, he thought. He doesn't know what I withheld from him, and he will never want to see me when he finds out. Rightfully so. For the millionth time, he asked himself the same question: Why didn't I give him that then? He still didn't have an answer.

He then pulled hand away from her to put out his cigarette. He knew he was wasting them, terrible of him, but they felt off no matter how fresh they were. Half expecting her to make a comment on how terrible it smelled, he pulled another one out, without taking his eyes from Jennifer. I am after the harm, it's death I'm not chasing. Maybe it was the opposite this time.

It was yet another snap of his fingers, out of pure habit, but this time it worked.

"Look," Jennifer said, clapping her hands. "A plot twist."

*

Thyren threw his head back, staring at the ceiling. "I honestly don't know what I would've wanted," he said. His voice was strained. "I think I still want Axel back, but I want my Axel back."

"That to me," Isabel said. "Sounds like you've solved your dilemma."

"No, because — I know none of us are one hundred percent the same, but maybe it would've been enough of a similarity. And that possibility really hurts me."

"Do you blame Damien for it?"

Thyren groaned. "He was in love with that other Thyren already, so who can blame someone for trying to do a favour for the person they're in love with?"

"Question isn't what someone would think. It is how you feel."

He raised his head, looking at Isabel. "I don't know. One part of me wants to know why, the real reason, but then..." He sighed. "I don't know what I feel or why I feel the way I feel. Part of me just wants to travel to other timelines, and I don't even know if it's possible."

"Because you still want Axel back. Which is a normal sentiment."

"No, the worse part is that I've somehow moved on a little. I got used to this life without him thing. I at least managed to spend days without feeling like going for a swim in the River fucking Lethe. But now? Now I know there is a small possibility that there's an Axel, alive, and well. And I am not there. We're just mourning for each other, and not even trying to reach to each other." He looked at her. "I am going to ask a question that I know I shouldn't ask, but help me out please."

"I think I know what follows, but do go ahead."

"Do you think he would've wanted this?"

Isabel closed her eyes for a second, and slowly breathed in. "I think you know the answer to this better than I do, Thyren."

"He wanted me to stay alive, after him. I know that. He wanted me to move on. But I just can't shake the feeling maybe he would change his mind if he knew about other timelines and the possibilities."

"What makes you think that he didn't?"

He had no answer to this. Really, how do I know he didn't know?

"Just, walk me through it," she continued. "You'd rather finding an Axel, who is not the person you know, not the person you shared the memories that make you miss him, and you'd rather try to build a relationship with him at the risk of being hurt, disappointed — or rather, at the risk of hurting his memory — to moving on as he intended you to?"

"When you put it like that I sound like a dick," Thyren chuckled.

"That's not my intention. I am just trying to understand how you see it. Because, from what you've told me, there's no scenario except for one very bad one by your own admission, you two manage to come together to the finish line."

"Yeah, that bad scenario gets me confused as well. I cannot imagine myself knowing the definite answer to saving Axel, and not doing it." He frowned. "I would've offed Alexei years ago if Axel had let me. Maybe that would've been better for all of us, but I would have done it. Would I be really that blind to seeing someone else suffer when I can just, I don't know, save everyone?"

"The answer to that is within you."

"I don't think I could have. Even if I didn't know Damien."

"Do you think Axel would let that happen? I mean the Axel you knew?"

Thyren's lips twitched upwards. "Oh, even if I was out of my mind enough for that, he'd put me in my place. Seeing a suicidal kid and exploiting his pain? No way. And I hate myself for wondering the same for him. Would he actually do that as well? Because I know he wouldn't."

"I think," Isabel replied. "And I'm taking my psychiatrist hat off for a second here, what divides this universe into parallel timelines is our choices. And, I believe if any of you were able to make those choices, this would be a very different timeline."

Thyren narrowed his eyes. "Do you take other gods than me as your clients?"

"Even if I do, I am not going to confirm or deny that," she laughed. "It's subject to privacy, and you know that."

"Yeah, but that was a damn good explanation that would've confused the living shit out of me if, for example, Martyn had done it."

"I am accepting your compliment, but focus on the task here. Knowing what you know, about all the choices, and all the scenarios, would you really risk that?"

"I would still rather shooting myself in the head and trying to find Axel in the afterlife, and even if I get therapy for a thousand years it won't change — but he literally forbade me from that so, my hands are tied." He sighed, loudly. "I think I am not mad at Damien as well."

"Oh. Why is that?"

"I asked him once if it was really only a moment of insanity that differentiated me from his King of Ashes. Maybe it really is. Maybe it's a moment of desperation that separated my Axel from the Axel who kept his own child in coma, just to save the universe. They could understand each other, making difficult decisions, under difficult times."

Isabel took some notes into her notebook, and raised her head from it. "Did he reply?"

"To what?"

"Is it a moment of insanity that made you two different?"

Thyren shrugged. "He didn't. I think it was because we both knew the answer."

*

Damien found the waiting room of the therapist really boring. The walls were painted with a boring beige, decorated with some nature paintings. I should've brought a book with me. He looked at his hands, moving his fingers simultaneously. I could conjure one. But the clock on the wall told him it would be meaningless, for his session was starting in ten minutes.

He knew Martyn's intentions were good. He knew the therapist was in all these, and it wasn't her first time working with gods — which was a red herring on its own. How would a mortal psychiatrist land a job as the official therapist of some gods, anyway? Though considering Jennifer's quips about how everyone in the Pantheons were one way or another mentally ill, the lady must have realised she hit a gold mine.

He had no idea what he was supposed to tell her. How his first suicide attempt was more akin to euthanasia instead of a full blown depressive suicide? How he died over and over again, countless times? How —

Stop. Stop, don't go there unless you absolutely have to. Just don't.

The secretary, a sweet young lady named Erin, walked towards Damien, interrupting his thoughts.

"She's going to see you in a few minutes, please come with me."

He followed her without much thought, and when she instructed him to wait for a seconds, he didn't even question it. Think of something else, he was still saying to himself. His throat was closing on itself, his heart trying to mimic a jet engine — working fast, and loudly. He is not here. He is not here.

The office door opened, and as Damien was very busy with fighting an internal battle with his thoughts, a very familiar figure appeared in the door. Humane concepts like door frames really underlined how tall, and how large he was — always a giant, sometimes gentle.

Thyren was right there, and they both stared at each other for a while that felt like an eternity.

He knows, Damien thought. He knows. It made no sense, he couldn't conceive how, but Thyren knew and maybe this would be the final death, this place would be ruined. His cheeks were on fire, his ears unable to hear anything else than the river of iron and oxygen. I think I am going to faint. Maybe then he would show mercy.

"Hi."

It took Damien a few seconds to realise he heard that, and he was still alive, conscious, and standing. He first closed his open mouth, then lowered his eyes.

"Hi," he said back.

"Glad to see you alive. And well. Well. Not bad, at least."

With that Damien looked at him, trying to see anger in those eyes. He was there, they were both standing, but he was also on the ground, staring at the same pair of eyes, same scars.

It's less lonely with you here.

Do you think you have a say in this?

"That's a surprise to me, too," he heard himself saying. In a part of his mind, he knew he was supposed to be struggling, trying to escape the iron grip. But I am standing. Thyren was silent, a silence that carried no expectations. But he's also standing there. Not letting me go. Let me go. Everything and everyone was screaming in his head.

From the corner of his eye, he could acknowledge the therapist - at least, it was supposed to be her, leaning to the doorframe, doing what everyone would, just like the secretary was already doing: Looking at both of them, expecting a combustion any second.

There wasn't a combustion.

"I have your knife," Thyren said, in a low tone. "I must admit, it's a beautiful piece. You should come and retrieve it sometime." A pause, and Damien finally tore his attention from the pure terror, and focused on the man in front of him. "I would love hosting you as well. I could use a partner in sparring."

Damien nodded. "That would be lovely."

"It's settled, then. I'll see you when I see you, Damien."

With a slight bow of his head Thyren walked away.

"Welcome Damien," Isabel Larkin said then, and only then, putting a hand on Damien's shoulder and gently nudging him towards her office. "It is so nice to meet you."

Chapter 14

"It is a strange feeling," Damien lamented. "I can't quite explain it, not fully at least. It fills you with an emotion that is nameless, brings out a lot of questions that wouldn't have been asked otherwise."

"Seeing your own grave?"

"Not just seeing, because, it could have been empty. An empty grave brings the sorrow of disappointment if you see it. However, this is not an empty grave. I know I am in there, a version of me, decaying. That is extremely human, if you ask me, a good reminder of our fragility that we often forget."

Thyren looked like he was considering it. "I don't think we are fragile," he said. "At least we're not made to be. To act otherwise would be a betrayal to our own nature and purpose."

"Maybe not physically. Our minds, however, quite fragile if you ask me."

"We would not be able to survive if we were fragile."

"Survive what, though?"

"Passage of time," Thyren replied, his voice low. "We're presented with two options there: Either we lock ourselves up in our planes, refuse interacting with anyone else, or we risk getting hurt by who aren't like us — those hourglasses, with each wind losing a part of themselves to the point of non-existence as we know it."

"Would you say we are cursed?"

Neither of them were looking at each other, their eyes were fixated on the gravesite, that was marked with a young yew tree. Damien wanted to break a branch, to carry with himself. Would it be disrespectful? To me?

"Some of us are," Thyren replied. "Some of us were never meant to live as long as we did."

"Or as many times," Damien murmured. "Or in as many places."

"Do you remember them all?"

"Unfortunately. It comes and goes in waves. You never know when the next episode will hit, so every waking and sleeping moment is full of thrill." He turned to Thyren. "Should we go inside? Winds are not kind on me these days."

"Of course," the host nodded, pointing towards the palace with an elegant hand wave. "We must have something warm to heat you up from the inside."

"Not going to deny, I would kill for some mulled wine."

They walked in silence, with a hand's distance between them. Damien wanted to ask how many months it had been, exactly, since they were up there, looking at the same scenery from above, even though he knew. It felt like a lot less time had passed for him, less days, less nights, but he carried with him one thing he didn't before: A thousand years' worth of memories. All the bodies he occupied, all the timelines he had been in, they were all there, they were all with him.

A small table was set up for them in front of the fireplace in the grand living room. It wasn't mulled wine, but rather a small teapot that was kept warm by a tiny candle beneath it. Damien could taste the memories in his tongue. Hold on, he chastised himself. You're going well enough.

"No wine," Thyren interrupted his thoughts. "My staff unfortunately takes more interest in my health than I do. They're afraid of me falling back into old habits."

Damien laughed at that. "Chasing the harm is not that of an easy concept to grasp for those who never felt a compulsion to do it," he said, pouring himself a cup of tea. "I know, I tried to explain once. It took me a very long time." When exactly did that happen? How many deaths, or how many lifetimes ago? "It's not addiction to the materials, it's addiction to how it makes us feel."

"I think that's precisely why for me," Thyren laughed too. "I am a very intolerable person once I get into that mindset."

"I knew you then. You were very pleasant."

"Does that mean I am not, now?"

"Of course not. And I say this as someone who has met countless different versions of you." Maybe with a certain exception. He realised his hand was on his throat, as if to get rid of something there. I am not there. I am here, on my own accord. "You were perfectly tolerable then as well, is what I'm trying to say."

"Thanks," Thyren replied. "I must admit, your presence was greatly missed."

"Now, you're just being kind," Damien said. "At best I was an imposing guest, at worst I was catastrophic."

"If that was true, I don't think I'd have invited you back." A pause then, they exchanged glances. "You took a long time to take me up on the offer, though."

"I have been avoiding you," Damien admitted, looking away from Thyren. "I am sorry for that."

"You're still avoiding me," Thyren replied, softly.

"I know. And I'm sorry for that, too. But it's only recent I've found my footing in this reality, and I don't know how strong it is. It feels quite fragile."

Thyren nodded. "I know the feeling. But I don't know your reason behind it."

"Do you want to know?"

"Tell me yours," he shrugged. "I would have tell you mine in return, but I don't think I have a story I haven't told."

"Do you really want to know?"

Thyren sighed. "Ignorance is rumoured to be a bliss, though unfortunately, blisses were never my thing... So, what happened?"

"After I died, or before I returned back?"

"After you died."

Damien put his cup on the small table, leaning back.

"I went back..." He started. "Back to where I started. Where it all started."

"Where the threads pulled you." It wasn't a question.

"Where the threads pulled me," he repeated. "They didn't pull me somewhere good." His hands were shivering, he flexed his fingers to get rid of the tremors. "I found myself returning from dead, but not in the I killed myself in this timeline, and reappeared in that timeline sense, no. There was that too, but apparently it all started because I was already dead there in the first place."

He told him. He, of course, told him the story of his Main Timeline, as he grew to call it. How everything was dying, and how Haylen made a call, and how he had no say in this.

"I wouldn't have left it to you," Thyren said, finally, when Damien had to pause, to drink from his now cold tea. "I wouldn't have left killing Alexei to you. Or to anyone."

"I know."

"I want to punch that bastard in the throat," Thyren added, as if he wanted to clarify.

Damien let a shaken chuckle. "I would love to watch that." His eyes looked somehow darker, solemn. "But I escaped. I don't know how. Someone saved me, some version of me that wasn't a version of me. Then it became worse. My own mind turned against me."

"I know the feeling."

"Then I did something... That I did not think was possible."

He paused, his face in pure agony. Thyren decided to put him out of his misery.

"You merged two timelines."

"You know."

"I do." He smiled, weakly. "I do."

"I am sorry."

"For what?"

Damien took a deep breath. "For not giving you a life with him."

"I am not sure if that's something you should be sorry for," he said. "That wasn't my Axel, and I wasn't his Thyren."

"That's—"

"I know. You could've made it so. You could've woven the threads into each other so seamlessly, or so I've been told. Issue is, then

I wouldn't be myself. Axel wouldn't be himself. We would be two very different people, maybe happy, maybe not."

"You don't have to forgive me over this."

"Forgiveness, I believe, requires a crime or an offence first, Damien. I don't think there's either of them here. Not against me, at least."

The young god remained silent.

"I have one question, though."

"Sure."

"Why him?"

"A good question," Damien said. "One that I've been asking myself ever since I did it."

"Were you able to find an answer?"

He nodded, curt. "He couldn't have moved on otherwise."

Thyren leaned back in his chair, without saying anything. Go on. Tell your story.

"It was the same reason I couldn't go back to him. He didn't want me there. Laying under the same sky, every day, waiting for a death that would never come was easier for him. But you..."

"Me?"

"I wanted to come back to you. This you, the one who called me back."

It's less lonely with you here.

"I would understand if you don't want to see me anymore, ever again," he continued. "A lot changed since that day."

"A lot changed, indeed," Thyren murmured. "But I doubt if my feelings about your existence changed alongside the circumstances."

Damien raised his head.

"Given my track record," Thyren continued. "If they did, you wouldn't be here, comfortably sipping tea while wishing it was wine, and more like... I would have killed you on sight and Martyn would be here, giving me his talk for the fourth time. Maybe even worse, now that he basically adopted you."

"What talk?" The relief was too great to ignore first part of that sentence.

"He didn't give you that whole speech on how we should preserve the mechanisms?" He laughed. "I've had to hear it thrice. First time when I found out that I was a god, the second time when I wanted to kill my birth father, and the third time when I killed Alexei." He shrugged, a mischievous twinkle in his eyes. "Y'know. Track record."

"Oh, he tried."

"Tried?"

"Then he remembered I was chaos, and I had no business in preserving anything." Damien shrugged as well. "Disrupt and corrupt, that's my motto."

"There might be several people who might disagree with you if you want to actualise that."

"Is one of them you?"

"Of course not." He sounded offended. "You would pour gasoline all over this stupid place, and I would at least hand you the matches, if I didn't set it on fire myself."

"I always forget you used to be a leytian," Damien said. "Rather I remember that, but I can't be certain if it was the case here as well."

"Oh, right," Thyren replied. "In at least one I was already a prince, right?"

"Born and raised one," he laughed. "Quite the different flavour, I must say, but somethings never change." Damien's eyes drifted to the windows, to the night sky outside. Time flies. Stars looked so close, so warm. Wait. His eyes turned to Thyren again, still avoiding eye contact though. "It's so late, isn't it?"

"Late? For what?"

Damien shook his head, smiling. "I really wish we had wine. We had it the last time." He got up, and walked to the windows. It didn't look like the garden he was in hours — hours? — prior. He felt so small, all of a sudden, so very inconsequential.

Screams filled his ears. Oh, right. End of the universe as we know it. The room got crowded all of a sudden. Everyone was there, even Sylen, they were all looking through other windows and saying things, screaming, trying to find a solution.

Damien turned his back to the windows, walking to the middle of the room. There weren't any chairs or couches now, the room was empty besides the cocktail tables. From the corner of his eye, he saw Jennifer there, in her butterfly dress. Sorry, we're all dying. He focused on Thyren, who was watching his movements. Isn't this Antenyr? Where am I?

He felt something wet on his face, and he wiped his nose with his fingers. Oh, a nosebleed. How long has it been since I got one? The room felt extremely hot, almost suffocating. With his bloody fingers, he unbuttoned his shirt's collar. Why am I so overdressed?

"Damien?"

"We're all dying, aren't we?" He smiled. His eyes didn't react well to the sudden brightness of the room. It had to be actual stars falling on top of them. "Do you think it will be peaceful?" He half expected to be on fire already.

"What are you talking about?"

"Stars," Damien said, all feeling slowly walked through his limbs to his heart. "Stars are raining upon us, don't you see?"

He faltered before he could take yet another step. Thyren caught him an exact second before he collapsed.

*

Damien was walking for what had to be for days.

He kept walking, and he kept walking, and he kept walking, until finally he saw a building that looked like it was hardly standing up. Damien raised his left wrist to look at the time, almost out of habit, but he saw that it was all rusty and cracked now. Okay, seriously, what is going on?

Against his better judgement, he walked in. It felt like a trap with each step, but the interior impressed him as well. Everything was dusty, but underneath that dust, there laid some pretty marble. It had to be a palace, he was sure. Or a museum. It must have been all so pretty, so carefully made before it was turned into rubble, and dust, and rendered unrecognisable.

He walked in with careful and quiet steps until he came to a staircase, and even though the correct course of action was to run away, to get out of this building and keep walking, he started ascending it. The steps carried him without giving beneath his feet, they didn't turn into rubble, which was welcome. Maybe I'll find somewhere comfortable to sleep.

Eventually he reached to a long corridor, at the top of the staircase. There was nothing but a door at the end of it, nothing but empty and dusty walls and a carpet that had to be red once. He turned his head back, to see nothing but a wall behind him. Walk forward Damien. Don't look back. So he did.

The doors, heavy, wooden doors with beautiful ornaments carved on, swung open in front of him once he reached them. The throne room. He had been in there countless times before. I died here many times before. He wasn't sure if a similar fate expected him here.

"Welcome home, Damien."

He sat upon a rusty, dirty throne. No doubt it was made of the prettiest metals once, shining. Now, neither the man sitting on it, nor the throne itself was glorious — far from it. Though the man had a certain allure, it felt like he was a forgotten statue. Time wasn't kind on him, with a face full of wrinkles and skin as thin as paper. He rusted along with everything else, or maybe he was the source of it.

Home? But this isn't my home.

"See your what selfishness has caused?"

"Haylen," Damien realised. "Not extremely comforting to see you alive."

"You should've killed me yourself."

"As you should, but that has never been your thing."

Haylen laughed, half of his teeth decayed and broken. "I survived," he said. "You failed."

"One for one," Damien shrugged, noticing the actual statues around — people he knew, people he maybe even loved. "So, what, did you kill your boyfriend as well?"

"Where do you think you are, Damien?"

The room changed. It was clean, brand new, so shiny, so beautiful. He found himself sitting on the throne, one hand holding a sword, and the other holding a stick — both of them adorned with gold. In front of him was a leytian, dressed as a legionnaire, standing tall. Damien counted the lines on his shoulder. Second Commander.

"Anthyren?" He called.

"At your service," the leytian replied, his voice hoarse. Damien heard a ringing, barely there.

"Where are we?"

"Why, in Flerketer, of course."

His hands hurt, he lowered his eyes to see both his sword and his stick were on fire. He couldn't let them go out of his hand. I need to let them go.

Anthyren, as if he heard his thoughts, shook his head. "No," he said. "You can't. It's part of the grand plan, you must play your part, Ashren."

"I don't want to."

"You have to." The leytian put his hands on Damien's, not affected by the fire. "You have no say in this."

There wasn't anybody there, and Damien wasn't sure if it was his own body he was occupying. He saw himself from outside: A terrified boy, screaming in agony, holding onto two ablaze ropes, as tight as he could. He wanted to look away, but someone forced his head there, to stare. He couldn't close his eyes.

"You have played with things you shouldn't have, son."

"Father?" Damien wanted to turn his head back and look at him, but he failed. Do what you have to do, he wanted to yell at the kid. Weave. Weave until everything burns. A warmth covered his chest, there was a cold wind in his ribcage. I am on fire, too. It was less of a surprise. He looked at his hands, to see the melting threads. I am doing this to myself.

"You're exhausting yourself, Damien."

"I have to do this."

"Yes. It's your duty. You don't have a say in this."

"It's my decision."

He closed his eyes. Now take a deep breath, little fish. Flames engulfed him, yet he didn't flinch. Weave. One knot after the other. His fingers didn't feel like his own anymore, but he moved them. He was only breathing in an out, through his teeth. If you scream, you'll give up. Weave. Weave until everything burns.

He knew he was spending all the power he had. His very essence of being was feeding the flames, but he didn't care. Weave until you burn to ashes.

Then everything came to a screeching halt. Flames died, lights died, and the pain stopped. His hands were empty, it was so dark he thought maybe he went blind. I am still here.

"Yes you are," a whisper sneaked up behind him. Damien closed his eyes. "You're on your own."

"As I usually am."

"Who takes care of you?"

"I take care of my own."

"Tsk tsk tsk... Who cleans your wounds?"

Damien turned back to see the owner of the voice, and visibly startled when he realised there was nothing but a mirror there. There he was, his own reflection, smiling a bloody smile, his clothes drenched in blood. He wasn't standing, or even sitting — he was there, on his bed, surrounded by endless shards of glass shining like tiny diamonds. He saw the blade in his hand.

"Right back to where we started," he murmured.

"Right back to where you left," his reflection answered. "Where is your knife?"

Damien tried to lower his head, but he couldn't. His throat hurt, his face was too sticky to move. I am smiling. Did he know that intrinsically or did he see that? I killed myself. His hands were empty, still. Where is my knife?

"Don't you remember where you left it?"

"I have been to a lot of places, so forgive me if I'm a bit forgetful."

"Close your eyes, Damien."

"I entrusted you with it, didn't I? I told you to hang on to it."

"Until you needed it," the voice reminded him. "Then you took it. Was it helpful?"

"It was supposed to be my light home."

"It still can be." The tone was a lot more compassionate now. "Close your eyes."

"I am dead," Damien said. "How can I close my eyes when I'm dead?"

"Why did you die with your eyes open?"

"I don't know."

"Close your eyes, then."

He did. But his own reflection didn't stop smiling at him.

"Now," the same voice said. "Wake up, Damien."

"I am dead."

"You are pretty much alive."

"I slit my own throat. I am fairly certain that I am dead."

"Open your eyes, and see it for yourself."

He opened his eyes. "You were the one who..."

It was middle of the night, and he was in an unfamiliar place. There was not a mirror above, nor he was covered by broken glass. Wait—

"Morning sleepyhead," Thyren, his Thyren, said. "Or I should say nighty night. Welcome back amongst the living. You scared us all."

Damien looked around. The room wasn't dark, moonlight allowed at least some level of vision, but even with that low level of vision, he could see how the bedspreads and pillowcases were stained with blood. Wait. Almost instinctually, he threw himself back in bed, pulling his legs to himself. "Where-"

"Nosebleed," Thyren clarified. "A lot of episodes of nosebleeds. Ferran should be here any second, I had just taken over the night shift from him."

Damien took his hand to his face. No, no, this is me just waking up. I am back where I started – it wasn't his room, but he definitely died – it's all his grand plan. He was too terrified to actually panic, too terrified to actually speak. I need to get out of here. Before — before —

He looked at Thyren, who was sitting very still, and looking at him with a great intensity. No, not again. Not when I'm powerless. Not when I can't even defend myself. "I don't even have my knife," he said, loudly. Why am I telling him this?

"I have your knife, and you were actually here to retrieve it. Remember?"

I don't remember anything. He looked at his hands, just to look for the burn marks. They have faded fast. He moved his fingers, reminding himself of marble spiders. There was no pain. Didn't that just happen?

"I wove," he said. "I wove until everything burnt. I was on fire."

"That was six months ago."

"Six months?" That had to be a lie. No, any minute Haylen was going to burst in and they were going to try strong-arm him into killing Sylen. "I cannot do that," he said, shaking his head. "I cannot do it."

"Do what, Damien?"

"I cannot kill Sylen." He sounded like he was begging. He didn't want to sound like he was begging. I am begging. I cannot do that.

"Nobody expects you to. He's been dead for over a year."

The door opened, and he heard Ferran's voice. "Who are you—" Their eyes met. "Princeling?"

"How long?" Damien asked. "How long since I killed myself?"

"You what?" Ferran paused. "Wait, didn't that happen in that other timeline?"

"What other timeline?"

Thyren sighed. "Ferran, please tell that stupid boss of yours that it's time to involve Juventas."

Damien sounded frantic when he spoke. "What does she have to do with any of these?"

"Ferran," Thyren repeated, impatiently. "Please. Or, I will bring my people here and he won't like that."

"You're here, with him?" Ferran asked.

"Yes."

"Where are you going?" Damien asked, shocked. "You're leaving me here, with, with—"

"I'm leaving you here with a good friend," Ferran said, in his best reassurance voice. "He will take good care of you, then I will be back with Martyn."

"They will worry." I can handle this myself. If only I can understand where I am and when I am... "They will worry out of nowhere."

"Damien," Ferran raised his hand, and Damien stopped rambling. I can trust Ferran. Right? I can trust him. "Can you please take a deep breath?"

He did. What if they got to him as well? What if —

"Now. Stay here, and don't move. I will be back in an instant. I promise you."

"Okay." Damien nodded. No. They could never get him. Maybe it's an elaborate thing, maybe we have an angle here. To expose them. So that the others can understand. "I am waiting here for you."

"Great."

Damien wished he had his powers back. I burnt through them. I have left with nothing. He closed his eyes, putting his head on his knees. Focus. There must be something I can do. He wanted to reach inside, to that familiar tingling at the top of his fingers. Focus. I am an entity, I am still chaos. His mind was filled with fog, thinking felt like walking through mud. Focus. All he could think of was colour purple, and that made no sense. Think of something. Something nice, and comforting.

He thought of the evening sky, then. Stars as small as they should be, evening breeze gently caressing his sunburnt skin. He thought of a man who stood next to him, as they both downed as much wine as they could. Their fingers brushed, just for a second.

Come back here. It's less lonely with you here.

Damien closed his eyes so tight, light exploded beneath his eyelids. He felt the strength of the fingers gripping his throat, pressuring his trachea just the right amount. He couldn't breath. But you hurt me, he thought. You hurt me, when I did nothing to you. Wasn't it you?

The door swung open again. This time, it was not only Ferran who came, but Martyn and Juventas was there as well. He raised his head.

"Wait," he asked. "Where is my mother?"

"Your mother?" Martyn frowned.

"Yeah — you're here, Aunt Juventas here, where is she?"

All four of them looked at each other. Juventas was the first one who got out of the shocked state, to come near him.

"What is your mother's name?"

"Madison," he said. "Syleren. How do you not know that, she's your sister!" His eyes got bigger, looking at all of them. "Is she— did something happen to her?"

"Damien," Juventas said, very calmly and softly. "Please look at me."

Damien turned his eyes to Juventas, in desperation. "Did Haylen do something to her? Because I—" The possibility physically pained him. I should've played my part, he thought. I should've shut up and played my part, and then my mother would be alive and—

"Look at me," Juventas said, once again. "Keep your focus on me."

It was an intense sense of deja vu. "I shouldn't blink," Damien said.

"Smart boy," Juventas murmured, one hand on his temple. Her eyes suddenly turned glassy. "Oh, you've been confused through and through."

"I don't know where I am," whined Damien. "When I am."

"Slow down..." She took a deep breath. "And close your eyes when I tell you to, okay?"

"Is it going to hurt?"

"Not at all, little nightingale, not at all," she tried to smile. "Tell me about your mother... Anything you remember about her. What did she look like?"

"She had long, blonde hair, a smile like sunshine. She would always say how it's a shame I didn't get my hair from her, and my father would say how it should be enough that I got my eyes from her."

"Oh, really?"

"Yes..." Damien's speech slowed down, along with his breathing. "When I was a kid, she would play with me. Let me braid her hair. I think I would hurt her too much, pulling too strongly..." Tears were rolling down on Damien's face, and unbeknownst to him, Martyn was wiping the tears on his face as well.

"Did she..." Juventas' voice faltered, tears were wetting her cheeks. "Did she ever sing to you?"

"She did... When everything screamed, she would sing to me to drown the screams... And I would sing with her... until... the... screaming... stopped..."

"Close your eyes, Damien."

"... the... screaming... never... stopped..."

"Close your eyes, please."

Juventas pulled her hand away the second Damien closed his eyes, and gently laid him onto the bed.

"Plot twist," she said, her cheeks wet with tears. "Did you know about that, Martyn?"

"Parts of it," Martyn replied, he sounded like someone was choking him. "Some parts of it."

Ferran and Thyren, the uninvited guests of the family drama, cleared their throats, almost simultaneously.

"Pardon me for interrupting the sadness," Thyren said. "Who exactly is Madison?"

"Well," Juventas said. "He was right about the part about her being my sister. You could call her that."

"You had a sister?"

"But not Order," Juventas ignored his interruption. "Ashren. Madison was Chaos, a perfect one at that."

"Roll back," Thyren said. "I didn't listen maybe half of those stupid history lessons back when I was a leytian, but I am pretty sure I've never heard of another sister before in my life, until right now."

"She was killed before the first leytians were created," Martyn explained. "And then it was decided that if nobody knew or remembered about her, it would be better. Aside from the six of us, of course."

Thyren sighed. "Alexei, right? Alexei killed her."

"Unfortunately."

"Well, explains why there was so much money on me killing Alexei."

Juventas cackled. "This is why you were one of my favourite leytians."

"Because I hated Alexei so much that I almost set myself on fire?"

"That was a factor, too, I am not going to deny."

Eventually they looked at the boy on the bed, sleeping somewhat peacefully.

"What's going to happen to him?" Ferran asked. "Or, first, what happened to him?"

Juventas' cheer faded rather quickly. "Well, remembering so many lives at the same time isn't easy. He was confused."

"And what did you do?"

"Put everything in somewhat of an order," she explained. "Eventually, he will be able to adapt to that in his head, and hopefully this will never happen again."

Martyn put his hand over Juventas' shoulder. "Thanks, Juve," he said. "Thank you."

"You played that card way too well, Martyn," Juventas leaned towards him. "Makes you wonder, doesn't it? What we could have had, what different lives we could have lead..."

"Don't go there," Martyn said. "You'll lose your mind if you do."

Thyren sighed, his eyes still on Damien. Tell me about it.

Chapter 15

The coastal city of Erthenca, population of ninety-thousand plus two deities, was known for its close proximity to Hysseren, its beautiful beaches, and of course, the calmness of the night life. Not that it didn't exist — but instead of the exploding music and non-stop hard drinks of Hysseren, they had somewhat a fair-like approach to spending the evenings: Walks near the sea, restaurants that stayed up very late to provide the best food and the best products of the local wineries.

Neither of them were alone this time. In the pathway around the beach, one of them was listening to the other talking about how he enjoyed small trips to the beach as well. They both were forgoing something they liked, today: For one, it was the sunbathing in the beach, and for the other it was fighting the waves, as he wanted to go as far away as he could. Coldness of the water contrasting with the afternoon sun above, the muffled sounds, and the salt pricking his eyes — all the more reason for him to enjoy.

"Can I ask you a question?" Thyren said eventually.

"Anything," Damien replied, his eyes on the horizon. A small boat was floating to unknowns, its sails all blown up with the wind.

"How does it feel?" He paused, signalling Damien to wait. Wait. "How does it feel knowing they are out there, but not being able to reach them?" The words were heavy, the implications heavier. Ignorance is truly bliss, Damien thought. If only none of us knew about other timelines.

"Heartbreaking," Damien offered, still. "I want to drop everything and go there, to make sure they're alright, alive, happy. But I know I can't. Not physically, but I'd pick death over going there." He turned his head towards Thyren, with a smile. "Maybe if I decide to finish myself, I will go there. As a reunion before ending it all."

Thyren didn't say anything at first. Damien saw him gripping the rails they were leaning on, until his knuckles were all white with the effort. "Is that a thought you entertain?"

"Suicide? I think once you actually go through it, you can never take it out of your mind. It was you, wasn't it? You told me about the yearning?"

"Yeah."

"I am not going to ask you how you know it. But the yearning is there, always. I guess the trick is never giving an ear to it."

"More or less," Thyren admitted. "Or even if you do, treating it like an obnoxious child speaking without considering the meaning of their words."

"Oh, that's something I have experience in," Damien said. "I always ignore the voices in my ear. Just one more won't make a huge difference."

"Whose voice do you hear?"

"My tormenter," he simply said, the name still wasn't easy to get out of his lungs, his throat, his mouth. "He's still shouting how every move I make is a part of his grand plan. At this point, I don't even know if I'm imagining him because I got used to him, or there's some abnormal explanation of it. I've stopped questioning."

"Does he keep you up at nights?"

Damien laughed. "You very well know it does."

They were sharing a house, together, for a while — a short one, in that. A small lakeside house in Lanenketer, with just a few bedrooms and nothing more. Martyn, of course, had Ferran come and check up on Damien every once in a while, but that was fine. It was alright.

It was Thyren's complaints about how the palace was as lonely as it could get, and how he missed visiting Lanenketer, that brought them here. "If you want you can join," he then offered. "It would be a change of scenery for you."

And what a change of scenery it was.

They established a routine together. Thyren was relentless when it came to trainings, even though there was literally nothing to train for anymore. In addition to sparring, they were duelling, fighting with knives — the whole nine yards. Damien oftentimes would complain about how he was not a leytian.

"You need to be prepared," Thyren would reprimand him.

"I can snap my fingers and render anyone ineffective."

"Imagine a scenario in which you don't have your powers." That would be the end of discussion.

They went on walks, they cooked — and despite the impressions, Thyren was excellent at that. They learned how to share things, which was even better, for Damien wasn't sure what he knew and what he didn't anymore.

That morning, straight after breakfast, Thyren started the sparring session. Damien, at this point knowing resistance was futile, followed him in silence — though he was thoroughly distracted. I don't want to fight anyone. Not anymore. But, in all honesty when push came to shove, what alternative did he have? Oh, some alternative, alright.

So they exercised, going through the same motions. But in a second, Damien found himself on the ground, staring at the man who pinned him to the ground. Wait. He stared at Thyren's eyes. "Let me go," he said.

"You can make me let you go."

"Let me go, Thyren."

But Thyren, without moving a single muscle, kept on staring at him. No. What is going on? Damien's heart started beating in a marathon mode, as if it was too big for his ribcage. Every breath he took burnt his lungs. I am not back. I am not back. He closed his eyes.

"Look me in the eye, Damien."

"You can't make me."

"I can't. But you need to look me in the eye."

Damien shook his head. No. I am not going to go through that again. "If you want to kill me, just go ahead."

"If that was my intention, my hand wouldn't be on your chest but on your neck. I want you to look at me. My eyes."

After a moment passed with reluctancy, Damien opened his eyes to look at Thyren's greenish blue ones. In the corner of his mind

where he couldn't keep quiet, Haylen was screaming at him how
he had no say in this, in any of this.

Even if I don't... I like where I ended up at.

"I'm not him, Damien."

"I know."

"No, you don't. And it's okay. But I'm not him."

"You're not him, because your Haylen isn't here," Damien blurted.
"If he was here, asking me the same thing—"

"I told you," Thyren replied, calm as the morning sea. "I wouldn't
let the honour of killing Alexei to anyone else."

"You wouldn't think it like that. It would be something Haylen
asked of you—"

Thyren sighed, but his pressure on Damien's chest didn't change.
All of his replies were squandered by the tears rolling from
Damien's eyes. "You're not there," he said eventually. "This place
and that place isn't the same. You know that."

"I do." This time he sounded less convinced, but more like whin-
ing.

"It's because we made different choices."

"Why are you doing this?"

"Because you're still not looking me in the eyes, Damien. After
all this time."

"I can't," he said, tears still rolling. "I still..." He couldn't finish the
sentence.

"I know. But you cannot let him torment you forever. Look me
directly in the eyes, Damien."

He did. He pulled all the strength he had, and he did look him
in the eyes.

"I am not him," Thyren repeated, his voice calm, but strong. "You're not back there. You never will be. You are here, safe, with me."

He released his hold on him, laying right next to him on the ground. They both laid down, in silence, their eyes in the ceiling. Damien couldn't stop the influx of tears.

"Last night was rough, wasn't it?" Thyren asked, eventually.

"Did I talk too much in my sleep?"

"You were rather wailing and screaming." He sounded rather nonchalant about it, as if screaming in one's sleep was so normal for him. "I wanted to come in and check up on you, but then you said my name."

"Oh..."

"Begging me not to kill you."

Damien didn't say anything.

"So... Sorry for taking you off guard. Though not sorry for doing it."

"Why are you helping me?"

Thyren chuckled. "Ah, princeling," he said. "You remind me of a twenty-six year old, banging on a door, talking about how he lost his mind. Someone told that twenty-six year old that they would find it together." He paused. "I want to be that someone for you."

"I didn't bang on your door."

"Yeah, you crashed into my backyard. Not that I'm complaining. I told you. It's less lonely with you here."

He lifted himself off the ground, and declared he was going to have some tea. "Do you want any?" He asked.

Damien, still laying on the ground, muttered a "yes" before getting up himself as well.

*

Beach was Damien's idea, because after a particularly hard night of seeing funerals of dozens of people he knew, or he didn't know, at least it would be a good change of scenery. I missed my mother. When he woke up and inadvertently started singing while plugging his ears with his fingers, he realised way too late that he was being loud. This was his way of trying to make it up to Thyren, for a lost night's sleep.

"Do you want to swim?"

"I do, actually."

"Then why don't you go for it?"

Thyren frowned. "Do you want to be alone?"

"Does that matter?"

"I think it should if this is a trip we're taking together."

"Go and have a swim with the sharks, Thyren," Damien laughed. "And I will take my top off and lay on the beach, then probably sleep."

"In the broad daylight?"

"Never stopped me."

He couldn't really explain what attracted him to the passivity of it. Enjoying the sun as he sat on the dry sand near the sea... That was something else. The calm breeze taking away the harshness of the sun, his bones getting warm under his skin, and different colours underneath his eyelids as he laid down and closed his eyes — all the more reason to enjoy it. It was something stationary amidst all the constant flow of things, and Damien wanted nothing more than that.

"Come swim with me," Thyren said, with a smile so sweet Damien actually wondered if he was really the destruction. He knew the man in front of him could bring ruin to everything, with a snap of his fingers. Yet, here he was, smiling so wide, so happy. "Then we can both sleep under the sun."

"Oh, you don't want to have me swimming," Damien laughed.

"Why is that?"

"I usually end up drowning."

"Drowning?"

"Yes. Unfortunately."

The smile was now replaced with a confused frown. "You don't know how to swim?"

"No, I do. I do," he insisted. "It's just — I don't know why actually. I think in one of my past lives, I died by drowning. Maybe that's why."

"Come swim with me," Thyren repeated. "I won't let you drown."

"I don't know..."

"Do you trust me?"

Yes. I said yes to this question a million times, with a million different version of you. I trusted you'd do the right thing so many times. I would hand you this universe if you asked me for it, of course I trust you.

"This silence is becoming quite hurtful, I must say."

"Oh — sorry. I was replying to your question internally. I do trust you, and I think you already know that."

"Then," Thyren extended his hand towards Damien. "Swim with me."

Swimming in the sea wasn't exactly Damien's favourite activity, he had to admit. Even the most tranquil moments floating would suddenly turn into him finding himself in the depths no matter how shallow, and struggling immensely to breathe. The aching relief of his lungs, that was the only thing came to mind when he thought of swimming.

I won't let you drown. And he trusted Thyren.

Water was cold and too salty, but something about the waves coming and going had a very soothing effect. He wasn't actually swimming, but rather just laying flat and leaving himself to the waves, but it was calming. Comforting. I could sleep here, he thought. I could lay there, and sleep.

But he opened his eyes. "Thyren?" His own voice came so far away.

"Yeah?"

"Go and swim."

The man laughed. "Are you sure about that?"

"Yes." No. Never let me go, maybe? "If that will comfort you, let's swim together."

"I think you are the one who should be getting comfortable." Still, he was submerged in the water till his neck. "You are the one who's afraid of drowning."

"A very real threat, by the way," Damien laughed, and he swallowed sea water. "Fuck, my throat-"

"Take it slow, princeling."

"You, too?"

His hands looked like ghosts under the water, less sharp, less deadly. "Suits you, doesn't it?"

"I used to be one," Damien said, hoping his low voice would disappear between the waves. "Not anymore."

"I think you'd find Martyn disagreeing about that with you."

Instead of answering, Damien took a deep breath, and dived in.

The water burnt his eyes, it was hard to see anything at all. But seeing something wasn't the point. He looked at his hands, his fingers, so different from the surroundings, they resembled the skeleton beneath all the skin and nerves and muscles. Water filled his ears, pressure actually comforting him. There were little, tiny fish swimming around him in lightning speeds. Avoid me, avoid me. He found it so funny how close they were, so within reach but so impossible to touch.

He wasn't drowning, even though he desperately needed to go up and take yet another deep breath. Just a little longer. Just a little longer. But before he could make his plea to himself, Thyren held him from his neck, gently but strongly, and pulled him upwards.

"As much as I approve you enjoying the water," he said, with a smile. "You need to breathe, too, Damien."

"Oh, bother," Damien scolded him, taking a few deep breaths. Deeper. Deeper. Breathe in deeper, then go deeper. He dived in, once again, without any movements. Quiet. It's so quiet. With each wave he could hear the pressure in his ear shifting just a bit, then it was back to normal, back to quiet again.

He stared at the fish, treating him like a rock, swimming around him. They were wary of any movement, tiniest of them to switch their directions completely. Don't be hunted. The next group of fish stood still for a while, before they all scattered. Why did you do that guys?

A face entered his line of vision, and Damien smiled. Saltwater was burning his eyes, but he didn't care as he held on to Thyren, them staring at each other in the infinite quiet of the sea. Don't let me go. Don't let me go. Thyren squeezing his hands in return was a promise, in that moment: I won't let you go.

Deeper. Deeper. Breathe out slowly. He wanted to stay here, to sleep here, to live here forever. You need to breathe, too, Damien. He wanted to argue. Do I really? Maybe this is where we belong. A cemetery that moved constantly.

They slowly rose to surface again, which didn't take very long. Even the water dripping from his hair was salty enough to set his eyes on fire, Damien rubbed them just to get the water away — but his hands were also wet, which didn't help. Thyren on the other hand, seemed like he was having no issues at all.

"How do you do that?"

"Do what?"

"How aren't your eyes burning?"

Thyren let a hearty laugh, standing tall. In that moment Damien noticed the scars he had on every inch of his body. The enormity of the number of them actually irked the young man. Tell me yours and I tell you mine. "I don't feel pain."

"None at all, or do you have a high tolerance?"

"None at all. Lost the ability a very long time ago."

"That's something you should tell me," Damien said, still half submerged in water. "The story behind that."

"It's a long one," he warned him.

"Don't we have eternity?"

Thyren didn't reply, as he slowly let himself in the water as well. He threw his shoulders, and his head back at the same time.

"We should have dinner in the city," Damien said, in an attempt to change the subject.

"I know literally none of the places in this city. Axel used to drag me around, but we would mostly hang out in Hysseren."

Damien tried very hard not to flinch upon hearing Axel's name. This one is not him, this one is not him. "I think I know some places, which means we'll get to see if they stay in the same level of quality through timelines."

"As you wish, princeling." Thyren reached and ruffled Damien's hair.

"Saltwater!" Damien yelled, blinking rapidly and fanning his eyes with his hands to stop the burning. "Oh, you owe me one for this."

Their laughter echoed through the sea.

*

"Pain is an odd concept," Thyren started, swirling his wine in his glass. It didn't smell as good as the ones he had home, but still, good for ending the thirst. "It's a good defence mechanism: If it gives you pain, you know you're supposed to avoid it. Simple enough. But subjected to it long enough..." He sighed, Damien actually could see the veins in his neck distending. "It messes with you."

"You don't feel it anymore."

"It's been a long while," he admitted. "A very long while. There were so many fights I continued despite — apparently — life threatening injuries. Back in Academy, they thought I was cursed."

"That's interesting." Damien finished his glass. "One would thought under Sylen's ironclad indoctrination, there wouldn't be anything such as being cursed. Or was that not a thing here?"

Thyren laughed. "It was, of course. And the curse, not officially maybe. But everyone kind of thought it was the gods' way of punishing me for my rebellious acts."

"Most scars originate from those acts, I presume."

"Oh, like you wouldn't believe."

Damien sighed. I think I counted them once. There was a part of him that wanted to tell all of it, differentiating between all those versions of the same people was getting extremely difficult with more time he spent with him. They are not the same people. "It's amazing to me how you're telling that with a smile."

"To be completely honest, I only realised it was a sob story after Anthony's freak out when I first told him. Before that, it was just another day for me."

"Were you gradually desensitised to it?"

"Absolutely not," Thyren laughed, this time even louder. "It actually has nothing to do with me — it's entirely on Geoffrey. By the power vested in him by being the God of Pain, he decided to take the ability from me entirely, because apparently, it was getting too much for him."

"Wow," Damien said. "Really?"

"Yeah, he has this whole I've always wanted a son, and you're it approach to me — it's his house actually that we're staying in. I mean, it was his, but after I killed Alexei, he decided I should have it. I didn't question. Though I'm pretty sure it was about their bet."

That reminded Damien of something. "Oh, they had it here as well?"

"Where else did they have it?"

"In another timeline, Sylen was the one who told me about it."

"He knew?"

"Yeah," Damien said, leaning back. The waiter was taking their plates, so he waited. "He found it funny when I told him you were the one who killed him, in a different timeline. He wasn't surprised at all."

Thyren's jaw dropped. "For real?"

"Oh, yeah."

"In no way I would have imagined that would be his reaction."

It was complete silence between them until they were served dessert, and their wines were replenished. Then, Thyren shook his head.

"I'm still in shock. Unbelievable."

"Yeah... But that's not the main thing here, is it?"

"What is?"

"Since we know about the bet, and that Geoffrey won it," Damien said, then he leaned forward as if it was a secret he was sharing. His voice was dropped to a whisper. "What did the ones who lost bet on then?"

"I am guessing Lionel bet on me not killing Alexei. Honestly," Thyren said, after laughing so loudly some other patrons got startled. "That guy had a different affection to Alexei, which explains the dagger gazes he throws my way whenever he sees me, but well... Who gives a fuck?"

"That leaves Gerard." Damien narrowed his eyes. "I think I can ask Jennifer about that, eventually."

"There's a possibility he didn't bet," Thyren shrugged. "I mean, with Geoffrey picking the winning option."

"That wouldn't be fun, though," Damien whined.

"Not everything in life is fun, princeling."

Damien looked offended at that. "You know, when you call me princeling, I don't know if you mean it in an affectionate way, or an insulting way."

"I find it cute," Thyren said. "Now, I know that statement is vague, but it's the truth."

"Cute usually means affection, though."

"Usually is the key word there. If anyone called me cute to my face, I would ensure they lost the privileges to several functions of their faces, for example."

"So it's an insult for you?"

"It's rather something I never want to be defined as."

"Oh, that definitely makes sense." It didn't. "What do you want to be defined as then, my liege?"

"Oh, fuck off," Thyren chuckled. "I know you're definitely insulting me."

"Aren't you a literal king?"

"One of two, thank you very much."

"Then it's factual. Now," he said in an excellent imitation of Thyren. "I know that statement is vague, but it's the truth."

"I am repeating my reaction. Fuck off." But he was laughing.

"In my lost traveller days, I always referred to you as the King of the Mountain, by the way."

Damien's way of speaking stopped Thyren's laughter. "You're serious?"

"Mmhm," he nodded. "King of the Mountain, King of Ashes. Two different kings, two different domains, but royal through and through. It was easier to differentiate you two in my head that way, because unfortunately, you share a name and most facial features."

Thyren opened his mouth, then closed it, then spoke. "Most?"

"One of his eyes was scarred. Not important. My point is, for me, you are first and foremost a King. Not directly my king, and even that's debatable given you've literally killed the defacto ruler of Flerketer."

"Herl'en Verketer," Thyren reminisced. "The King Above."

"You know, I think I've never heard that epithet for Sylen before."

"Which ones did you hear?"

"One, actually. The Puppet Master."

"Oh, definitely." He nodded, all serious. Then his face brightened up. "I wonder what yours were. Any interesting names?"

Damien smiled, bitterly. "Haunted," he said. "Or Steel Prince."

"Steel?"

"They called my mother The Starlight Queen. Iron comes from stars, and all that spiel."

"That sounds sweet."

"Yeah, it was." He smiled. "What are yours?"

"Well, let me think…" Thyren started counting on his fingers. "Anastatēr after I got the crown, but we share that one with Anthony. After I killed Alexei, those in Leytianketer treated me as a scary concept, hence, Ashketyirlen." He paused. "Given most of them means destroyer in one way, shape or form, I think everyone just wants to call me a murderer, but they're either too kind, or too afraid to do that directly to my face."

"They all sound rather terrifying," Damien agreed. "But as some-one who would punch anyone who'd call you cute, you have no room to complain."

"Ah, here I thought you were on my side, princeling."

"I am, I am absolutely on your side. That's why I support the moniker selections, my liege."

Thyren shook his head. "I'll never be free of that now, will I?"

Damien shrugged, his eyes on his glass. "The moment you drop princeling, I'll drop my liege."

"Don't threaten me."

"Less of a threat, more of an offer for agreement."

"I wouldn't want to repeat myself a third time," Thyren laughed, raising his glass. "Cheers?"

"Mer Silantra," Damien replied, in the old language. To the stars.

In silence, they ate their desserts.

"Do you think we, deities or entities whatever you call us, are too used to have whatever we want, whenever we want?" Damien spoke up. "Or can we consider that a prize for standing still despite changing times and places?"

"Where did that existential crisis come from?"

Damien shrugged. "I just want to order a second serving of that cherry pie."

*

Nowhere near the afternoon, but it was hot in the night as well, in Erthenca. Opening the windows didn't help in the slightest. Even the thinnest sheets were too much, touch of them grating his skin. Damien opened his eyes in frustration, despite his body being tired as ever.

Some birds were chirping outside, with no intention to silencing themselves, they would have no care about how humans around them needed to sleep — made total sense, in a way, but it didn't make the chirping any less annoying. Damien decided to go downstairs to the kitchen, with the hopes that maybe a cold glass of water would take the edge of the weather.

Without wearing his shirt, he headed out of his room. Dim light of the kitchen was visible, even from the top of the stairs. An irrational part of his mind immediately went to the worst case scenario: An intruder. Someone broke in. Flexing his fingers, he ascended as quietly as he could. Tips of his fingers sent electricity through his arms. Yeah. You're there alright. Life was so much better without that emptiness in his chest.

Though once down, he let a breath he didn't know he was holding.

"Couldn't sleep, huh?" Thyren saluted him with his full glass.

"Way too hot," Damien agreed, going to the cupboards to get himself a glass. "I couldn't breathe."

"Yeah, I forgot how awful summers are here. Springs and autumns are the best seasons to enjoy Erthenca, but we both picked summer to be depressed."

"Worst season for it, really." The glass was cold enough that even holding it numbed his hands as he brought it to his lips to drink it. "Winter. Or autumn at best."

"Autumn more like it. With the fallen leaves."

Damien raised the glass as he drank it, but spilled some of the very cold water to his own chest. He shook his head as his brain felt like it was frozen, but as he jumped slightly to sit on the kitchen counter, he didn't look like he was much affected by it.

After his second glass of water, he decided to break the silence, just so he could stop thinking. "You really have a ton of scars," he observed, his eyes on Thyren. "That almost never changes."

"Oh, good to know all my other timeline versions were abused as a child."

That wiped Damien's dreamy expression. "Wait — I'm sorry."

"Oh, don't be," Thyren laughed. "All the scars we carry and all that bullshit... Find any Hyiressen that's older than forty, and you'll find scars." He paused. "Not more than me, though. I was a notoriously naughty as a child."

"Only as a child?" Damien asked, one eyebrow raised. It was at this moment he wished he poured that cold water over his own head.

"Depends." Thyren apparently had decided to play the game.

"On?"

"Multiple factors."

"Such as...?"

"What about you, Damien?"

So much for fair play. "Do I look like I play nice?"

"To be honest, in all the time I've seen you, you looked like you were a moody teenager."

"A hundred and more lifetimes worth of trauma does that to you, but I was — and if provoked, still am — a player."

"Playing?"

"The men. The women. Fler, leytian, and lanen alike. Also the odds." He smiled, wide. "Nothing is as easy as gambling if you can change the odds in your favour in the blink of an eye."

"Oh, you fucking cheater."

"At your service. Although in my defence, I never claimed to be monogamous."

Thyren finished his glass. "Does Jennifer know about it?"

Below the belt? Very naughty, Hyiressen. "Jennifer and I have a very clear agreement."

"Is that so?"

"Yeah... We both know what it entails, and we're not interested in asking for more."

"A honourable cheater."

"I would never break a promise." Damien replied, his voice intense, though his eyes were away from him. "I didn't break the one I gave to you."

Thyren responded with the same intensity. "You came back," he said.

"I came back," Damien repeated.

Without saying another word, Thyren got up and walked towards the kitchen door.

"Good night?" Damien said behind his back.

"Good night, princeling," Thyren replied. Damien could hear his smile in his voice.

He stood there, under the low light of the kitchen, his empty glass still in his hand. It was a calm moment for him, his mind finally silent, absolved of the screaming in his ear. He closed his eyes, he could almost taste the peace. I think it's over. Over. He felt his shoulders drop, as if it was tension that kept him so high. That's the thing about anchors, my dear boy, a familiar, but not hostile voice spoke in his ear as he looked through the door Thyren had just passed through. You can always make a new one.

Damien finally understood what it meant.

Chapter 16

"So," Jennifer said, throwing her bag on his couch, and then jumping right next to it. She let her high heels fall from her feet, crossing her legs right afterwards. "Erthenca. Was it as romantic as I hoped it to be?"

Damien rolled his eyes as he focused on the loom in front of him. Today he picked all the cold colours, blues and greys. He had no interest in determining a pattern, he was tying and changing threads as he saw fit. "It was nice," he said. "We went for a swim, even."

"Oooh," she giggled. "Underwater action?"

"Jenny—"

"I'm kidding, obviously, but I am going to be very surprised if none of you made a move."

"Why would we?"

"Umm," she narrowed her eyes, disbelief apparent in her voice. "Because you both make puppy eyes to each other all the fucking time? It's honestly so tiring."

"We do not do such a thing."

"Yeah, Damien, go ahead and lie to yourself. I'm pretty sure Thyren is giving a similar speech to Anthony right now. And we'll all pretend we agree with you until you guys can wake up and realise... Everyone was right!"

"No, you're mistaken on one part. I already know what I feel, my issue is I cannot tell if I actually feel them for him, or it's because I cannot differentiate between all the other ones I've fallen in love with." He pushed his loom on the table, and leaned back as he turned to Jennifer. His arms crossed, he stretched his neck and his shoulders. "An anchor," he said.

"An anchor?"

"I need an anchor. I cut off all the tethers, now I'm drifting like a leaf in the wind — I need an anchor."

Jennifer leaned slightly forward, serious. "Okay," she said. "How will you get one?"

"I have some ideas. Theories. Two theories, specifically." He sighed. "Still up in the air."

"Must be tough."

Damien didn't say anything.

Deep down he knew. There were a few points in his life, throughout timelines that never changed, and he knew they were the answer. It was clear to him, no matter how many threads he cut, there was always something that connected him to her, to Thyren, to his father, to Sylen, to Haylen. Haylen and Sylen were dead, so that left him only three people.

All of whom attended his funeral.

"How about you?" He decided to change the subject. "How is your life going?"

"Keeping secrets from literally everyone is harder than I expected," she said. "Hardest is my mother. Every time she stares into my
eyes, I get this feeling she's trying to read my mind in the literal
sense."

"I don't know why you're still hiding," he said.

"I just don't feel like it's the right time," she shrugged. "There
should be a party to announce, and then another party to cele-
brate."

He shook his head, laughing. "Do you think it will be a boy or a
girl?"

"I am hoping for a girl, but I'd be okay with everything at this
point."

"Any ideas for a name yet, or do we need a party for that as well?"

She threw her head back, her eyes on the ceiling. "Few," she said,
quietly.

"Want to run them by me?"

"You can even chip in with a few ideas."

"Really?" He raised his head at that. "You'd let me?"

That earned him a sweet laughter from Jennifer. "Let me ask you
something," she said, as she straightened in the couch. "Do you
really want to be involved with the kid?"

He stayed silent for a while, as silence put everything into
perspective. Saying yes to her was not a particularly decision for
him — not on the baby, not on her conditions. Even though he made
her work for it for a while, she didn't even need to argue, in his
admittedly twisted mind. In the end, she saw him getting buried.

"Yeah," he said. "As much as I can. I know, defeats your whole
purpose for picking me, but what can you do? Paternal instincts."

"I can have my father kill you, you know that, right?"

"You like me enough not to do that."

"I'm pretty volatile when it comes to emotions," she said, closing her eyes. "So I wouldn't bank on it, if I were you."

"Good luck with your child, then."

"Oh, fuck off, Damien." She laughed again. "Did you know the infamous Gentlemen's Club has a bet on you?"

"On me?"

"Not just you, you egoist. They're betting when you and Thyren will finally acknowledge what you feel for each other."

Damien dropped everything he was holding onto the table, and turned his entire body toward her. "Are you serious?"

"I'm not the only one waiting for the romantic conclusion to your love story through all timelines. So, if you could give a heads up to the mother of your child, I can make my father happy, and maybe," she smiled wide and innocently batted her eyelashes. "Just maybe, he won't kill you."

"I'm pretty sure Geoffrey will win again — which reminds me of one thing. What did your father bet on Thyren versus Sylen death match?"

Jennifer started cackling. "You know about that?"

"Oh yeah. It's a multi timeline thing, too, apparently. I've heard it from a Sylen."

"Damn it," she was still cackling. "My dad bet on... That Thyren would kill Uncle Alexei, and then fall. He technically didn't fall, though, but he burnt his wings and didn't kill Uncle Alexei for a long time — that's why Uncle Geoff win. He bet on first the fall, then the murder."

Damien stared at her, jaw dropped. "I cannot believe this being a topic of betting for them."

"You know the only reason your father cannot bet — and yes, Damien, he's your daddy, please stop flinching at the thought — is that he can see the future, right?"

"First of all, fuck you. I didn't flinch, and this Martyn is not really my father. Secondly, oh, he cannot see the future per se, but how certain choices might affect it."

"Semantics," she dismissed him with a hand wave. "The Gentlemen's Club is awesome, no matter what you sensitive little babies think. Personally, I think they ruin my parties, because they create themselves comfortable couches and sit on them and talk all night without even appreciating the decorations and the food, but they are amazing."

"No doubt there." He sounded so disappointed.

"In your bet," she continued, ignoring his comment. "Stakes are even higher, because this time, Herschel and his crowd are betting too. Herschel, you know, the twins' father? Or do you know?" She shook her head. "I am lost as to what you know and what you don't, but it doesn't matter. As per usual, your father is forbidden to bet, so I would suggest you to inside trade the information with me."

"Just to spite all of them, I want to declare my love to you and end their bet right then and there."

Her face got cold within a second. Her voice was a whisper when she narrowed her eyes and spoke: "You wouldn't need my father for killing you then, and I am not going to work as clean as he does, just for your information."

"I am not certain," Damien started, leaning back. "If I should find this reaction offensive, because I am a terrific lover, or confusing, because you're repulsed by the idea of me telling people I am in love with you, yet you're having a child with me."

"I'm offended that you think I would disrupt their bet by being a part of it."

Damien nodded, all serious. He pulled his loom back to himself, and continued with his weaving as he spoke. "You know, if this is hereditary, I might enjoy having a daughter way too much."

"Oh, dear," Jennifer shook her head. "I take it back. I want a son, that's for sure."

"Doesn't matter, I'll spoil the kid to the high skies, and they will love me more than they love you. You should prepare yourself for that."

"Already trying to steal my kid, unbelievable," she shook her head, but she was smiling. "I want the throw the announcement party next week, you might want to get ready for it."

"Get ready?" He frowned. "I will get dressed, Jennifer, what other preparation should I make?"

She shrugged. "I have way too many ideas, but when I clarify I'll let you know."

"Will you at least tell your parents before everyone else?"

"Should I?"

"Jennifer," Damien sighed. "Don't you think they deserve to hear it before everybody else?"

"Will you tell your dad?"

"Martyn already knows."

"He — what?"

"Yeah. So does Thyren. Well, he knows we have a deal. Not the specifics."

"Damien," she opened her mouth, and closed. She pinched the bridge of her nose as she inhaled deeply, then tilted her head on right. "Why?"

"You do realise I'm as mentally unstable as you can get, right? There's no guarantee I won't wake up tomorrow thinking I'm back in my origin timeline and think all of this is a dream. Someone has to know."

"Unbelievable," she shook her head.

"I'm pretty sure neither of them have told anyone. You'd know otherwise."

"The fact that you let people know about our sexual activities..."

"What do you think people will deduce once you say you're having a kid with me, for all the gods above and below?"

"Still!" Jennifer threw her hands in the air. "I hate you, but what's done is done. Any tips on how to say something like this without bringing down the wrath of a parent?"

Damien shrugged. "I theorised the kid might be my anchor."

"You lucky bastard," Jennifer murmured. "I know the card I'll play with dad, but currently I'm at a total loss with my mom."

"Jenny," Damien reached and held her hand. "I don't think she will get angry. Just, be calm, and explain."

"You think?"

He nodded, letting her hand go. "Would you get world shatteringly angry?" He started, as he turned back to his loom. "If our kid came to you and told something like this. Would you?"

Jennifer didn't say anything.

"See?" He smiled, wide, as his attention were still on his threads. Weave until everything burns. "It is going to be alright."

*

In all honesty, Damien knew this was going to happen. When he told Jennifer to tell her parents, he knew he was going to get reprimanded. He mostly expected Juventas, and he was even ready for it mentally — as much as one could be ready for it. No matter the timeline, there was always an edge to her that terrified Damien, yet, he was determined he wasn't going to waver. It was Jennifer's call. I just helped her.

But when it wasn't Juventas, but Gerard — the scary, cold, Flerl'en Frea, he felt every bit of the resolution he had disappearing. Oh he's going to kill me. But a part of him was fine with it as well. At least this time it will be permanent. Probably. His hair so blonde that looked like snow white under the correct lighting, his eyes so cold blue, he as a whole reminded Damien of winter. Freezing to death in your sleep, he found himself thinking. Not that bad of a way to die.

When they took their places, sitting across each other, Gerard didn't look angry. He didn't even look sad. His face was the pure peace and comfort, as he leaned back and sighed. "So," he said. "You and my daughter."

"Yes, sir," Damien said, his voice croaked. He immediately cleared his throat. "Should I call you sir? Never mind — I mean to say yes."

"I think I should congratulate you."

"Um..." His brain froze. This wasn't a response he was expecting. "Congratulate me?"

"Being a father is no small feat. I am fairly certain you jumped into it without thinking about what it actually entails, but something tells me you'll succeed in it."

"Thank you." His posture straightened, confidence was leaking into his heart now. "I will do my very best."

Gerard chuckled. "You thought I was going to kill you, didn't you?"

"You're Death, so... With all my respect, yeah, I did."

Gerard's chuckle turned into laughter. "Damien, Jennifer is thousands of years old. I would more worry about her corrupting you."

"I can assure you, no corruption took place."

"Oh, fuck off," his cheery dismissal came with a smile. "I know my daughter. She can be very insistent when she wants to be. Under normal circumstances, I would worry about her being tricked, but yeah... Doesn't make sense to worry about it under these circumstances."

"I see."

"Is it true that your mother was Madison?"

Damien stared at him. Was? She's still alive. She should be. Everyone should be alive. Even Haylen. His voice was nowhere to be found, no strength in him to open his mouth even — as if someone pulled the batteries and left him like a broken toy. He managed to nod, but no sound came out of him.

"Syleren," he continued. "Tell me about her."

"I—I don't know," Damien started, almost too quiet to be heard. "I don't know what to tell you."

This time, Gerard's smile was anything but cheerful. She's dead here, he thought suddenly. She's dead here, because Sylen killed her. It was a familiar story that he should have never heard. I should have never lived through this. But here they were.

"I knew her," he spoke softly. "I've known her as chaos, I've known her as order, I've known her as an advisor, as my mother."

"You are very lucky," Gerard replied. "To know her."

"I feel lucky," Damien said. "I feel lucky that she was my mother. That she protected me, as best as she could. That she was always there, for everyone, standing tall and proud." He paused, raised his head. "She taught me about my powers once, when I was in another timeline, and she was only a ghost. She was there with me, as much as she could be."

"I've always wondered," Gerard said, blinking a few times, fast. "How it would be, if she was alive. Where we all would be. We have suffered a lot after her, without her. Though," he leaned forward and invited Damien to do the same. "Can you keep a secret, Damien?"

"I think so."

"She's a ghost here, as well," he was whispering now. "Though, I find the term ghost quite offensive, in all honesty. A presence, is what I would call the phenomenon. She's a presence here, as well."

"Is she here? Right now?"

"Oh, unfortunately not. Although, for the father of my grandkid, I might do a little favour. If you want."

The question, the one single question everyone asked him, stood right in front of him now, like a brick wall. Does it matter? She isn't the same person. He wondered if it would be akin to substituting water with wine — quenching the thirst then and there, only to have a bigger quench later on. Would I have anything to share with her, when it isn't even her? He looked at him, questions floating in his head still. "I don't know what I want," he said, quiet. "I don't think I ever will."

"What I've come to believe, Damien," Gerard started, leaning back. Damien didn't move. He couldn't move. "Is that we're given too much power. Great enough to do great things, no denial there. But we are not equipped to handle those powers. It takes a lot of falling on our knees, getting up, and marching on without letting the scars heal."

"It feels like that," Damien nodded. He couldn't see anything now, his vision blurred by the tears. "I should've never gone through all that."

"You shouldn't have. There is a reason we don't resurrect people after their deaths, no matter how much we want it. No matter how much we need it. It's too much."

"I don't even know how many times I've died." He almost pleaded. There was now the inherent understanding that amongst all the people he came to know, he was now talking to the one who would understand him. "It's... a lot. More than I can handle."

"I have wanted to bring her back," Gerard said, in response, slowly. "When she died in front of our very eyes. We were all there, we all watched her dying, listened to her final words. I wanted to bring her right then, right there. I didn't want to put her through this. But she didn't want to move on. She wanted to stay, at least long enough to see her killer's demise."

"Sylen," Damien murmured.

"Sylen," Gerard nodded. "Alexei, as we call him. Then, she couldn't move on still. A presence, is the only thing that's left of her." His bitter smile returned to his lips. "We don't know what we want, Damien. None of us do. We don't know, we will never know. Until it is way too late."

"Does she..." His voice trailed off. "Does she know?"

"Yes, she does. She knows your story, as much as we know. I haven't seen her that upset in a very long time."

"I didn't mean to upset her."

"She knows. I know. We all know." He sighed. "We might not be the family you had, Damien. But we want to be. We can be. Martyn wants it more than anyone."

"He does?" He looked at Gerard, directly into his ice blue eyes. "He really does? Not because of my mother and—"

"We have this thing in our Gentlemen's Club," Gerard answered, softly. "One way or another, we find ourselves wayward sons, and we adopt them."

"Yeah," Damien couldn't help himself but interrupt. "You also bet on very serious issues."

Gerard started laughing, almost in a roaring fashion, and Damien couldn't believe how similar he looked to Jennifer when he laughed like this. "That, too. But to answer your question, no, it's not about your mother. Not entirely. I cannot deny the weight Madison's name carry, but one way or another, you're his wayward son, and he wants to help you. We all do."

He got up, and ruffled Damien's hair before walking towards the door.

"Gerard?" Damien said, trying to sound clear.

"Yeah?" The man turned, looking at him.

"I would love to." He paused. "I would love to talk to her."

Gerard smiled. "Then, I'll see you when I see you."

EPILOGUE

It wasn't until after dinner Damien sought Martyn, and found him in the library. Which wasn't particularly surprising, the library acted less like a library but more like Martyn's study, even though he already had a designated study. Damien figured it was because the library had a better view of the backyard, which oversaw the winter garden as well — after sunset, fairy lights would come alive and would make the garden look even more magical.

He didn't say anything at the beginning. He took one of the chairs, quietly brought it next to the large window, and sat there. He knew Martyn was aware of him, but even then he paid no heed, which Damien welcomed. I don't know what to say to you. That was a lie. He knew what to say, very clearly, he just couldn't bring himself to it. Come on. What do you have to lose?

Martyn was reading a book, his focus so intense, Damien wondered if it was possible to burn through the pages simply by staring at them like this. Don't distract yourself, Damien. He wondered what book it was, what about it was so interesting. Can you please focus? He couldn't. His focus wanted to play hide and seek, and he had no choice but to chase it. Currently, it was in that book.

He cleared his throat, and turned his back to the window, facing Martyn directly. He remembered a different Martyn, in a different library, reading a different book — with the same intensity, with the same care in each page turn, with the same eyebrow raise every time he read a sentence that interested him.

"Reading," he started, he was surprised how clear he sounded. "Reading feeds our minds in a way we cannot replicate with our powers."

Martyn, without raising his head from his book, nodded. There was no eye contact, but he still responded. "It keeps the mind sharp."

"A sharp mind is dangerous."

"How so?"

"Eventually it might try to cut the skeleton it's confined in."

That got Martyn's attention. With the low light coming from the windows, the man's wrinkles around his eyes looked so much like spider webs. Weave, weave until everything burns.

"Why would it try to escape?"

"Within the same prison for all eternity," Damien shrugged. He had no idea he was saying. From hundreds, and maybe thousands, of thoughts in his head, he was trying to pick something that made sense. It didn't work, just like one couldn't get a cup full of water with their hands from a river. He still tried. Maybe not in one trial he was going to fill it, but ten. "I think minds get bored. Or, they finally realise none of it is real, but a mass delusion and try to wake up."

"Is that how it feels for you?"

"Nah," he shrugged. "I am not that sharp minded. I am mainly confused. Trying to find differences between things that should be the same. For all I know, they are the same."

"That is difficult," Martyn agreed, closing his book. "Did you find a way to manage it?"

"Stopping resisting," Damien replied. "However, in the end, what puts context into things, and people, is the shared history with them. It gets difficult trying not to resist when you have a whole different history, histories, with someone, who doesn't even know you." Again, he shrugged. He was afraid it going to become a tic nowadays. "Yet, I tried to go resistance is meaningless and all that spiel."

"What stops you from creating a new shared history?" Almost an academic interest, there was in Martyn's voice. "Surely, you can create something new out of the remainders of the old."

"I think what scares me is that, creating that new history is harder than resisting." His eyes travelled from bookcase to bookcase, shelves full of collective history of everyone. "I trust you, because I've always trusted you. But I don't know if I should trust this you, right in front of me, within my reach. That means forgetting the trust I've harboured for you, even though it was based on a history you don't share with me, and start anew. What if I can't build a new thing, after I demolish the already existing structure?"

"You think that's a risk not worth taking?"

"I think it's terrifying. I don't think anybody can make such a distinction without driving themselves mad."

Without saying anything, Martyn continued watching Damien, a silent invitation to continue. Go on. Tell whatever it is you think of. At this point, Damien was tired of telling. He just wanted someone to look at him, and then understand everything — including the things even he himself didn't understand.

But that was not possible, so he continued, trying to slow down the stream of thoughts in his head, trying to strain all the dirt to get to the gold with only his fingers. It was hard work. But then, what was ever easy?

"You're not my father," he started, trying to keep his voice as even as possible. He didn't want to sound in denial, it was just a fact — a fact they both knew. "You haven't shared with me what my own father shared. We shared different things, you have seen me at my worst, and you've taken care of me. Thing is," he raised his hand once he saw Martyn's shoulders getting tense, as if he was getting ready to argue. Let me finish. If I stop, the river will flow through and I won't be able to speak about it again." I am afraid. I am afraid of admitting you are my father, the fact that we're from different timelines damned, because if I do that, if I do that for everyone, I won't be able to tell where I am anymore."

"Is it really that important of a distinction for you?" Martyn asked, softly.

"I killed myself, where I am from. I killed myself, because the pain, the screaming, the insanity of it all was too much for me. In every other timeline, where we were still father and son, I died — sometimes gently, sometimes horribly. Admitting you are my father brings back all that. It brings back a fear of death I don't want to cloud my days with."

A strange, annoying, headache manifested itself in his forehead. As if something wanted to get out of his head, by pounding from inside to break his skull. Make it stop. He took a deep, calming breath. Go on. Pour all the poison out. Never stop.

"Every night," he continued. "I wake up, trying to understand where I am. Which of the Damiens I have been I am, and how I will die. When I say it like that it sounds like it's not a big deal, but the disorientation, I have to say, is a bitch." He didn't mention how he looked for the cracked glass around him, how he looked for the remaining pieces of the mirror above his bed — to see himself, surrounded by blood, his own blood, dried. "I have to hang onto something to remind myself that it's different. This place is different, I am different, and alive, and not dying at the end of this story. That's why I need it to be different. That's why I try so hard to hang on to the small differences, the non-existent history, that's why I feel guilty whenever I call you my father, when in reality, there's nothing I want more." Maybe one thing. One person.

"You're looking for an anchor," Martyn clarified.

"I am looking for an anchor." It was that simple. It was so much more complicated. "To stop me from drifting."

In all honesty, Damien wanted to applaud himself for being able to say all of these without crying. He desperately wanted Martyn to be impressed by it as well. I am sorry, he wanted to say. He didn't know what for.

When Martyn finally spoke, in his own calm way, Damien realised he wasn't talking to the man he'd come to know for the past year, on top of all the other Martyns he had ever known. It was the normally-should-be-terrifying God of Fate, who held all the strings and wove them like a very patient spider, seeing everything, every angle.

"Fate is a weird thing," he started, softly. "People think it's prede-termined, forcing us to play less than ideal hands, putting every-thing we have on the table, when in reality, it's just us trying to go with one of the few ropes extended to us. It's the tether that connects us to the universe, because after all, that's what universe is: Many million, billion beings that are inherently interconnected one way or another." He let a breath out, then continued. "Fate is how we are connected, and how our waves affect others."

Damien nodded. He didn't feel like he was understanding what Martyn was explaining on a conscious level, all the understanding was happening not in his mind but in his heart. How we are connected. How our waves affect others.

"Your problem, dear boy," Martyn said, looking Damien directly in the eyes. "Is that you aren't connected to anyone. You are looking for an anchor, when you don't need one. You need to be connected, to other beings, and that is something only you can do, only you can build those tethers. The past doesn't matter. You are the master of your future, and for that, you need to focus on your present. That's where you're failing, currently: You try to hold onto a past that doesn't exist, not anymore. It's a past you have no tethers to. You are not extending your hand to the future, as you still try to catch the burned and frayed ends of that past."

"I don't know how to let go of my past," Damien murmured. He couldn't look away.

"You don't need to do anything about it," Martyn said. "You just need to focus on the present. To you that stands here, in this moment, your own surroundings, and connect to the people in front of you."

Getting up from his desk, he walked to the big windows. Magical, Damien thought as he watched Martyn looking at the view outside. He went next to him, without another word. Past. Present. Future.

The tops of the trees were swaying slightly under the evening breeze. Left. Right.

"I am going to be a father," he said, slowly, savouring each word. "It's something I've never experienced before, so any tips and tricks are much appreciated."

"Would love to, but I don't have any as well," Martyn let a soft chuckle. "Though I can redirect you to those with experience."

"Come on," Damien dismissed, cheerfully. "Nobody would believe that after seeing you dealing with me, certifiably the worst person to be a parent figure of."

"Dealing with an adult kid is much much easier than dealing with a baby, I must say."

"How did you find out about me? Before I came here, I mean."

"You were creating waves." Was it really that simple? "Waves that are my job to notice."

"You're not giving away all your secrets, are you?"

"Never," Martyn laughed. "Otherwise, there's no point in keeping them."

They watched the garden for a while. Every now and then, there would be small shadows scurrying across the yard, only seen in the lights of the small torches and the fairy lights of the winter garden. Inherently interconnected. Stars above were shining like tiny diamonds.

"You loved her," Damien said. It was less of a full-stop sentence, but a question. "You wanted to protect her."

He didn't need to say her name. For Damien, this Madison, The Chaos Before Him, was almost a myth, one that he could witness to some facets of. A ghost, a presence, that haunted them — both figuratively, and literally — to this day, eons after her death. She fascinated him.

"Yes," Martyn agreed. "I did love her. I failed at protecting her."

"I still cannot believe you've built a whole separate place, a separate domain for her."

"She deserved the best of everything…" He sighed, eyes far away on the horizon. "I begged her, many times, even the day before her death to let it all go. To come here, and rule this place as she wanted." He shook his head, sniffling. "Tell me about your mother."

"She was…" Damien didn't know where to begin. "She was the sunshine. She was the starlight. Main difference was, though, she wasn't chaos so none of the associated insanity. And since she didn't need to, this domain didn't exist. You were also in Flerketer. And we were all happy."

"Happy is good," Martyn said.

"It was good. I think she wasn't that different from what you know your Madison to be. Nobody is. Granted, with a few exceptions." He found it funny. He couldn't believe how funny he found it. "You were in love, really, like teenagers. After thousands of years."

"Good to hear we've made it in one place at least, obviously with a glaring difference." Martyn didn't sound upset. It wasn't even yearning. "Chaos and Fate never sounded like a good match. Like disaster, ready to combust, any second."

"If you think about it, Chaos and Fate are a great match."

"You think so?"

"Yeah." Damien closed his eyes, smiling to himself. "Fate is the hand that guides Chaos to throw the wrenches where necessary. The reason you didn't work out was the reason this timeline almost imploded on itself."

"You shouldn't hang around Thyren this much," Martyn mused. "Normally, blaming Alexei for everything is his forte."

"After many timelines where he killed me, or he killed the universe as he knew it, I can safely say Sylen is the knot that cannot be undone. So much that, to save the rest of the thread, you have to cut him out. With one exception, it was always too late for that."

"Which exception is that?"

"He killed himself. Thing about him is that, he didn't do it out of malice. Granted, he was an asshole when he wanted to be one. However, he had one purpose. To bring balance. That eventually means the final. No in, no out. He was either too good at doing it, or too bad at preventing it."

"Damien," Martyn said, turning his head towards him. "Do you believe our impending doom is far away now?"

"I wouldn't be able to tell... Help me with throwing the right wrenches to the right places and we should be safe and sound." Damien turned to him, and smiled. "I mean, it's your fatherly duty after all, dad."

With that, Martyn pulled him in a hug. Damien hugged him back, even tighter.

*

To be completely honest, Damien had scoffed the idea of a baby shower. Jennifer, on the other hand, jumped at the opportunity of throwing a party, and even though it meant she couldn't drink through it, she still persisted. And so, just a week after telling everyone who could reasonably expect to be told earlier, she went ahead with it.

Last time a convergence of the same crowd had happened, it was a week of events Damien remembered quite vividly, for after its end he killed himself. Suicide was one of those things he could never succeed at, as he kept getting resurrected. Right wrenches, right places. He had no complaints about where he ended up.

"Long live the King," Damien announced as he entered the balcony. "Still the avoid everyone routine?"

Thyren laughed as he raised his glass. "Oh, you're gracing me with your presence, princeling." Damien wanted to stare at his smile forever. "I take it as you're tired of the endless river of congratulations?"

"More like half of the pantheon threw dagger glances at me, because aside from Juventas and my dad nobody knows me there. Maybe Gerard, too, but only a little bit."

Thyren shrugged as he drank his wine. "I do."

"My association with you is also a grave concern for them. Though, you vouching for me to Gerard is I presume, why I'm alive."

"Oh yeah, Gerard loves me," Thyren nodded. "Not as much as Geoff, of course, but once upon a time I dated his... I'm gonna say his son, because that's who he was. He was very okay with it."

"How did it end?"

"I almost died so he broke up with me."

"You literally just said Gerard was okay with it."

"And I didn't say he was the one who almost killed me." He smiled again, and Damien felt his heart flutter. "Leytianketer was a ruthless place, princeling."

Damien laughed at that. "You sure made a habit of dating princes, then. Any other ones I should know about?"

"I made a habit like that, but we couldn't exactly call Kyrean, the aforementioned infamous son of Gerard, a crown prince. Granted, he should've been one. A crown would've looked good on that bastard."

With that Damien turned his back to the view, leaning on the balcony rails. "That's a leytian name."

"It is. Kyrean was the very second ever Leytianl'en Frea."

"Oh, boy," Damien threw his head back. "Your other habit was clearly chasing literal death, then."

Thyren did the same, and let a hearty laugh. "Did you ever doubt that? I've been suicidal since I was five. I still am, but promises made, promises kept."

They both watched the kerfuffle inside for a while, distance between them, distance between their hands. Damien finished his glass, and threw it over his shoulder. When Thyren looked at him, in disbelief, he shrugged.

"It's Jenny's palace," he said. "She can have it cleaned."

"Man, I guess I am lucky you haven't brought down my palace on top of my head."

"I like your palace. The always blowing breeze, the beautiful backyard that I crashed into, also the food — just , simply amazing."

"Nothing else?" Thyren raised his eyebrows.

Damien looked at him, straight in the eye. "Maybe one more thing, but I'm still on the fence about that."

"Let me know when the debate ends."

"Will do for sure, my liege," he laughed. "You'll be the first one to know."

There was laughter rising from the room inside, glasses clinking, the chatter. Damien felt like he belonged there.

He knew he didn't.

Does it even matter where I belong?